CW00766896

TobyJo

Alice Scott

authorHOUSE®

AuthorHouse™ UK Ltd.
500 Avebury Boulevard
Central Milton Keynes, MK9 2BE
www.authorhouse.co.uk
Phone: 08001974150

First published by AuthorHouse 7/2/2009

ISBN: 978-1-4389-9350-8 (sc)

This book is printed on acid-free paper.

ACKNOWLEDGEMENTS

TO ALL WHO ENCOURAGED ME AND
READ VARIOUS DRAFTS

JOYCE STEVENSON, MY SISTER

PAULEEN LANGRIDGE

WENDY MC KECHNIE

TELMA BIAZ

DAVID FOWLER, FOR HIS GENEROSITY, HELP, AND
ADVICE

GILLIAN MARTEN, MY FRIEND AND COVER
DESIGNER

DEDICATION

TO MY REAL FAMILY WHO HAVE LIVED ALONGSIDE MY IMAGINARY ONE FOR TWO YEARS AND NEVER KNEW.

Contents

CHAPTER ONE

THE WAITING ROOM

On the night of March 15th 1956 the railway station in Edinburgh was a depressing place. The relentless rain and snow poured down without respite and there were few places to shelter.

I am seventy now and I remember the details so clearly. The events would replay in my memory for years like one of those black and white films set in dreary railway waiting rooms in wartime.

I was twenty and had discharged myself from a nursing home in order to escape from my wealthy Italian stepfather Dino Grimaldi.My main luggage had been secreted out of the home the day before by my friend Katie. Jim her boyfriend had volunteered to take me to the station in Glasgow to connect with the Edinburgh train. My valuables were in my holdall which was to stay by my side throughout the journey. He met me at the back of the hospital near the fire escape after visiting time. After the drama of the previous week it was a great relief when I finally helped me into his car. From then onwards my arrangements were flimsy. I had to rely on people I hardly knew who had made promises they may or may not be able to keep.

I had over an hour to wait in Edinburgh but managed to find a porter to escort me to the nearest waiting room with my two cases. I tipped him and he seemed amused.

'Thanks miss these lads will take care of you won't you boys.' he said pointing to groups of soldiers drinking beer around the coke fire. One of them shouted back

'Of course we will thank you mate, come on in sweetheart.'

I knew I was overdressed as Dino expected me to always wear expensive Italian clothes especially when I was out with him. As I had been expected to go to Milan after my discharge he had sent me a cashmere camel coat and some Italian leather boots. They made way for me. I could hardly see it was so thick with smoke. Conversation stopped as I went through the door. Some of them whistled and two of them grabbed my luggage and made room for me on a large bench by the fire. In a panic I took back the holdall and put it between myself and the wall covering it with my scarf .They pushed the rest of my cases under the seat. I was the only woman and within five minutes there was no way in or out without having to push past the new arrivals.

The noise was deafening. Trains hurtled by at unimaginable speeds. Some were shunting and the railwaymen were loading coal and blowing their whistles, frustrated as the snow turned to ice jamming up the points. That was nothing compared to the noise inside. It was a place I did not want to be in for five minutes. I felt dizzy and faint as the men's' faces all seemed to fuse into one for a while and appeared to be spinning around like a kaleidoscope. I was acutely aware of my designer clothes and expensive luggage and quickly began to realise that I would have to pay a price for my freedom and this was only my first day.

It was a filthy room. The floors were covered in beer bottles, cigarettes and chewing gum. There was a smell of stale urine from the half-open toilet door. The tea bar with half-closed shutters was covered in unwashed cups and plates with half-eaten food and cigarette stubs. The men made a circle around me. Some of them sat on my table and tried to proposition me. One of them came and sat beside me and told the others to move away .They did so quickly but stayed in a circle like an audience at a boxing match. The man had three stripes and took his place as if it was his right to sit there.

At first he didn't speak but placed a full bottle of whisky on the table. He started to drink and wiped his mouth with his fist. Turning towards me he moved a bit closer running his eyes up and down my body as I pulled my coat tighter to keep warm. He was a strong well built man who towered above the others. He spoke slowly and carefully, weighing his words as some men did when they had too much to drink.

'What's a beautiful girl like you doing at this time of night on your own are you going to London?' I nodded. 'Well you need an escort; there are a lot of wild Scotsmen out there. We have three carriages booked you'd better to come with us. What do you think boys should we make room for this gorgeous young lady.' he looked around for a response and there was laughter from the boys nearest to us.

'That's ok with us Serge we'll look after her, she can come in our carriage anytime'. One of them shouted.

These faceless men started getting bolder with their remarks.

'You'll be alright there serge' one of them said. 'We know why girls go down to London don't we, look at her gear.'

He handed me the bottle 'Have a drink of this sweetheart you are shivering.'

'I don't like the taste of whisky' I said.

3

I was fearful that he would insist but he put his arm around my shoulder instead.

His breath smelt of stale beer and cigarettes. He had just stubbed one out and it was still burning falling into a pool of beer making a sticky mess. I felt nauseated. He tightened his grip. His moustache was neatly trimmed and waxed. It was thing a senior NCO often did. It was like a passport to seniority. He grinned at me and his teeth were brown and nicotine stained.

'Has anyone ever told you look like Bridget Bardot.? We have a 6ft pin-up of her nude over the bar in the Sergeants mess.'

He waited for the men to react watching my face. I froze like an animal trapped waiting for worse to come. I was already cold, tired and afraid. He leaned back in his seat and stretched his legs putting his thick boots on my expensive leather cases. Lighting another cigarette he paused, preparing to entertain his audience at my expense. His arm tightened. He started to whisper to me but it was so noisy I could hardly hear what he said.

'Come on Serge tell us what you are saying.' ? The men shouted.

'I am just telling how gorgeous she is. A bit of class, just what I like. I thought she might like to know a bit about the night life in Glasgow where we were last night.

You know when I went on the raids with the police looking for my lost boys.

And the privileges we get for our pains. It was a good night for all concerned particularly the girls. They encouraged him to tell them more but the noise outside drowned his voice to my relief. I could not move. I turned away from him with my back on my hold all and leaned against it trying to hide it. It was no place for a three week old baby. Safely under his mattress were my passport, bank book and birth certificates. I did not want to explain his presence. I wore no wedding ring and was worried that any moment the police would come looking for me.

'Come on come on. Give me a smile, say something. I won't hurt you.' he said.

I gave him a watery smile 'Sorry I have just had a long day and am very tired.'

'That's better your warming up a bit, now have some whisky. You need to relax sweetheart we like to have female company don't we boys. You see those lads they trust me, they do as I say and they know I can make things happen.'

'Please I don't want a drink it makes me feel ill.'

'Now don't get above yourself darling with your fancy accent.' he snapped.

He paused for a moment and looked at the men.

'But I can deal with that can't I boys?'

They started laughing as if they knew he what was coming next.

He went quiet. 'I think I will tell you what I do with my girl recruits when they act up. They are about your age and full of fancy ideas. Why you must only be about eighteen.

You have a lot to learn yet. Should I tell her what we do.?

They shouted 'Yeah tell her about the gym Serge;'

He stared at me closely watching my face as he continued.

'I put them through their paces in the gym after dinner and then work them hard for an hour. Afterwards I give them a lecture on the evils of VD. Then they have to watch a film on Sex Education When they understand that after viewing it twice I show them a special one from our private collection.'

There was applause from the men at this remark.

'It is an experience they never want to repeat especially if it becomes necessary to put a couple of them on stage to help us demonstrate a few points. By the end of the session they know exactly where they stand as women in the army and who to respect and who to please.'

They all started laughing taking up the theme boasting about how they humiliated and degraded new recruits of both sexes. It was nasty and violent and I felt sick.

Ignoring them he continued to stare at me. He seemed mesmerised.

Then he pulled off my silk scarf and watched my hair fall to my waist. He stared at it as if in a trance.

'You really are a beautiful girl. What's your name'? 'Jo.' I said quietly.

'Jo, well Jo I am Ken your next dance partner.'

One of the men shouted.' Go on Serge get on with it. There's no one here but us. The porter won't be back. We tipped him again.'

By now my coat had fallen off my shoulders and they whistled as they noticed my tight sweater. I had dressed hurriedly and I was fully aware that it was clinging to my figure as my baby was breast fed. His face was getting redder as he reached for another drink. Then he put the bottle down and went very quiet. The whole room seemed to go into slow motion as the men stopped talking, waiting for his next move.

Then he let me go and slowly stood up taking back his authority swaying and waving his arms.

'Right out all of you, go on all of you get your kit and go. The show's over. Come on I mean it out, the train will be here soon'.

They muttered as they started to pick up their kit bags. I tried to get up but he grabbed my arm clenching it behind my back hurting me.

'No not you young Jo, you are staying here with me to dance the night away.

We are catching the mail train. You will get cold out there. I am going to stack up that fire. Where's Snowy? Tell him I want him.' he shouted.

There was a scuffle outside and a good looking black soldier walked through the door. His greatcoat was soaking as he had obviously been standing in the rain for a long time.

'Snowy is one of my best Sgt's.You've have never met a black man before have you? 'Well don't look so worried he likes white women don't you Snowy. Just look at this young filly, she's called Jo. Long legs, blonde hair a true thoroughbred and she has just walked into our stable. Look at these curls all over the place isn't she gorgeous. He lifted some of my hair up and stroked it.

Snowy smiled at me and bowed.

The sergeant roared with laughter and swayed again holding on to the table. His uniform was stained where he had spilled his whisky.

'He does that to all the ladies, they love it. He had to practice for the Queen. He's been to Buckingham palace, got a medal so you'll have to be nice to him too.'

'Now Snowy I want a favour. I am staying here with Jo. She and I are going to finish this whisky and get close by the fire and then we are catching the mail train in an hour. I want you to stay behind with me, get our kit together and do bit of guard duty. When the train comes we will grab a first class carriage and enjoy her company in comfort. Then we can all have breakfast together. I will need some sleep at some point as I have to meet the Col tomorrow at the MOD. Whilst this is happening you can take care of her for me. You can do that can't you my man for Queen and Country.'?

Snowy pulled him to one side and said something. The sergeant let me go and shook his head and searched his pockets for more cigarettes.

Whilst he did so Snowy leaned over to me and whispered.

'I'll be back in a minute get your bag. I will deal with this.'

Later I found out who they were. One of the nurses had talked about the beach being sealed off for army training near Edinburgh. Her brother worked for the forestry commission in the forests and mountains beyond. They were a special service unit.

The Staff Sgt was their chief instructor who taught them how to survive in the mountains and live rough. He also taught them to kill mercilessly, anything when they were hungry, and anybody who got in their way when their politics put them on the wrong side of the lines.

The room emptied as the men went out into the snow to catch their train.

I was alone with him. He started to shovel coke on the fire and after laying his greatcoat on the floor tried to grab me. I sidestepped him and picked up my holdall. As I did so a large presence in the shape of an army Major came through the door followed by Snowy just as Toby my baby started to cry.

CHAPTER 2

THE FLAT IN EAST SHEEN

Snowy had brought in the Major as he had felt powerless to break up the situation on his own. I was to learn later that Snowy deserved his OBE.

I was put in the next compartment to the Major who arranged for blankets, drinks and refreshments making sure I was comfortable and private enabling me to feed Toby my baby. Snowy and another trusted Sgt stayed in the corridor thus preventing any further disruptions.

I was amazingly calm as I allowed myself to fall asleep to the rhythm of the train.

I had survived so many precarious situations during the last year that this latest incident in the station waiting room made me more determined to go ahead with my flimsy plans in my search for freedom and independence. I drew my strength from the knowledge that the only strong person in my life my mother would have wanted me to do this, to fight for my survival and that of my son Toby. I slept fitfully and so did he. As he was only three weeks old I was lucky in that he was undemanding and content with his routine of sleeping and feeding. He had been with me day and night since his birth and I was tuned into his needs.

I had planned my escape well and had enough supplies with me. Instead of carrying dirty linen and nappies I disposed of them in waste bins. I had enough money to replace them and in that I counted myself lucky. In the morning we were still in the midlands somewhere as there had been a delay in the night. Snowy knocked on the sliding door and offered to look after Toby whilst I washed and freshened up. When I returned he had him on his knee and had managed to entertain him.

'What a great baby and good looking too' he said as he handed him back grinning from ear to ear.

'The Major said I was to ask you where you wanted to go in London as he will get his driver to take you in the staff car. He is to be met at King Cross and after he has been dropped off at the Ministry of Defence the driver will to take you on to your destination. He suggested I accompany you if that's all right.'?

I hesitated, as my plans were very sketchy. All I had was the key to a flat owned by one of the nurses sisters who had agreed to help me until I found somewhere else or could locate my cousin. It was in East Sheen. I knew I had to sound confidant and assured. Snowy had rescued me and appeared to have the Major's trust so I felt that perhaps I should trust him. I agreed to the plan and asked him to thank the Major.

He left the carriage and arrived back a few minutes later with a waiter from the 1st class restaurant with a tray of breakfast.

'You will share it with me Snowy'

'I thought you would never ask' came the reply'.

He smiled again with the large generous smile I was becoming used to. I had never met a West Indian man before as there were few black people in the Northwest where I had been brought up. I had always loved jazz and he reminded me of musicians I had seen in films. I asked him if he played an instrument.

He laughed 'I am a pianist, my grandmother taught me. She wanted me to play classical music and go to Music College but I prefer jazz and I had to do my national service. I am being discharged soon and have a scholarship to study law.'

He paused and then quietly said

'Do you want to tell me about you and Toby and why you are on your own on a winter's night?'

'I can't' I said.

'The Major asked me to ask you, if you needed any help.'

'I will be all right when I get there I have some money'.

'Well the he wants me to give you his card and I will give you a contact number.'

I looked into his steady brown eyes and I knew he meant it. I ate all of the breakfast and Snowy had some toast and coffee. He told me stories about when he had first come over to England when he was twelve and how his father had encouraged him to study and go to University to study law. A few minutes later the Major joined us. I was able to see him properly for the first time in the morning light. He was tall and broad shouldered with sandy hair. He had soft pale blue eyes that suddenly sharpened and became alert at times almost changing colour with his mood and state of mind. I felt like a schoolgirl in front of the headmaster waiting for an interrogation.

'Good morning Jo I hope you and the little chap slept well and that you feel better today. My Sgt may have told you that we have organised some transport across London if you agree.'

'Thank you I am very grateful for all your help' I said.

'Well it's the least we could do after your ordeal and believe me there will be an investigation'.

With that he left. I was to learn much later that he was a very highly respected officer who was to be promoted on his next tour to Malaya. I did not see him again until I was escorted to his private car by Snowy who held Toby for me. A porter followed with our luggage. The rest of the men were a long way down the platform so fortunately I missed them. I wondered how they would treat Snowy when they met up again.

There were two policemen standing by the ticket office. I do not think they noticed me as I walked alongside the Major. They were silent and formal during the journey to Whitehall and when we arrived at the Ministry of Defence the driver removed the Majors luggage. He nodded to me as he got out and said 'Well, goodbye you have my card if I can ever be of assistance'.

He told Snowy to take a couple of days off and report to him later.

The driver took his instructions from Snowy and carried on with the journey towards Richmond and East Sheen. I asked them to drop me of at the nearest tube station which the driver agreed to do as he had another urgent pick up.

Snowy jumped out piled our luggage onto the pavement and said

'I have to make sure you will be ok where is the flat'?

'I think it is round the corner on the main road.'

I had written the instructions carefully and drawn a map and had a key to the flat, which was over a shop.

Mary who owned it was in New Zealand and was away for six months. She however decided to stay over there and I eventually bought it. I still own it today.

We found it between a coffee bar and a second hand book shop.

The entrance was in between and clearly marked 21A. The shop below was boarded up.

I'll see you inside' said Snowy dragging my big case and his kit bag.

He seemed superhuman and no doubt he was. He was over six foot tall and reminded me of an Olympic athlete. He told me later about his sporting career in the army, Athletics, rugby, squash and downhill skiing in Germany in which he had won championships.

I must have looked a forlorn sight in the rain clutching the key and Toby.

He smiled at me. 'Don't look so worried I will be off later once you are settled. I am here to help. My orders from the Major are to make up for the way you were treated by our Staff Sgt.'

He opened the door clearing the post and newspapers letting me lead the way up the dingy staircase. He quickly found the kitchen and some heaters. Once they were on we explored my new home. I suddenly burst into tears and hugged my sleeping baby and my six foot hero in relief.

'It's not that bad' said Snowy.

'It's wonderful, wonderful! I said. In spite of the scabby paint on the stairs it was better than I had ever hoped for. The kitchen was white with blue gingham curtains with a window a overlooking a large park. It had a large dining table and six chairs. There was a gas fire and a double stove with brass pans hanging over it. A welsh dresser was stacked with blue and white crockery .There was an enormous bathroom with an airing cupboard complete with white towels and a clothes-drying rail. It even had a little electric washer with a wringer and a new-portable spin dryer. In the sitting room there were two sofas, a record player and records. There was a sideboard with a drinks cabinet and four bookcases packed with books. In the large period fireplace was a modern gas fire, which warmed up the room instantly. The bedroom contained a white four poster bed with floral drapes and lace bed linen. There were two built in wardrobes and a white dressing table. More bookshelves lined the room and the large window overlooked another part of the park. There was a smaller bedroom with another large bed in it and ample room for a cot.

Two hours later the flat was warm and cosy. Snowy had been to get groceries. Toby was fed and fast asleep and we sat down by the fire with our warm soup, and egg and bacon sandwiches. As it began to get dark Snowy said

'I really have to go now to visit my parents. I would like to call again tomorrow. Perhaps I can make myself useful.'

I hesitated 'Yes I would like that if you have time; you have already been so kind and helpful.'

He left leaving me a phone number and shouted.

'Don't forget the hot water bottles.'

Next morning I was surprised to find that I had slept until 10 am. Toby had slept even longer and before he woke up I had lit the fires and had a bath and unpacked my belongings. I found a locked drawer and put my bank book and the documents in it and hid the key. After I had fed Toby we ventured out and explored the neighbourhood. Everything I needed was in walking distance. I bought food and then went to the park with Toby in a sling. I watched the children on the swings and tried to imagine Toby on them when he was older. I liked the area and a suburb of a large city seemed an ideal place to get lost in. As I sat on a bench I began to feel calm and felt able to work out a few survival strategies. It felt exhilarating to be free, to think for myself and take charge of my own destiny at last. I banished any negative thoughts and replaced them with thoughts of my mother Ruth who had died the year before. I felt she would guide me out of the tangled mess that had been my life in the last year. I blessed her for the importance she had put on saving for me for just such a day as this.

Snowy arrived at midday. Bounding up the stairs he seemed to bring the sunshine in. No longer in uniform he wore a navy duffle coat and a multicoloured scarf. From behind his back he produced the largest bunch of daffodils. I gazed at them and thanked him. They gave me a feeling of renewal and hope in the spring and the future.

He said. 'You both look fresh and bright today did you sleep well?'

'Yes thank you we slept until ten. We also went for a walk to the shops so I have got my bearings. It is an interesting neighbourhood I have a good feeling about it.

Thank you for coming you have been so kind. Come through. I have lit a fire and I will make some coffee'.

As I carried the tray through he was reading a paper and as I sat down he looked at me and said

'Jo I think you should read this. It is an article on the second page and there is a small picture of you.

The headline said. *'Millionaire Searches for Stepdaughter.'*

Josephine Grimaldi step daughter of Dino Grimaldi left a private nursing home in Glasgow and is believed to have travelled to the South and of England. Mr Grimaldi says she is in an unstable state of mind and suffering from severe depression. He is offering a reward for information of her whereabouts and has informed the police.'

He handed me the paper. I froze when I read it and panicked as I tried to explain.

'Yes it's true but I had to leave as they were taking Toby away to Italy to be brought up by the family. I am not unstable but upset and disturbed by the situation they have placed me in. I come of age soon and should have a legacy left to me by my mother. I suspect that there may be a problem with that and this nursing home story and my so called *'instability'* is an excuse on Dino's part to prevent it from happening.

He threatened to commit me. There may be a lot of money at stake. He wants total control and his new wife is extremely jealous of me and likes her own way. I am relieved to be out of their reach. I hope you believe me. During my pregnancy I made friends with my fellow students. They supported me and one of them found me this flat. I am determined now to succeed on my own.'

I realised that I was going to have to trust Snowy.

He replied, 'I have nothing planned today. Why don't we have another drink and a sandwich and you can relax when Toby has his rest and tell me all the details. I already have some experience of the law. Perhaps I could help.'

CHAPTER 3

MY CHILDHOOD

During that chilly March afternoon whilst Toby was asleep I gave Snowy an account of my life up until our meeting.

'It's a long story Snowy but I will start at the beginning. My father died in the war and my mother Ruth ran a large haberdashery shop in the town in the Lake District. My grandfather started the business and when he died it was left to my mother to manage. She had grown up working for him and when she married she continued. My father was a teacher. He taught maths at the local high school for a few years before he was called up. He had always liked sailing so he chose the navy and served on submarines. He died in the Battle of the Atlantic. It was a sad and dark time for us but we had become used to living on our own. It was the way it was for all of us then, not many children had a father around.

Ruth was only in her late twenties and was pretty, smart and clever. She managed the business successfully all through the war and it sold just about everything. It was a large building on four floors and we lived in a flat above. In spite of shortages and clothing coupons she managed to stock clothes and materials for dressmaking and as much other stock she could acquire bearing in mind it was war time. She had mostly women on the staff but employed a handy man cum cleaner for the heavy work. From an early age she encouraged me to help and taught me all she knew. I was aware that I was privileged. I never went without as some of my friends did. We also escaped the bombing as our town was ten miles inland. We had no other relatives only a distant cousin in the South of England who sent us a Christmas card every year. She is my father's brother's daughter and is ten years older than me. I want to contact her.

I went to the local school and later to a girl's boarding school. I did have friends but when school was over I was needed to help at the store. On Saturdays when we closed we always had a special meal and listened to the Radio. Sometimes went to the Cinema called the 'Rialto' which was an unusual name. When we read Shakespeare at school I found out that the real Rialto was a bridge in Venice and much more glamorous than a rundown wartime cinema. I could never imagine that I would stand on that bridge and become fluent in Italian.

Sometimes Ruth would bring some of the new clothes upstairs and we would try them on. Fridays we would wash our hair. She loved brushing and combing my long fair hair. Hers was dark and also long almost to her waist but she always wore it in a bun. I longed to see her with it combed out but she said she was too old. She had a beautiful face and bone structure but she liked to look severe and businesslike. She was proud of mine and encouraged me to wear it in different ways but at school I wore it in one thick plait. Sundays was our day off and in the summer we often caught the bus to the countryside or the sea where we would picnic and lie in the sun as we had no garden. We would talk about everything and she would discuss my future.

'One day this business will be yours and I want you to learn as much as possible   about finance so try and do well in maths at school. Your father taught Maths and would have encouraged you go to University to study economics. I was only eleven then but knew instinctively that she was right. For as long as I can remember I had a bankbook and when the wages were done on Fridays she always put money in it for me. I still have it and hopefully it will provide me with all I need until I decide what to do next.

Snowy asked me several questions throughout my preamble.

'And did you do well at maths.'

'Yes I always came top of my class and did go on to University to study economics'.

'Did she have any men friends?'

'Not really, she loved my father. They were childhood sweethearts and went to the same school. When he died I was only five yrs old. She missed him and tried not to show her grief openly but I heard her crying at night sometimes. I would often creep into her bed and cuddle close to her. She devoted all her time and energy to the business and my education. We had we six years on our own until Dino came along.

'How did that happen and where did they meet'? Snowy asked.

'He was an Italian prisoner of war in a camp about two miles out of town. Two of them were allowed to help on one of the local farms and they brought the animals to market. He used to come into the shop to buy materials as he was allowed to do some tailoring as a sideline on the camp. He was very popular and the prison staff often asked him to make clothes for their families. Sometimes parachutes were available and he did make some remarkable outfits. He designed and made a wedding dress once for one of their daughters. He was very handsome and he and his younger fellow worker Tony created great excitement with the girls when they came to town. Even in their work clothes they had style and smart haircuts.

It was quite a while before he met Ruth as she spent a lot of time in the office or the stock room. Also her clerk and cashier Gloria monopolised him when he did come in and would not let the other girls serve him. She told them that he was a prisoner and that they were not allowed to 'fraternise' as she called it. She was a plump blonde girl and very glamorous. She wore lots of make up having access to our stock as she took charge of the demonstrations. She also ran a successful corset fitting service. Her rooms were on the second floor. Like Ruth she wore the latest styles when they came in. She also entered beauty pageants and often won prizes. Soon after the war when they opened up the restaurant in the back of the shop she organised fashion shows twice a week. She loved life and spent every weekend going to dances at the local army camps. She longed to meet an American serviceman as some of her friends had done. The odd one or two became GI brides and that was her dream too. Her destiny however like ours went in a different direction.

Once when Dino came in on his own she invited him up for a cup of tea in the main office when Ruth was out. Bob Gray the caretaker saw them once and was not very pleased. He had been wounded in the early part of the war and knew my father and grandfather so he was protective of us. He clearly did not like Dino from the beginning. We put it down to jealousy. Ruth was the sort of woman everyone seemed to like and admire.

Mrs Myra Lee Dino's employer was a widow in her fifties. She was very grateful to him and found both men good and reliable workers. Dino had an eye for business and got her the best prices. He also did a few odd jobs around the house and made her some curtains for her kitchen and covers for her chairs. After the war she wanted him to stay on and help her but Dino had other plans. Myra often came into the shop on market day and was a friend of Ruth's having known her father and mother. She often had coffee with her.

One day they were both outside the bank manager's office chatting. Dino was with her with the day's takings. He was very charming and Mrs Lee introduced him to Ruth as 'my saviour and my right hand man.' People seemed to have forgotten about his status at times, as he was very popular around the town. The camp was about to close so the rules became very lax. I think my mother must have looked lovely as Dino always said that she dazzled him with her beauty and her smart clothes. Dino knew about such things.

'I would like to see her picture', said Snowy.

'I have one in my bedroom, I take it everywhere. I will show it to you later.

Once introduced Dino lost no time in contacting her. Two days later Gloria feeling very put out escorted him up to Ruth's office on an appointment he had made with her. He explained that as the war had ended he was due to go back to Italy during the next few weeks but wanted to return and start up a tailoring business in the town.

He said that he there would be a market for demob suits.

Being a self confident man he lost no time in putting a business plan to her and asked if he could lease a couple of rooms in the shop and set up in business. He said would pay a rent agreeable to both parties and hopefully help increase her trade.

He explained that his family all had contacts in Italy in the fashion industry.

He also had two brothers who would want to join him at a later date.

Funds would not be a problem and after a while they could expand moving into their own premises maybe opening a factory.

Ruth was excited about the idea but being cautious said she would think it over and would meet him again when she had consulted her solicitor. A month later Myra Lee allowed them to meet in her sitting room for a business meeting. He had already told her about his ideas and much as she wanted him to stay on with her she approved and offered to let him lodge with her on his return.

He had also talked to her about getting her some help. He asked around the camp for a likely man who on being demobbed would need a job nearby. She was very grateful to him when he found her a couple who had not been married long. In fact it she was the girl for whom he had made the wedding dress. Her new husband needed a job and was used to farm work. There was a cottage so it was a perfect arrangement.

Again Myra Lee felt beholden to Dino.As she was included in his future plans Dino allowed this to happen. It worked out very well for all parties as Sonia and her husband Jack stayed with her for years and became like her own family. When they had children she quite happily fell into a grandmother role.

About this time Dino found out about the terms of his repatriation and was given a date. Within in three months he was gone and Ruth was busy reorganising the third floor using the plans he had drawn up before he left. He was to use the rooms adjacent to Gloria's fitting room.

I was told nothing of this until he arrived back and was asked to Sunday lunch.

At that time they sat me down and explained it all to me. I knew then that our lives would change. I always wondered why she never discussed it with me. I think it was too personal. She must have been feeling confused and disloyal to my father. This turned out to be the case as she had fallen in love with Dino.

I of course knew a little bit about Dino as I had seen him come into the shop and heard the girls talk about him. To them he almost had film star status. The months back in Italy had obviously done him good. He was relaxed and sun-tanned and seemed even more handsome. No longer a prisoner he exuded self-confidence. He talked non-stop about his plans and new ideas.

In some ways I was pleased as he was friendly and nice to me and brought some fun into our lives. Even on his first visit he sang to the radio when he heard something from La Traviata. 'Opera you will learn to love it as we Italians do. One day I will take you both to LA SCALA in Milan.'

Ruth seemed to light up when he spoke and as he brought plenty of Italian wine even I was allowed a glass occasionally.

'How did you really feel', said Snowy.

'At first I experienced some strong feelings of bewilderment and jealousy.

When other shops struggled with coupons and supplies Dino magically had them imported from Italy and many ready mades too.'

'I wonder how legal that was' said Snowy.

'Probably highly illegal but Ruth was very naive. He was right about the demob suits however and word soon got around the county. Men travelled long distances to have a suit made by Dino.

'He had it all planned didn't he.'

'Yes and he soon became impatient and wanted to hurry the marriage along and take charge completely. Ruth stood firm at first but her simple upbringing and unworldliness was no match for his charm sophistication and powerful personality. He bought her flowers weekly and we always had wine with our food. He also bought her the most exquisite clothes from Italy even though we were still using our clothing coupons.

His brothers played their part as they came and went on their trips to and from Italy. There were three of them in all Dino, Paulo and Roberto. All took part in the charm offensive. They visited the flat made magnificent meals, drank lots of wine and danced and sang to us. They included me in all of this.

Later I saw photographs Roberto had taken of us all in the early years laughing and dancing with the staff at the Xmas party. The girls in the shop loved it and Gloria in particular. She always favoured Dino when Ruth was not around.

Bob Gray the caretaker was retired soon after Dino arrived but to keep Ruth happy Dino saw to it that he had a financial reward for his loyal service.

Dino was meticulous in business and just as meticulous in his relationships with people. His determination to be respected and liked matched his determination to make his fortune. They finally married a year after Dino had arrived back from Italy to the day. I was eleven and the only bride's maid. The townspeople had a lot to say at first but generally they were welcomed as everyone seemed to want their goods. In time Dino very cleverly supported all the charities and became a member of the Round Table and golf club.

He was soon in a strong position to further their interests and made many business contacts. Within two years he had negotiated with The Ministry of Defence to buy some land and hangars on the old camp where he had been interned. Also the airfield and the landing strip which would prove very useful to them. They then opened a factory with Paulo in charge. Unlike his brothers he was an introvert and very serious. He was an accountant and had been interned near London but had managed to study during this time. He married much later to a local sports teacher called Helen.

His younger brother Roberto lived in America during the war with his Uncle Jo who was a dentist in New York. He went to university and studied journalism and photography. He was a talented photographer. At twenty four he was put in charge of setting up the mail order business and the 'in house' catalogue. He was very good looking with black curly hair and the whitest teeth I had ever seen. When he smiled I wanted to smile with him because he lit up the room when he walked in. I suppose people in England at that time did not always have access to good dentists and their diet was poor. When they visited he would always come over and talk to me. He taught me to play cards using pennies.

'Let's pretend we are going to a big casino in Italy.' he would say and often let me win. I loved him dearly and still do. At the time he was married to a girl called Rosa who was American. They had two daughters aged one and two. They joined him later and I enjoyed going to see them when they moved into their new house.

Dino bought some land from Myra Lee and helped him get planning permission to build a large house overlooking the lake next door to her farm. All of this of course affected my life greatly and I began to feel an intruder in our home as Dino monopolised Ruth who adored him. Handing over most of her business interests she retained the ladies fashion part herself and managed her own books. Then even in that area Dino seemed to surpass her and helped her make it more successful.

The fashion dept became a magnet. They attracted buyers sometimes from London who came to look at their stock and see their monthly fashion shows.

They also ordered from their catalogues which were an astounding success. Gloria was included in this expansion and her loyalty was rewarded. She however was never popular with the staff but was a good businesswoman working closely with Dino. She had got to know him well working on the third floor together.Dino wisely needed to keep Ruth busy to allow him freedom to pursue his ambitions. In the end she lost track of all of his business dealings and had to trust him. She gradually did less and less but did keep an eye on her own accounts and always made sure my bankbook was topped up.'

Snowy said 'You sounded as if you were all one happy family. How old were you then?'

'Coming up for seventeen and yes we did have some good times. We went to Italy a lot and I became fluent in the language. They had lots of relatives and large family parties in Tuscany.'

'What happened next.' said Snowy?

'We moved into the new house by the lake designed by Dino. Roberto bought an old house next door adjoining Myra's farm when his family finally joined him. In my eyes it was the perfect house. It was Edwardian with dormer windows and wisteria growing up its walls. It had views of the lake and the fells .The kitchen had an Aga and the life of the house seemed to revolve around that warm log burning stove. I still love it today it is like a poem in itself.'

'I would like to see the Lake District. I hope I will one day and go fell walking.' said Snowy. 'But tell me about your life in the new house.'

CHAPTER 4

THE HOUSE

The house was finished a few months before Ruth's fortieth birthday and she was very excited. It was very large with eight bedrooms, a dining room, breakfast room, games room and two sitting rooms. It had a swimming pool and a cottage attached.

Gloria moved into our old flat. This suited her as she had started to take over some of Ruth's work and even went on buying trips to Italy with Dino.

When we moved in Dino wanted Ruth to take more responsibility in the home and play golf and tennis. He wanted to have dinner parties and improve their status in the community. They also entertained people from London who were in touch with the large fashion houses. Directors came up and often brought their models.

Ruth would do anything he asked of her as she adored him till the day she died.

She was a good hostess and enjoyed her new role. She had a few secrets though and one was my nest egg.

The house was always full of people when I was home. Dino's family kept coming and going there were lots of parties and outdoor meals. Ruth embraced their way of life and spoke fluent Italian.   By this time I was at an exclusive girl's boarding school. I was awarded a scholarship and was determined to do well with the opportunity. It was I suppose my father's legacy as it was his wish that I had the best. I knew it was important to Ruth. It was a relief to go in the end as our old life was finished and our new one was dominated by Dino. Occasionally one of my friends from school would come and stay which led to talk at about our exciting life particularly the parties and the glamorous people.

Roberto by this time had set up a photography studio in the hangars and had started to develop the in house magazine and mail order Company.

The two hangers were extended and more land was bought from Mrs Lee who was still a friend and a shareholder.

Once day Roberto was talking by the pool to a director of a model agency who was organising his next shoot with for the summer catalogue. I was quietly studying in the corner at a table under an umbrella. I was wearing my swimsuit which was still wet. He asked who I was. Roberto explained that I was Dino's stepdaughter. Jack the visitor said. 'Jesus Rob why don't you introduce me to the most beautiful girl I have ever set eyes on. I bring them the best of them up here from London and you have a star in your own back yard.'

Roberto brought him over and introduced him .He looked at me as if he had never seen me before. He stared at me as if he had never danced with me, played cards with me, swam with me and sat under the stars at outdoor parties in Tuscany.

He had watched me play with his children, cook pasta and laughed at my Italian accent.

'I will give you my card young lady, as I would sign you up anytime.' said Jack.

I felt uncomfortable with this as I was in the middle of a maths problem. I quickly pulled my towel around me.

'Thank you but no. I want to go to University. I don't want to be a model. We have much better looking girls at my school who would love that as a career.'

I excused myself quickly and ran to get changed and rushed upstairs to see Ruth who was getting ready to go out. I didn't tell her. We ended up going to town together in her new red sports car which was her birthday present from Dino.

Roberto must have told Dino what Jack had said because one evening when Ruth was getting ready to go out he came to my room and sat talking to me. He often did this I was used to it. I had just got out of the bath and was wearing a dressing gown. My hair, which was normally tied back, was hanging loose and wet. He picked up a towel and came towards me.

'Let me dry your hair like I did when you were young. Remember when you and Ruth used to have your girls night in washing and grooming your hair.'

I felt strange as he said this and slightly nervous. I was on the stool in front of the mirror and he came up behind me. He lifted my hair and rubbed it vigorously.

'It's gorgeous; it's like gold' he said I have not seen it loose for years you always plait it.' He started smiling 'Jo when did you become so beautiful, Roberto said Jack wants you to join his model agency what do you think.'

'Dino please, it is not the life I want. I love studying and I want to go university and get a degree. The headmistress thinks I have the ability to get a first.'

With that he said 'Yes you are right you are your mother's daughter and she is proud of you as am I your stepfather, I shall have to protect you from the Jacks' of this world.'

No more was said as their life was so hectic. Dino had decided to open up another shop in Edinburgh so they were always busy coming and going. The next time I saw Roberto was at our big Xmas party. I had just had my seventeenth birthday and he wanted me to dance. We had a jazz band and I loved dancing to jazz. He often danced with me as we liked the same music.

Being the youngest son he was about twenty six whereas Dino and Paulo were nearly forty. He was also the best looking of the brothers. Dino was short and a compact, a powerful looking man with strong features and piercing dark eyes. Paulo was tall but severe and businesses like and had cultivated English ways. He was polite and well mannered. He was successful in the stock market and managed the company's finances.

Roberto was tall and handsome with curly black hair. He was always dressed in black and wore expensive sweaters and leather jackets. Sometimes he wore a scarf in a bright colour. Even when I was young he dazzled me. When we stopped for a drink he said.

'Jo come over one day to the hanger and let me take some shots of you. I could take a special one and present it to Ruth for her birthday. Bring some pretty clothes.'

I had had one glass of champagne and felt quite giddy so I agreed.

I had been given my horse Bonny the year before by Dino and loved riding out.

The brothers were developing a taste for racing alongside their new business ventures. I kept Bonny in Mrs Lee's stables. She knew a lot about horses and I agreed to let the other children ride her when I was away at school.

I said I would call in the hangar during the following week as I went riding every day during the holidays. I often had coffee at the farm. Mrs Lee was happy with her new family and would still do anything for Dino. In a way she had been partly responsible for some of his success as she had invested in his company and allowed him to buy her land at rock bottom prices. He had rewarded her buy getting Paulo to advise her on other investments so she had no longer to rely on farming for an income.

On the way to the hangar I remembered that I said that I would take some clothes for the photographs. However I did not think it significant as I only wanted one taken for Ruth's fortieth birthday the next month and my riding outfit would be appropriate.

I had never been in the studio before. At one time the upper floor of the shop had been used. Roberto had made quite a lot of money taking poly photos where a whole sheet was taken for a minimum price encouraging the buyer to invest in larger and more expensive portraits. A lot of my friends had had them done and I assumed that's what Roberto intended doing picking out the ones we liked for Ruth.

I tied up my horse and went in. I was amazed by the size of the place and the equipment. It reminded me of pictures I had seen in magazines of film sets. There were several large cameras, lots of furniture and props and sets laid out a sitting rooms and outdoor scenes. There was a bar and several sofas with hundreds of books and magazines lining the shelves.

Roberto was there alone and came to greet me. He stroked Bonny my horse and helped me tie him up outside.

'Jo it's great to see you but seeing your horse gives me an idea I could take some shots of you riding. I like the white breeches, they are very smart and your blue tweed jacket matches your beautiful eyes.'

He showed me around. There was a dark room where several hundred negatives were developing. The catalogue was circulated throughout the country and it was from the offices next door they were printed and sent out. I had met several girls from my old school who had managed to get work in the office. Roberto poured himself a glass of wine and offered me one. Although everyone in their family drank wine regularly I was still at school and Ruth only allowed me to have a drink at dinner parties. I refused but Roberto put his hand on my shoulder challenging me and gave me a glass of Vino.

'Come on drink up there is only the two of us. We can have some fun like we do on the dance floor. We do have music here too. I will play you some Dizzy Gillespie later, now where's your gear'.

'I haven't any I forgot'.

'No matter we have wardrobes full and the very latest models you could try some on.'

'I thought perhaps you could take a few of me with my horse, Ruth would like that'.

'Of course but promise me you will let me take one or two others whilst you are here. Come and look in the wardrobe dept.' he said leading me up to another floor which housed the stock. He encouraged me to try on several dresses. One was dark blue silk, an off the shoulder evening dress, three quarter length.

I looked at myself in the long mirror and had to admit that it did look pretty. I suddenly felt shy and apprehensive about exposing myself. I did have some expensive clothes but they were country clothes mainly suits and separates. As I came out of the dressing room holding on to my modesty Roberto stood looking at me in surprise. He stroked his chin and paused and then looked me up and down and told me to 'do a twirl.'

"You look ravishing but come and sit down I need you to put on some lipstick and rouge and pile some of your hair up. I am going to make you look fabulous'.

He found some combs and pinned half of my hair up and showed me how to apply makeup. I had only been allowed to use a little before. We often experimented in the dormitory but Roberto knew how to apply it professionally. I did not recognise myself when he had finished. It did not look like me in the mirror anymore and I wasn't sure how I felt about my new image.

He put on some music Dean Martin an American crooner. Then he sat me down in an antique chair and posed me as if I were a member of the royal family. He then brought out some imitation jewellery and put them round my neck and at the same time he pulled down my sleeves and neckline.

He then took about ten shots from different angles. He talked all the time suggesting what I should be thinking about as I smiled.

'Listen to Dean Martin *Amore Amore.* Think of your boyfriend Jo look excited and happy'.

'I haven't got one' I replied shyly.

'What! Well there's a surprise you will have them falling at your feet one day.

Dino will make sure Ruth takes care of you no doubt. Girls in Italy are still chaperoned and he takes his stepfather role very seriously.'

This touched a raw nerve as recently Dino had finally persuaded Ruth to let him adopt me and take his name. I did not like the idea but Ruth could see no harm and liked being the wife of such a successful businessman whom she loved very much.

She seemed to have forgotten about my father and how important it was to me to cling to his name.

'Get up now Jo I want you to pretend you have just arrived home after a ball. Lie on the sofa and stretch out your legs, kick of your shoes and laugh. Hold the glass of wine, the boring ball is over and all the old men who ogled you are long gone'.

I did as he asked and he took lots of shots laughing as he did so.

'You're a natural Jo'.

I realised it was getting late so I got up and began to get changed back into my riding clothes. As I came out of the dressing room he said.

'Don't put your jacket on yet and leave your hair down. I want to take a shot of you like this, sit on the chair. Here hold your whip like this'. He sat straddled across the chair and then sat me down in the same pose.

He pulled my hair around my shoulders and unbuttoned the top three buttons of my shirt. I was embarrassed but stayed there trusting his judgement knowing full well that Ruth would like my princess pose for her birthday portrait.

'That's going to be something', he muttered under his breath.

I held the whip as he said and watched him smile and then raise his eyebrows.

'A very successful shoot indeed Jo, it all looks good. Thanks for being such a good model. Shall we take you on your pony now'?

I put the rest of my things on quickly, took some of the makeup off and became myself again a happy open air girl sitting on my horse. Roberto took several and then helped me down locking the hangar as I took my pony back to the stable.

He waited for me and gave me lift home.

"I shall get these developed as soon as possible Jo. I will let you choose the one you want for Ruth. It's our secret. We will enlarge it and put it in an expensive Italian frame. I have been importing some lately and they are selling well. People like them over their fireplaces. I can just see your mother and Dino giving it pride of place.'

He put his hand on my arm as I came out and kissed me on the cheek.

'Don't forget you are a lovely young woman and I could get Jack involved anytime you say the word'.

I smiled at him. I did have a good time and it had all seemed so harmless. Roberto was fun and had been really nice to me. On the way home I smiled to myself. He had that effect on me.

I began to think that perhaps one day when I had finished my studies I could earn some money as a model after all but not yet. My headmistress had high hopes of me and had talked to Ruth about going to Edinburgh University for my interview during the month ahead.

I saw the prints a week later. Roberto called in one evening when I was alone.

Dino and Ruth were at the golf club. It was a two weeks before Ruth's birthday. He helped himself to a drink and then sat down on the sofa next to me with his portfolio.

'They are very good Jo, Ruth is going to love them'.

He handed them to me.

'Which one do you like? I love the one on the sofa it is very sexy? he said but Ruth is going to like the princess one best don't you agree.'

'Yes but I like the one on my horse too'.

'Well yes you look like the girl we know and love. We can frame them but knowing Dino as I do this will be the one over the fireplace believe me the dress is the same colour as your eyes and your hair looks in magnificent condition. I must say I did rather well combing it like that, you look like Veronica Lake'.

'Where is the other one?' I asked?

'I don't know, the negatives weren't there. Sometimes they get mixed up and are sent to Italy by mistake, it's a pity I was looking forward to seeing them. But we achieved what we wanted to do. I will get them framed and perhaps you can wear the dress at the party what do you think'?

He got up to go taking the prints. He put his arm around me as he walked out singing quietly to himself. At the door he pulled me to him and kissed me on the cheek but he stayed holding me for a few moments looking into my eyes and I was unable to release myself. I was confused 'Save the last dance for me sweetheart.' he said as he left.

CHAPTER 5

RUTHS BIRTHDAY.

I was leaving school around the time of Ruth's birthday and was waiting for the results of my sixth form exams.

I had been accepted into Edinburgh University to study Italian and Economics.

Dino suggested that during all of my breaks I learned a bit more about managing a store. He was opening one in Edinburgh and had already acquired a flat there.

He was very keen for me to join the business one-day.

Ruth agreed and persuaded me to do as Dino suggested so again I gave way and we were taken to look at the flat. It was very elegant and across the road from the new store in a modern block. The windows at the back overlooked the river.

Ruth was as thrilled as I was and Dino let us furnish it the way we wanted.

We chose some Italian furnishings which Dino had imported, from Milan.

He said that I might be able to use the flat when I went to university.

Ruth seemed so happy since she married Dino and although I missed our days together I did not have many regrets. He had fulfilled all of our expectations.

The birthday was a surprise for Ruth. Roberto rang me to say that he had framed the picture and would take it with him. His call was short and to the point and I had not seen him since he left the house that night. I had picked up the blue dress from our store as Roberto had left it for me with the costume jewellery. I dressed quickly and put a cape over it so Ruth did not see what I was wearing as she was laughing and joking with Dino in the bedroom.

She was putting on her on new silver evening dress and Dino was about to present her with a sapphire necklace to go with it. Their suite was at the other end of the house and they did not meet up with me until our chauffeur arrived in a limousine.

Ruth looked radiantly happy. I kept that memory of her that evening always.

She looked everything she was a beautiful raven-haired successful woman with a kind heart and a loving husband by her side. For once she had her hair combed out in a pageboy style bob which was fashionable at that time and it suited her.

We were taken about fifteen miles away to a large country hotel tucked away in the Lake District, the most prestigious one Dino could find. When we arrived the family were waiting. Some had travelled from Italy that day and were staying there. The hotel matched anything Italy could offer in style and grandeur.

I had told Ruth that I was going to give her my present in the evening. However I had bought her some *CAPE DE MONTE* glass she liked which I gave her in the morning. I had bought it in Naples on a previous visit.

She remarked on my dress and said how beautiful and grown up I looked in it.

The ballroom in the hotel was lit with candles and there were two bands playing one after the other. There were ten round tables ready laid for us all with ornate flower arrangements of pink roses and white orchids. We were given champagne when we arrived and then we were served. The meal was Ruth's favourite a Scottish salmon dish followed by fresh strawberries and cream. A very large birthday cake followed and a ceremony to mark the occasion. Dino made a charming speech about how much Ruth meant to him and how his life had changed once he had met her. He also included me saying that to make it all extra special he was officially adopting me and from that moment I was to be known as Jo Grimaldi. They had discussed it for months and in the end I gave in as Ruth said it meant so much to Dino as they would never have children. Everyone cheered and hugged me and welcomed me into their family. I accepted it all with a few misgivings as really I wanted to have my own name and my own identity.

Afterwards Ruth opened her presents and finally unveiled mine, which was on an easel. She was surprised and thrilled, as she looked in awe at her daughter in the large portrait. It did not look like the real me in the same way that being Jo Grimaldi did not feel like the real me. The sophisticated girl in the portrait confronting us had discarded her glasses and a plait had her hair hanging in golden curls and was wearing her first evening dress, which was low and revealing. She was cool and composed with skilful make up highlighting her high cheekbones.

The room applauded and Dino stood back in amazement. He at once declared he had the perfect place for it and commissioned Roberto to take one of Ruth also saying that he wanted the portraits of his two beautiful women together over the fireplace for posterity. I still would have preferred the one on my pony but everyone seemed delighted especially Ruth who at the end of the day loved fashion and clothes.

Everyone congratulated Roberto. He had already made a name for himself in Milan and London and was commanding high prices. I watched him dancing with his wife and he only had eyes for her. She was an artist and had started to design children's clothes for the catalogue and was in touch with several American stores and Art Directors as her family were dealers. As they finished their dance they came over to our table.

Rosa sat and chatted to Ruth and then Roberto asked me to dance. The jazz band in the next room was playing traditional jazz. The two women laughed at him and Rosa said jokingly

'Behave yourself Rob she has to come down to earth tomorrow and come home with us, not to Milan or Hollywood.'

Roberto laughed and actually blushed like a small boy as if being chastised by his mother.

The band played all the music I liked. We had some records at home of Miles Davis, Dizzy Gillespie, Fats Waller, Ella Fitzgerald, and Billy Holiday. My father had collected them and I listened to them all the time and over the years had picked up the rhythms. I could play the odd tune myself as I had piano lessons over the years and had achieved good grades. Roberto was a good dancer and we enjoyed ourselves. He laughed when I threw off my shoes. He shouted at me over the music.

'You're born to dance Jo you should do it more often'.

Then they played the blues something haunting and sad about love and heartache. Roberto held onto me and tightened his grip.

'Come over sometime again Jo to the studio before you go. I have some more ideas for another shoot. We could go riding together. I like being with you we have become good friends haven't we.'

I pulled away and said and 'Sorry Roberto I can't, I really can't, but I knew I wanted to.' He had a powerful effect on me and it felt uncomfortable.

I left him on the dance floor and went back to Ruth and Dino.

'Look at you" said Dino as I approached, 'Now I am a proud father I want to dance with my new daughter in her beautiful dress. With that he got the band to play and waltzed me round to a delighted crowd.

We ended up drinking champagne whilst Ruth and Dino finally danced together for the next half-hour. It was the end of a perfect evening for Ruth but within a few weeks she was to get some news that would change all of our lives forever.

CHAPTER 6

THE NIGHT BEFORE.

I started helping stock the new store in the summer before I was due to start University and stayed at the flat. It was to be a very expensive designer store in the city centre to attract a new generation of fashion conscious women.

Gloria managed our other store most of the time and had become reliable and trusted by both Dino but she was not popular with the staff however and tried on many occasions to undermine me if I had been given any responsibility. It was almost as if she was in league with Dino against Ruth and me. It was subtle but a reality as she reported everything to him when he was back from a trip. Sometimes I felt I was the grown up and Ruth was the child as she did not seem to understand that Gloria was not all she made herself out to be. She had always valued her and declared she would never have managed without her. We had many suppliers, beautiful clothes and a beauty shop and a hairdresser. Gloria and all the models were allowed discounts in these departments as they had regular fashion shows in the shop and after hours in hotels. She made sure she was first in line for new products when they came in and she made herself look smart and fashionable at all times. Unlike Ruth she had a voluptuous figure and was popular with male businessmen on sales trips. She liked the Italians and made sure she picked up as much of the language as possible. She would often stay late with Dino and his brothers discussing business

Dino did not seem to think this odd or unusual but the rest of the staff talked.

In their eyes Gloria had always had a reputation and they remembered the days when she young and out and about with the American servicemen spending nights away from home. Ruth chose to ignore all of this as Dino professed to all his great love for her and her only and I believed this to be true. He liked to think of her at home waiting for him. He wanted her by his side be at dinners at the golf club or at the big hotels when important customers travelled up from London. He showered her with presents especially if he had been away. In five years he had changed from an apologetic, polite, but ambitious prisoner of war to a smart, clever and very rich business man. He worked tirelessly to achieve this and changed our store into one of the most respected institutions in the North of England. It was also the first to operate a clothing catalogue service.

The week after her birthday Ruth decided to visit her Dr. I was in Edinburgh and Dino was in Milan. She was concerned as she had found a lump in her breast and not being too worried decided to quietly get it dealt with whilst Dino was away. She was to come up to visit me at the weekend and was not seeing Dino for another two weeks. She was at the flat when I got there. When I walked in she was sitting on our new expensive white sofa looking out of the window at the spectacular view of the river and the bridges beyond. She wore a black suit, a cream silk blouse and patent shoes. I shall always remember the way she looked that day, so smart and elegant. She had opened a bottle of wine and I was surprised to see that she had already drunk half a bottle. She never did that and I immediately realised something was wrong. She did not see me come in. Her face said it all as she turned to look at me, whatever it was it was bad news.

What I did not know until that moment was that the biopsy was positive and that she had to have a mastectomy as soon as they could schedule it.

I was the first person to know and she refused to tell Dino on the phone. He rang every night.

I hugged her and we both clung to one another and cried and cried and finished the wine and another bottle straight after.

'You've got to tell him' I said.

'No it will be all over and done with before he gets back. He will drive me mad with his fussing'.

'But he will never forgive me for not telling him and he will be hurt.'

'It's the way I want it Jo please do not tell him. I have to go in tomorrow here in the Royal Infirmary. I have told Dino that you and I are going to the Highlands for a few days and to call us when we get back. The builders are in this week here so you can make yourself scarce and come to the Infirmary with me if you want to.'

'Of course I will. I will be there day and night for you. I will never leave your sight, you're my mother and I love you.'

'I have written a letter to Dino just in case there are problems. I have said that it was my idea to go in and get the operation done secretly and that you resisted it but he was not to blame you for anything. If I don't survive I want him to make sure you are looked after. I want you to hold on to your birth certificates, and adoption papers.

Dino will have copies. I also want to give you your savings book now.'

She handed it to me. 'No one knows about the money not even Gloria or our accountant. As you will see there is quite a lot as I sold a property just before I met Dino so that has increased the balance. I love the Italian family but there's always been a lot of wheeling and dealing going on so I could never predict what the financial future would be. They could go bankrupt for all I know.'

I took the book and was amazed at the balance. It was quite a substantial sum.

It was a relief to have it however as it immediately made me feel more secure.

I hugged her and thanked her through my tears.

She then said 'Dino has done well for us. I do love him but he never replaced your father in my heart. I am not blind Jo I am aware that he is an attractive man and men like him and his brothers are not always faithful to their wives. It is accepted in Italy and they are after all in the fashion business and always surrounded by beautiful girls. Roberto is typical. He is charming and extremely lovable and such fun to have around. I have noticed that he is very fond of you. He watches you all the time. My birthday portrait was his creation and one of his best but it was not the real you.

He loves Rosa and the girls so try not to get too entangled. I think he will leave the business and move into films or maybe photojournalism as he is very ambitious and has had lots of offers.'

I had never realised that Ruth had picked up on this but she knew me well and probably noticed how I behaved around Roberto. I would have liked to have talked to her about it.

'Try and stick to your plan and finish your degree. It's your route to a great future and hopefully you will not lose track of our business and let the Italians completely take over.'

'You talk as if you everything will go wrong you're frightening me.'

'No I have to say these things they are important. When I come out of the operation I may be ill for a long while. I need to tell you now whilst we are alone and can share our thoughts.'

She spent the next hour telling me about my father and grandfather and told me where all the photographs were kept. When we finally went to bed she tucked me in and kissed me the way she did when I was little.

That time together was precious and loving.

CHAPTER 7

RUTH

Ruth did not survive. She did not even come around after her operation.

I held her hand until the last minute and I was the last face she would ever see before she went into theatre. She was happy and smiling as if showing me and telling me how to be brave in adversity. She was my beautiful mother full of love for me and it broke my heart when they told me the awful truth.

We had both been so optimistic and had started planning a trip to Italy as soon as she recuperated. Having had few symptoms apart from tiredness, which we put down to her hectic business and social life she was riddled with cancer which had metastasized everywhere.

Alone and cold at 2 am I was comforted by the nurses and Drs who explained everything to me. My thoughts were with Dino. He would be devastated, shocked and furious that he had not been told about her operation.

They contacted Roberto first for me who was at home a hundred miles away.

He sounded calm and expressed his sorrow but mainly he was concerned about me. He said I had to go to the flat and he would talk to Dino in Italy and drive straight up arriving hopefully at dawn.

It was a cold rainy night reflecting my gloom and despair.

I shivered and could not get warm. I wanted to go to sleep and wake up in last week when things were good and Ruth was there. But the realization came to me that I had no one else in my life to turn to. I could not predict how Dino would be. There had been alienation in his attitude to Ruth and myself recently. He had always declared how much he loved me and how proud of me he was doing so well at school but I had always had unease about these elaborate proclamations. He had created an empire since he met and married Ruth and his life seemed to be dominated by money and acquiring a good name for himself. Lately he had been away from home a lot in America and Italy and when he was home he had worked late. Ruth had never complained but after her birthday she seemed to spend more time alone. Dino wanted her to focus on opening the new branch for a while at first and let Gloria run the old one but in the end she became superfluous.

Roberto had been away too in America where he was anxious to get into filming and photojournalism. He had studied the management of the three main superstores Montgomery Ward, Sears Roebuck and JC Penny in the USA learning about their distribution methods and their pick up services in most towns using catalogues.

All of this information he had passed on to his brothers who had begun to train managers and create new outlets.

He had several times mentioned that he wanted to go back to New York to concentrate on his photography but at the same time keep his share and input into the business in England. The portrait of Ruth had never been done in the six months, which had passed mainly because Roberto and Ruth were never around at the same time and Dino seemed to have lost interest. Dino had also insisted that Gloria who now also managed the model agency they had created should take on more responsibility. She had a large pay rise and there was talk about her being a director. The mail-order business was going so well they found it more convenient to recruit their own models.

Ruth had been my best friend and having left school any friends I had made in the sixth form were already at University. There had been such a turnover of girls in the shop as it had modernised that some drifted away to other jobs. In fact the only member of the old staff was Gloria. I found her difficult to engage with particularly in the last few months. She had always been off hand with me and probably thought I was a spoilt child but I knew I worked hard and in spite of my privileges intended to do so always. Rosa was Ruth's best friend and I knew she would support me.

I had grown fond of their children. However it turned out that she was on a buying trip to London and they were staying with Paulo and Helen.

I brought Ruth's personal possessions back to the flat. I found the letter for Dino from Ruth. Then there was a package for me who included the sapphires and a copy of her will, my bank book, my birth certificate, my adoption papers and my passport.

I was surprised that she had the forethought to do all of this but she was a good businesswoman to the end. Her letter was simple but insightful and so very painful to read.

'My Darling Jo,
I may be ill for a long time when I come round so it is important for me to write this to you.

My will is with Mr Deverell and there is a large bequest to you as the major part of the business is in my name and Dinos'.

However my department always had been intended for you to run or to sell to Dino.

Dino has always been good to me and brought love into my life. I love him dearly although as I always told you your father was the true love of my life.

Dino is not without faults and the Grimaldis' may be up to all sorts of business dealings I do not know about.

I know he has his ruthless side which he never allowed us to see so you must turn to Mr Deverell in an emergency.

You could try and find our cousin in Surrey.

I am so proud of you. You are very beautiful, talented and have been a perfect daughter and friend.

Dino and the family think so too but they may want to exploit your looks and talent and encourage you to go into modelling particularly Roberto.

Since the portrait he has asked me several times to let you sit for him again.

He is very engaging, handsome and flirtatious but he is married. He makes it no secret that he thinks you could go far but please think seriously before you enter that murky world. I know I talked to you about this but it is important you take it seriously.

I hope I live to see you falling in love and getting married to some nice man who you will love forever. I want you to have children.

What a joy that would be and I would love being a grandmother.

Read everything you can that will advance your business knowledge in any way including the law. If you decide to carry on in the fashion business remember there are other outlets you could explore France, Sweden and America for instance. Look at the young people around you and go into an Art School and look for talent.

It is possible to conduct a business ethically but you already know my views. Value and respect your staff and hopefully they will respect you.

Remember me always if you are on your own, as I shall always being with you in spirit. Be strong and keep your own counsel.

We have never been religious but I have had faith in God all my life and still have. Hold on to my love and think of me always.

All my love forever
Ruth.

It broke my heart.

I took a taxi to the flat I and had no sooner arrived when the phone rang.

It was Roberto to say that he would be with me early in the morning. He had spoken to Dino who was already on a flight to Edinburgh. He also said that he was in deep shock and very upset that he knew nothing about the operation so I had some explaining to do. I did not even undress but collapsed on the sofa and fell asleep.

CHAPTER 8

GRIEF

I awoke to banging on the door and quickly orientated myself. It was 6 am in morning. It was Roberto looking tired and unshaven.For all my misgivings it was wonderful to see him. I realized that he was the nearest I had to family at that time and the only one who could help ease my pain.He had driven all night in his fast car.

He put his arms around me and I sobbed, grateful to be held.

'My darling girl what you have been through but I am here for you now and Dino is coming later'.

He held me for a long time and then I made him some coffee whilst he showered and changed.

As we sat in the window watching the dawn break over the city I tried to explain Ruth's attitude to her unexpected illness. She felt it was best to keep the news from Dino to stop him getting upset and stressed unnecessarily.

'It was so like her. Do you think Dino will ever forgive me? He never had a chance to say goodbye'. I said looking searchingly at Roberto for an answer.

He put his arms around me.

'Look at me Jo. You did not know this would happen. Dino will understand and will be sorry that you have had to deal with it on your own. You are only nineteen how could you have known it would end like this.'

After a while I had a rest until Dino arrived. Roberto found a mild sedative in the bathroom cabinet and made me a drink. I did sleep and woke up at midday to hear Dino and Rob talking in the sitting room.

I quickly dressed and went to join them. Dino stood up and greeted me. He looked grey and unshaven and had a bottle of whisky in front of him. He clearly was in a state of shock but hugged me tightly saying

"Jo why has she gone my beautiful Ruth. Did she talk about me- did she love me'.

'She loved you very much and told me so when she went in for her anaesthetic.

There is a letter for you. She wrote to us both.'

He stayed for about an hour finishing the whisky and going in to a trance like state staring at his glass his letter on his lap unopened. After a while he got up and booked himself into a hotel and said he would go to the hospital on his own to see Ruth's body and ordered a taxi. However Roberto insisted on going with him and said he would come back later to stay with me at the flat.

I found out later that Dino had also phoned Gloria to ask her to come up straight away. The next day when we met she was already there taking complete charge of Dino. It was a sign of things to come and even in my naivety I realised that she would change everything as she had started to do in the last few months. Things began to fall into place as I it became obvious that she had some sort of power over Dino. It all came out later that she had been his mistress since around the time of Ruth's birthday. She had not been at the party, which was a subject of gossip. As she lived in our old flat people put two and two together. They regularly travelled together to Italy on business.

Whether Ruth had known I would never know but she did believe Dino loved her. I had very little knowledge of sexual affairs only gossip and what I read in magazines and saw on the telvision.Ruth and I had lived such a quiet existence. She believed in people and looked for their goodness. She was so unworldly.Dino had been charmed by this and wanted to keep it this way. However the brothers lived and worked in a competitive world which dealt in beauty, fashion and sexuality. They were also in a position to exploit people particularly young women which to them became like commodities to be promoted when fashionable and discarded when they had passed their sell by date.

I sorted Ruth's clothes out and packed them in to plastic bags, tidied the flat and did some shopping for milk and bread.

Roberto came back about eight and said that he would take me out to dinner.

We walked down the road to a small hotel, which had a jazz restaurant in the cellar.

'I thought this place might cheer you up a bit Jo, Rosa and I came last time we were here'. It was small and expensive with its own regular jazz pianist. I wasn't hungry but managed to eat a little. As usual he ordered a bottle of Chianti. He did his very best to say all the right things. He talked about how much they had loved having Ruth as part of their family and he hoped I would also look to him as a proper uncle figure whenever I needed anything. This was a different Roberto to the one I had become used to. He was thoughtful and kind and I could finally see why Rosa loved him so much. I picked at my food and ate mechanically but I did have one glass of wine. He suggested that I might want to rethink my future. We talked about Rosa and his children.

"Rosa wants you to come back with me and stay for a while the children would love it. They adore your pony and keep wanting me to buy them one what you think? Perhaps until you go to University. It would be better than being alone in that big house with Dino or on your own here now things are different. There was talk today about using this flat for entertaining when business people come up from London.'

'It's so nice of you both to ask me perhaps I will for the time being. I don't think Gloria will want me around much I seem to annoy her."

He made no comment but I knew he understood. We chatted for a while about nothing in particular but it was a strain for me and he suggested we went back. He held my hand all the way. When we arrived back he watched TV whilst I got ready for bed and then like a father tucked me in and gave me another sedative sitting for a while holding my hand as I drifted off to sleep.   I thought I heard him talking on the phone to Dino.I could have dreamt it. He was speaking in Italian. He was saying something like. 'She is fine I will take care of her she can stay with us when we get back until you decide her future. You are to stop blaming her. Ruth explained everything to you in her letter. The poor girl has lost her mother too we have to look after her. Come on now Gloria will be with you soon she will cheer you up When is she arriving, oh ten o'clock at Waverley. I see that soon well she hasn't wasted much time. I will see you tomorrow then Chow.'

When I awoke Roberto was lying on the bed next to me fully dressed looking at me? I sat up quickly holding on to sheet.

'Don't be alarmed Jo .I was just going to wake you but I wanted to look at you for a while. You looked like an angel lying there did you sleep.'

I nodded, and then everything came back as the sunlight flooded the room. I stared out of the window to the mountains beyond and said a little prayer asking for help to get through the next few days. I felt Ruth's presence in the room.

Then Roberto jumped up and said 'I will bring you some coffee and run your bath and we can face the day together, don't cry I will be here so be brave.'

I bathed and dressed and heard him on the phone to Dino again.

When I joined him for croissants and coffee he told me the gist of his conversation with Dino. Evidently Dino was needed for two or three days whilst they conducted the autopsy and made arrangements for Ruth's body to be returned to the Lake District. Gloria was staying with him and doing some hiring for the new shop. She was to be overall manager and was to train a locality manager to engage the rest of the staff. They were to use the flat and I was to return for good and help out where needed until I went to university.

Dino would talk to me later about this but if I did go to Edinburgh I was to live in the halls of residence and not in the flat Dino and Ruth had bought for us.

Already I was starting to feel uncomfortable and insecure about my future.

Roberto tried to be gentle with me.

'Jo Dino is so upset, it seems his therapy is to charge around planning things.

Don't take it personally he loves you dearly we all do.'

Ruth's words came home to me, as they would always do in the next few years.

'Keep your own counsel and watch the family. I knew then she was right but it wasn't the family I had to watch it was Gloria.'

Roberto then told me that we were to travel back straight away to the Lake District to his home. Rosa had been contacted and she would be home when we got there. Roberto had his Mazerati car and as he piled our luggage in he turned to me and said. 'I will always watch over you I promise. Remember that. I love you.'

I had allowed myself to believe the uncle story but I realised how much I was beginning to love him too. I always had. It was all mixed up with Ruth's death my loneliness and somebody to be there for me. Ruth had spelt it out before she died. He was married and I would be foolish to get involved. I had liked the odd boy at school but I was never allowed to go to parties and dances and was always chaperoned. I was to be sheltered and protected the Italian way.

In spite of that as I sat beside him in the car and looked at his hands on the steering wheel I was aware of him in a strange way.

I wanted to touch his hair that always fell over his forehead. I wanted to push it back out of his eyes as he often did himself. I wanted him to look at me the way he had done that morning on my bed. It had been a look of love.

All the way home he talked to me, flattered me and tried to cheer me up.

In fact he did when he pointed out a young couple getting into a car with a new baby.

They were oblivious to the world as they carefully passed their precious bundle from one to the other.

'One day I hope that's you Jo. It is a wonderful thing being a parent.

You are so like Ruth and look what a wonderful job she has done with such a beautiful and talented daughter. I want you to get to know my girls they are going to love you.'

As we stopped at a roadside café he was protective to me and held my arm sitting me comfortably whilst he went off for drinks.

He came back sat opposite me and said.

'You're looking much better after the fresh air with my hood down. Why don't you go and comb your hair put on some lipstick and make a grand entrance. Go on I dare you, make those lorry drivers jealous of me'.

I did as he said but kept my coat on and crept in through another door. I was after all my mothers' daughter,

He was very amused by this then he asked my about the horses at Mrs Lees.

He told me that he used to ride in the mountains in Italy and would like to do so again saying that we could ride out together on the fells.

He made it all sound so idyllic. He fulfilled his role perfectly and did ease the pain.

I still remember every moment of the ride back from Edinburgh from the moment he held my hand as I got into his car. In some ways he seemed like a hero in a novel.

It was dreamlike and unreal. It was unreal, a fantasy was it love? I did not know.

I knew that I was a young girl innocent and naïve and about to enter a new phase in my life. It would be a new world, out of my comfort and safety and into deeper water.

CHAPTER 9

CHANGES

So much happened in the next few weeks which affected my status, my future and my personal life.

Throughout my story Snowy listened carefully.

'That was so hard for you losing your mother. Please continue. Take your time. I am beginning to understand what you were up against. Tell me what happened next.'

'Well if things were bad the day Ruth died they got worse. After the very large funeral complete with hundreds of mourners we allowed Ruth to rest in the village churchyard close to her family graves. I tried to be brave and sat dutifully next to Dino.Rosa and Roberto supported me throughout the ordeal and Myra stayed by my side offering help and advice. I was grateful for that. We had a very expensive reception afterwards where Dino gave a fine speech about his wonderful Ruth almost identical to the one he had read out on her birthday. It sounded hollow this time. He vowed he would take care of his beautiful daughter who would he was sure live up to her mother's good name. He did appear to forgive me but I never lived in our home again.

Gloria gradually moved in and they were married within six months. My portrait and my possessions were moved out one day and there was never any mention of a legacy. Gloria even demanded the sapphires as his second wife.

I did not visit Mr Deverall as he too died unexpectedly. His son took over and he was Dino's solicitor. I stayed six months with Rosa and Roberto.

He was away most of the time spending weeks at a time in America. Rosa was an exceptionally nice woman who tried to welcome me as an addition to her family.

I kept reminding myself that my attachment to Roberto was ridiculous. I had been upset when Ruth had died and let my imagination run away with me. Posy and Poppy were great fun and I played a lot with them. I read them stories; baby-sat and put them to bed. I also helped teach them to ride. We saw a lot of Myra and it was a happy and healing time.

Whenever I was with Roberto he was thoughtful and kindly. If ever I was alone with him, which was rare, he behaved like a brother or an uncle the way he had always been for years. I gradually accepted this and relaxed with him and enjoyed his company. After his many trips he would bring all of us gifts home. We loved these times as he always had some treat or trip up his sleeve. He used to take us sailing on Lake Windermere and we had to play 'Swallows and Amazons.' and have surprise picnics. We would cook on a campfire. The children adored him and so did I.

Myra was also welcoming and kind to me for she had liked Ruth. She was a happy old lady of sixty surrounded by her grandchildren by adoption and got on well with their parents who ran her farm with great success. She was very wise and she seemed to understand how I was feeling. They all contributed to my partial recovery but I found that I was at my happiest taking care of the children. Rosa would disappear to her studio in the barn where she designed her clothes for an ever-increasing market. She and I had lots of nice moments together and she tried to fulfil Ruth's role. She allowed me the space to talk about Ruth and what she would have wanted for me in the future.

By this time Gloria had a large say in running of the shops and there was no mention of me getting involved at all anymore. When I did see Dino the conversations were mainly about me going to University. Gloria made it quite clear that she wanted me off the scene as soon as possible. I made no more trips to Italy as she became epicentre of their lives and Dino let her have her way on everything. She had a limousine with a driver and used Ruth's sports car. They entertained lavishly and had several servants who came in daily. I was never invited and almost forgotten about. She rarely spoke to me and if she could undermine me she would. I was playing tennis with Rosa and two Italian businessmen once. They were friends of Dino's

I had a short tennis skirt on and she complained to Dino that the men were making innuendoes about me and that I was drinking with them and encouraging them. This was not true. I left after the tennis match with Rosa whilst they continued talking to a group of models including Gloria. This happened all the time and she knew its effect on Dinothere would get very angry and banned me from being around when they had business meetings at home. He had strong feelings that I should be introduced to decent men when it was the right time. This was the Italian way.

There were also a lot of legal difficulties regarding my standing and my legacy. It was never mentioned but occasionally it would be alluded to and quickly forgotten.

I never signed any papers and in my simple understanding of business dealings knew that if it were important I would have to. I knew that when I twenty-one things would change and I made up my mind to wait until then before challenging my status.

I did not have anyone to discuss it with but I thanked Ruth for my secret legacy safe inside a locked strong box in a bank in Edinburgh with my documents.

Just before my first term in Edinburgh Rosa informed me that they too were all leaving for America. She had secured a lot of work there and Roberto was having great success with his photography. He as a free lance had so much work offered to him he wanted to pursue it. It meant him travelling worldwide. He was going to hand over most of the family business to his cousin Tony who was already over there.

This saddened me as they were all I had as family and I would miss them all very much. Paulo would move into his house with his family with a view to buying it if they stayed in America. They were always very pleasant to me but had always lived the other side of town and Helen had always carried on with her teaching. However she did make a point of saying that I would always be a welcome guest as I did not think she got on very well with Gloria either.

CHAPTER 10

MILAN

I enjoyed my first year at University. I had my own room but shared a communal kitchen. I made friends with two or three of the students but never went out much.

There was lots of work to do as our seminar commitments and our written assignments were strictly monitored. We had to work hard. Economics was not an easy option but I was determined to learn as much as possible to equip me for the business world. Italian was easy for me and the tutors looked to me for conversation and pronunciation. The girls used to ask me about Italian clothes and admired my wardrobe. They had seen Dino dropping me off in the Lamborghini and were curious about my life. The male students seemed friendly enough but gave me a wide berth.

I was basically shy with boys of my own age. Sometimes I longed to join them all and go out to one of the local pubs but kept to my study schedule so determined was I to succeed. I had a strong feeling that one day I would be on my own and have be self-sufficient. Maybe it was the way the family were silent about my inheritance and my shares in the company. I did realise that when I was twenty-one there may be a confrontation and I was determined to be ready with a degree and knowledge of business law. The words of Ruth were always with me. 'Work hard and keep your own counsel'. I intended to stand by her principles and succeed as an independent woman as she had done.

I was just beginning to make new friends when other things happened in my life curtailing my education. I used to send Dino a note every week and wrote to Rosa in California. After her first few letters she did not reply and I wondered what was happening. They had been in California for nearly a year and I heard from the others that Roberto was very in demand by most of the Geographical magazines.

I understood that Rosa was also very successful with her clothing range for children rivalling the leading brands. She had been to art school in New York and had many contacts with professional artists and designers.

There was never any mention of them coming home. At Christmas time Dino decided that we should all go to Italy. I had also been asked to Mrs Lee's farm and would rather have gone there. When I protested Dino insisted that I had no choice as one of his very important clients had seen some photographs of me taken by Roberto when I was sixteen and was interested in the possibility of using me for a photo shoot. I did not understand which photo they were referring to and assumed someone had seen my portrait, which was no longer in the house. He said that if I agreed and if they liked me I would be paid and was signed up with a contract in our own model agency that Gloria ran. Our company stood to make a profit from this, as it was a prestigious group in Italy with contracts for major top of the range magazines and publications.

Paulo was also going with his family. I had never really got to know him. He was quiet and businesslike, pleasant and polite but said very little in company. I got the impression that even then he was the backbone of the business and quietly stayed at the helm. I had begun to like his wife Helen. She had given up teaching as they had a young baby. She was not interested in fashion living mostly in sports clothes and had little in common with Gloria. Both of them had been very fond of Roberto and Rosa

We were to stay in a large hotel in Milan. Christmas day was to be spent with a lot of Italian relatives on a large farm in Tuscany.

We arrived three days before Christmas and I was taken to meet the head of the agency Antonio Greco in the City centre. I was used to grand buildings but there's' was a state of the art Modernist building only a year old. It was vast and had ten floors in all with large windows and lots of stainless steel in the latest style. It was designed by one of Italy's leading architects. Gloria and Dino accompanied me. She had spent hours making herself glamorous for the occasion having spent days in the beauty salon and the hairdressers. She wore a white suit from our designer store in Edinburgh. Dino as usual looked as if he had stepped out of Savile Row. He used a tailor there as he liked the idea of being dressed like an English gentleman. I was reprimanded by both of them for looking too casual wearing what the Americans called the 'Preppy look'. To me it was comfort wear a Polo neck sweater, an A line skirt and flat shoes. I wore my hair in a ponytail. I certainly did not want to look like a model and wore little make up. I was feeling uncertain and unhappy about the whole thing but reluctantly did as they asked.

As we went into the large vestibule there were gigantic murals of models and stars everywhere. There were blown up posters of LA DOLCE VITA a film which had come out the previous year. The company had handled all the publicity. We were ushered into a large office with the biggest desk I had ever seen behind which was a huge window overlooking the Milan Opera House. There were two leather sofas and at the other end of the room a round antique conference table and a cinema screen. There were amazing photographs around the walls all blown up to gigantic proportions. They were of leading figures in art, design, film and photography.

As I followed Dino and Gloria in and a second before I was introduced to Antonio Greco I came face to face with MYSELF.

A blown up portrait of me straddled on a chair exposing as much cleavage as possible wearing tight jodhpurs and brandishing a riding whip was on an easel in front of the desk. I was completely shocked and must have gone very pale.

An astounded Gloria murmured 'My God its Jo' and Dino clearly equally surprised tried retain his composure and did the introductions.

I felt angry with Roberto for having betrayed me. Not only had he not shown me the picture but he had also denied that it existed. It was obvious that Dino had never seen it before and I could imagine what both he and Gloria must have been thinking. Antonio came forward and kissed Gloria's hand. She clearly enjoyed his flattery and soon gave him the impression that the whole thing had been her idea.

He smiled at me looking me up and down as if he were buying a new racehorse of which I gathered he had many. He held my face between his hands and muttered.

'Perfect bone structure, and an empty canvas, no horrible make up. An 'English Rose' complexion superb! Bon journo young lady you are more beautiful than I imagined.'

He turned to Dino 'You have an exquisite daughter. This year we are looking at the English country house, the horse and hounds look she is perfect.'

I blushed wishing myself in England at Mrs Lee's farmhouse table eating her Xmas fruitcake.

He was a tall-distinguished looking man slim and elegant with fair hair unusual for an Italian. His blue eyes were sharp and piercing and disarmed me when he looked my way. However when he smiled his face changed and he was very handsome indeed living up to his playboy image which Gloria had made much of. Evidently he mixed with film stars, racing car drivers, and yacht owners and was part of the social set around the Mediterranean.

I was asked to sit on the sofa next to him. Dino and Gloria sat opposite.

She had a look of incredulity on her face but Dino having accepted the situation seemed keen to proceed. He listened carefully to Antonio as he outlined his plans. He was talking about a famous Calendar, which came out every year and was the most popular of its kind catering to a world market. It was usually contained the most beautiful models and stars in the world. One for each month. They were tastefully done but strictly for the male market.

These were never seen in service stations and offices and difficult to come by. They were often traded for high prices when the limited editions were sold.

To own one was almost like owning an expensive sports car and like many paintings were kept for posterity. Antonio was planning a similar calendar for a large company and being a sharp businessman felt he could compete and produce a much more desirable product charging even higher prices. He explained to Dino that whereas they would create unique photographs they would also engage artists to recreate the same photograph in a modernist style to go along side it.

He had been studying the Abstract expressionists in America an idea Roberto had put to him. They intended commissioning up and coming Italian artists to do the work. Dino appeared to be interested and went straight away into his business mode as I had seen him do so often. It was suggested that I had some photographs taken straight away by their foremost photographer who was world famous. If they were suitable there was a possibility that they could be followed by a full-length painting in the summer?

Contracts and finance were not mentioned at this point but I got the impression that everyone concerned was keen to proceed. Antonio had coffee served as Gloria and I was left to our own devices. She who I rarely saw and resented me and all and that I stood for tried to give the impression that we were close. She expressed her concern that I should not be exploited and be chaperoned always.

I heard her saying to Antonio. 'Of course we have to keep an eye on her she is still a student and has to finish her studies. She is a temperamental girl and a bit of a handful at times but she is Dino's stepdaughter and has to return to University next term. She is not to be treated like the other models. We cannot allow any of your male staff to be familiar with her.'

It was almost as if I was a commodity. She now owned me as it had been necessary for me to sign up with her agency. She insisted that she should chaperone me during the shoot.Dino seemed pleased that she appeared to be taking my part.

He was clearly very happy to be connected with this very prestigious agency.

It was agreed that after the Xmas break Gloria would stay behind with me for the photo shoot whilst Dino and the others went back to England. My term started late in January so I did not have a problem .I had brought books with me. I was glad of this as I would have an excuse to go to my room.

Dino and Antonio agreed to talk again the next day and we were all served with Champagne to celebrate. Little was said in the car but at the hotel afterwards they both confronted me and demanded to know when Roberto had taken the photographs and why I posed in such a provocative way.

I was in tears and could not convey to them how it happened when I had arrived at the studio on Bonny my horse to have the birthday shot taken. I seemed to twist myself in knots whilst trying to explain how Roberto had instantly posed me and quickly taken the shot. Dino shrugged his shoulders and appeared to understand knowing his brother but I knew Gloria would hold it against me as if it was my fault and my doing.

As I left them I heard her saying. 'See what I have been telling you all along Dino She is devious. Goodness knows what else she gets up to behind our backs. You will have to check up with her tutors. She has been thoroughly spoilt all her life. Its time she learned a lesson or two.'

Naively I was unaware of her insecurity and intense jealousy of both Ruth and myself. She disguised it when Dino was present but carried on with her verbal attacks on me when they were on their own. They left me in my room that evening and dined with Antonio and a woman friend.

Helen and Paulo asked me to join them. They wanted to played golf the next day and I offered to look after Jenny their baby. This suited me and in between taking her out for a walk and swimming in the indoor pool she spent a few hours asleep. This gave me time to study and stay out of the way.

Dino and Gloria were out all day again negotiating my schedule with the company without even consulting me. This confused me and I began to feel uncomfortable about my whole life and my place in the family.

The next day we were to go down the coast to join the very large group of relations for what promised to be a long drawn out series of feasts, wine and music.

Christmas Eve and Christmas day we all trooped to the Catholic Church and then opened the mountains of presents. I spent most of my time with Helen and Paulo. Jenny was passed around and mutually adored fussed over and fed by all the numerous female aunts and cousins. I saw little of Gloria and Dino who stayed out most of the night going to parties and did not get up until lunchtime.

I was given some expensive jewellery from Dino and Gloria. I was also given some new riding boots and a soft leather holdall from Paulo and Helen which I liked and still use today. The aunts and uncles all made me very welcome. The various male cousins all joked with me brought me drinks and wanted to take me out dancing between Xmas and New Year. Gloria put her foot down and Dino refused to allow me to go anywhere. We were to return to Milan on the 28th and the shoot would take place the next day.

Paulo and Helen decided to go back to England early as they planned to spend New Year with Helens parents. I went down to wave them off into a taxi at about eleven am.

Just before they left Paulo who had been paying his bill came up to us and put his arm around us saying that Roberto had rang. He had just received a phone call from him saying that he was arriving that day for the New Year. He also said that he was in a state as Rosa had left him and had moved in with an artist. She had already filed for divorce and was claiming custody of the children. I had not heard from Rosa recently. It explained the lack of communication. There was little we could say as Paulo and Helen had to catch their plane and only had time to leave a message at the desk for Dino.

I went to my room and felt so alone and cried for some reason. I was quite disturbed and wondered how Roberto would be when he joined us.Dino and Gloria called me in my room an hour later. Dino said that as he was due to leave the next day himself, as there was important business to be done in London before the New Year. He would ask Roberto to stay on with Gloria and myself.

I did not see Roberto until the day of the shoot. On his arrival Dino and Gloria had taken him out to dinner leaving me to dine alone in my room again. They excluded me on the pretext that they needed to talk to Roberto about his marriage break-up. I was uncertain how he would greet me. My feelings for him had never changed. I had begun to accept that it was just a teenage crush. During family parties we had rarely been alone. Rosa was an exceptional person and made me very welcome. In fact I had been truly happy there and loved the children. When they left for America and their house was left to Paulo and Helen it was a sad time for me as I had enjoyed real family life for the first time.

Dino was due to leave at ten the next day so called to see me in my room telling me to meet Roberto and Gloria later in the lobby. He was quite curt with me and said I was to listen to Gloria and do as she requested. I was not to go off on my own partying. They would fly back together to London where they were to pick up a car. I was to fly to Edinburgh on my own.

In the lobby I saw Roberto before he saw me. He looked thinner and taller and there was an air of sadness around him. He was buying a paper and I came up behind him and tapped him on the shoulder. He turned around and then he smiled.

He lifted me up and hugged me. It all came back, my heart almost stopped, I could hardly speak.

'You look wonderful Jo' he sunk his head into my shoulder for a second and then looked into my eyes.

'It's so good to see you, so good. I wanted to see you last night but Gloria said you weren't around.'

I smiled. 'I was in my room hoping you would call.'

His brown eyes had lost their light and mischief. I wanted to keep him there forever.

Gloria had left a message saying she would join us later at the shoot. Antonio would be driving her. They had a late night and she had a headache.

We found a taxi and Roberto held my hand for the twenty minute journey to the studio. I expressed my sadness about the divorce saying I was surprised as they seemed so happy when I was with them.

He said. 'It was our last chance Jo that is why I had to try so hard to keep it together. You see Rosa has known Will for a long time. They went to art school together. I knew him too we were all friends .One of the reasons she wanted to join me out there was that he had offered to help her promote her designs. He has always been in love with her. They are getting married. It is final. I loved her very much and adored the children. Rosa was like Ruth a perfect woman, beautiful, clever, and a marvellous mother and I was a faithful husband always. I never needed anyone else she was everything to me. I mix daily with many men who think nothing of sleeping with other women whilst they are away from home but I could never do that, it damages people and it's dishonest.'

'I am so sorry' I said and kept repeating it over and over again.

I did not know what else to say. I was young, innocent and naïve in a sophisticated world.

CHAPTER 11

THE SHOOT

We were taken by taxi to the studio of to the renowned photographer Christo Palmero. It was in an old warehouse by the river. We were met by Christo himself who gave us a quick tour. He seemed pleased to see us and immediately congratulated Roberto on his work. The large old warehouse was ten times larger than the hangar at home and there were multiple sets and cameras everywhere. There were several anterior rooms for makeup and hairdressing. There was a theatre and several catwalks. The walls were covered with murals and famous art works many by Picasso.

There were only a few members of staff present.

Christo called an assistant to bring us coffee and then took us into his private studio, He was in his fifties a large muscular with a mass of curly grey hair.

He like all Italian men looked sun-tanned and healthy but in his case he was a seasoned sailor and lived aboard his yacht.

He asked us to sit down and addressed himself to me and wrote notes as he asked about my life.

'Antonio told me all about you Jo but I want to know a little more. I do not regard my models as mere coat hangers I look for a real person behind a beautiful face. Roberto has done that already and I believe that one will be iconic one day. But I already have some ideas.'

I had seen his work as there were many albums and books around to look at. Most of the famous stars had been photographed by him. Roberto seemed to come alive there, as he was in a place that felt familiar and comfortable.

Christo then produced a large copy of the photograph taken from Antonio's office. He praised Roberto and told him that even though it was three years old and Roberto was still inexperienced it was of a high standard and reiterated what he said earlier.

I realised that I still had to have an explanation from him in relation to this picture. After all it was my portrait and I had never agreed to it being there in the first place. Roberto seeing my face and reading my mind came up with an explanation as soon as Christo left the room.

'I am sorry Jo but it's a long story.'

He cut it short and said that the negatives had got put in a pile of film that was in a box to go to Italy. In fact the cleaner had found it and presumed it had to go with the others. It was not until it had been developed in Italy that it had been discovered.

They had enlarged it and as it was so good one of the other photographers knowing Antonio wanted to do some English horse and hound type pictures showed it to him. I was relieved that there was an explanation after all and felt guilty for being angry with him.

Christo then asked me to change and put on a shift rather like the gowns patients wore in hospitals. He also asked me to wash my face and remove any make up. This was easy as I only ever wore a little lipstick.

He sat me on a podium and took many shots using different lights. He was very polite and discreet and although he wanted shots exposing different parts of my body he made sure I was comfortable and happy with what I was doing.

He asked me to dress again and took us both up to his office which was very spacious and comfortable and left us whilst the films were developed.

He invited us to help ourselves to some wine and so we relaxed and waited. Roberto seemed happier as he was involved in the work he enjoyed and was anxious to learn as much as possible. When Christo went into the dark room he repeated the story of my picture. I said that I was upset when I had seen it as I felt he had betrayed me. He held my hand again and said

'It was a series of mistakes I am truly sorry I would never do anything to hurt you. However this is a good break for you and even if you do not want to be a model you will be paid a lot of money and you can put it in the bank until you need it. Any way I am proud of you, you are my protégée.' After a couple of glasses of wine he became quite cheerful teasing me as the old Roberto used to.

When Christo came back he seemed delighted.

"My dear you have a wonderful face and body and extremely photogenic even without the makeup. We have our own brand and have skilful makeup artists. You young lady hardly need any but as Roberto found out you can look ravishing with just a little here and there. Now this afternoon I want you to put on the riding clothes. We have some new ones for you and we will get lots of poses. We will have the makeup artists and the hairdressers here soon and get down to business.'

He said that he was meeting Antonio for lunch but he hoped we would join him with that night on his yacht as he was planning a New Years Eve party.

Roberto and I went for a walk around the harbour and then had lunch at a fish restaurant overlooking the river.

It was a simple place and the fish had been caught that day. It was perfect touch to what was to be a happy day. Roberto was quiet and most of the time we just sat and looked at the view. He had another glass of wine but discouraged me from drinking buying me a soft drink only.

He became protective again saying that if we were going out tonight it would be wise not to, as it would also be a long afternoon.

When we got back to the studio Gloria had arrived and was perched on a director's chair next to Christo and Antonio drinking red wine and enjoying her.

She was smartly dressed in a black suit very much like the one Ruth used to wear. Her skirt was shorter and she wore black patent shoes. Recently she had also had her hair cut in a similar way to Ruth's'.

She greeted me effusively as if I were really her daughter.

Christo put his arm around us both saying 'Two beautiful women together hey Antonio a fine sight'.

Antonio chatted to Roberto whilst they applied my makeup.

He also congratulated him on his style of photography and they spoke about the work he was doing in Los Angeles. My make up seemed to take so long. They were all so skilled and knew exactly what would l would look like when the lights were on and the camera took over. My hair was piled up and dropped down again casually as if blown by the wind. I already had my riding clothes on.

Then Christo took over. He posed me in a similar way to the way Roberto had done but used a different type of chair. This was black and made of bamboo. I also wore black leather gloves and wore a yellow jumper which had a polo neck and was tightly fitting. Christo took around thirty shots running around me taking me at different angles. Several times they changed my hair and put more make up on using dark eye liner and mascara. He took one of me throwing my head back and laughing with my hair flying all over the place helped by a wind machine. Then to my amazement they brought a horse in and sat me on it in different poses. He was a white Palomino and very good tempered. I was surprised but thrilled, as I had never seen one like it before. He was exquisite. I couldn't wait to stroke him. A groom who obviously took pride in such a beautiful creature accompanied him.

Christo then asked me if I would allow him to take a shot without my top on sitting on the horse with my hair down. I saw him discussing the details with Antonio, Roberto and Gloria. Gloria did not appear concerned about me and was completely bowled over by Christo's' charm. I felt embarrassed and vulnerable and Christo sensing this said that I could wear a body stocking.

The shot would be in keeping with collections theme. It would be a pre-Raphaelite study with the painting done in a similar style. Antonio took a book over to Gloria to show her some famous poses by Victorian painters.

Roberto came over to speak to me and sensed my embarrassment. 'You can say that you would rather wear a body stocking it will look fine. Christo knows what he is doing he is one of the best in the world.' I will talk to him.'

Gloria nodded approvingly as after another couple of glasses of wine she would have agreed to anything Christo said. I wondered what Dino would have made of it.

It was agreed and the staff helped me with the body stocking. They then rearranged my hair into long ringlets combing it to cover my body and added some extra hairpieces to give it more length. Then I was ready to get back on the horse. It took him about two hours to get the shot he wanted with breaks for the horse to exercise.

Christo then thanked me graciously for being such a perfect model.

Antonio who had been in deep conversation with Gloria seemed well satisfied with the shoot. We left about four pm and Antonio took Roberto and I back to the hotel in his chauffeur driven car. Christo ebullient and happy with the shoot reminded us we were due at his party on the yacht later and held my hand for a second and said. 'You were perfect my dear.'

Gloria stayed behind, as he wanted to show her the studio and discuss the contract.

Back at the hotel Roberto suggested we had a rest before we went out in the evening and escorted me to my room saying he would pick me up at eight pm and we would meet Gloria in the bar. He looked exhausted as he had flown from America the previous day and he must have had a lot on his mind,

I had a bath and rested for a couple of hours while images of Roberto kept rushing around my head. I woke up with a start as the phone rang by my bed. It was Roberto.

'I will be with you in half an hour did you sleep. ?'

'Yes did you'?

'No images of Lady Godiva got in the way'.

'Come on that wasn't Lady Godiva it was me Jo.'

'Yes I know and that is the problem'.

CHAPTER 12

THE PARTY ON THE YACHT

Roberto knocked on my door at eight. He was nearly his old self but I could sense his sadness still.

'Come on I want to go and show you off and enjoy an evening with the rich people. You can be my first date in my new life and I shall be the envy of all, you look gorgeous.'

I wore a white linen dress with a halter neckline and a black stole.

Gloria was waiting for us in the bar and was already drinking. She wore a tightly fitting red dress and the sapphires. Even then I assumed that she was playing some sort of game with my emotions. She may not have known that Ruth had left me the jewellery in her will but it was more likely that she did. Her subsequent treatment of me bore out all of my suspicions. She was determined to enjoy herself from the outset and I felt she was competing with me for the attention of the men, a competition I wanted no part in. She very rarely went anywhere without Dino and appeared to be revelling in her freedom.

Roberto escorted us to the Yacht. It looked magnificent. It was fully lit with extra coloured lights and Chinese lanterns giving it a festive look.

There was a live band playing and as we went in there were already couples dancing. A buffet was laid out in the state room.

We were met by Christo who introduced us to his friends mostly other yacht owners and artists. Roberto got swept up with a group of them, as they wanted to talk about art and photography.

Although we had dressed formally many were dressed casually and in some cases had adopted a bohemian and existentialist look in common with the French and Italian style at the time. The women mostly wore black and lots of heavy eye makeup.

Christo had been divorced twice and had no partner although like Antonio had many women friends. This seemed to suit Gloria who stayed by his side most of the evening. Antonio joined us and said he approved of my outfit saying I had faultless taste. He also said he would like to have a dance later.

It was all very exciting and I saw many actors and actresses I had only heard of or seen in the papers. Roberto came over to rescue me after an hour as I was surrounded by a party from another yacht who were trying to persuade me to decamp to theirs. They were all around my age and tried to convince me that I would have a better time away from the older members of the party. They had guitars and were interested in the latest music from America namely rock and roll. I declined as I wanted to spend some time with Roberto at last.

We danced to our favourite music and stayed on the dance floor for a long time to be interrupted by a call for us to collect our buffet. Roberto was now in good form and laughed and joked with the many people waiting to get their food. We sat with Antonio and several models and their partners who told us a lot of stories about their life in Rome. They were interested in my story and curious about why I was there but as it was still under wraps we had agreed not to discuss it.

I only caught glimpses of Gloria as she got involved in a crowd who wanted a conducted tour of the yacht.

Roberto did not seem to want to dance with anyone but me. He seemed comfortable in my presence and was not interested in the beautiful women who were flirting with everyone at our table. Several came up to him as he was a stranger to them and a good looking one too. He chatted to them politely.

Finally Antonio came to claim his dance and took me into a separate room off the main dance floor where an American jazz pianist had just arrived and agreed to play.

I saw Roberto come in and he stood silently at the edge of the crowd. I was aware that he was watching me dancing. He stayed there a long time just staring.

Antonio told me how pleased he was with the shoot and said he wished I could stay on. He asked me if I would like to come out in the summer and sail. I said that I would need to talk to Dino as I would then only be twenty and would never be allowed without a chaperone.

He smiled down at me 'It will be arranged I assure you and you will have fun. We will teach you how to live the good life and meet exciting people. Anyway I am looking for an artist to paint you so we could arrange that also.'

Gloria came in with Christo and had obviously not stopped drinking as she was quite garrulous. She saw Antonio who by that time was holding me closer and made a loud comment to Christo about how I was free with my favours. He was very charming and calmed her down saying that I was young and having fun. He appeared to be enjoying himself and I did not see them the rest of the evening.

Antonio eventually took me over to Roberto saying he had to go and see if his secretary and her husband had arrived.

We took a walk on deck to see the lights and talked until the countdown to midnight. We took our own champagne with us.

I asked him how long he would stay in England.

He said that he had to go to London and then would fly up to see Dino and Paulo and the business. After that he had a hefty schedule in Africa.

"I would like to come and see you at University before I go. We could go up to the Highlands. What do you think?'

'Yes please do I would really like that?'

I smiled at him, I was happy that he had suggested it.

The festivities started and we stayed where we were. I was tired and Roberto looked strained. We wished one another a Happy New Year with a chaste kiss.

We then decided to go back wanting to miss the New Year madness.

Roberto went to look for Gloria but Antonio said that Christo was seeing her back to her hotel. He said he would drop us off as he was going anyway. He was flying to Paris and Brazil the next day.

When we arrived Roberto excused himself when Antonio insisted on seeing me to my room. I thanked him for seeing me back. He stood at the door for a few moments hesitating. At this point Gloria got out of the lift with Christo and I think they assumed that we had been in the room together. She muttered something to Christo and they both went into her room.

The next day we all travelled back to the airport together and Gloria hardly spoke to me. Roberto was polite and pleasant to both of us making sure we had all we needed on the flight.

They were to meet Dino in London and I was to fly back to Edinburgh on my own.

Roberto made sure I found my gate leaving Gloria to shop in the duty free outlet.

He said 'I am sure you didn't entertain Antonio in your room but Gloria thinks you did. You know she will tell Dino.'

I replied. 'Yes I am afraid she is determined to find fault with me on every occasion. I know better than to offer a coffee in a hotel room to a man twice my age particularly with his reputation. I do not think she was setting a good example to me either.'

He smiled and gave me a hug.

'Bye my darling Jo, I will see you very soon and I promise to be good company next time.'

CHAPTER 13

THE HIGHLANDS

I settled down and started to enjoy life on campus again.

The girl I was closest to was called Kathy. She shared our kitchen and we often cooked together. She had a boyfriend who was a medical student and they were always out together when he had time off. However I did share the odd confidence with her and she was the only one who knew about my life. She came from a wealthy family who owned a large estate in Scotland and properties in London.

She was there when I returned and keen to hear about my photo shoot and the New Years Eve party. I told her a little about Roberto but she guessed that I was hiding my feelings. I tried to explain how difficult it was as he was so newly separated and much older than myself. It all seemed so impossible and a little fanciful on my part. She suggested that the separation was good and only time would tell if it were to mean anything special.

We went out that evening with her boyfriend Hugh and some of his friends.

I had a good time and drank lots of beer. I forgot about the family and Italy for once.

Hugh played the piano as they had a successful Rugby match and won the game.

I joined in with their rugby songs for the rest of the evening. A couple of his friends chatted to me and asked why they never saw me around. They asked me to meet up with them again the next week but I didn't go.

I heard from Roberto a few weeks later. He wrote to me saying he was going back to America. He planned to reorganise the business there and was to slowly pull out of it leaving his cousin Tony as the manager. He said that he was enjoying filming and had been offered a commission in Nairobi with a unit for a famous geographical magazine. He thought it would be a good break away from everybody. He said he would come up for the weekend to say goodbye.

I had very mixed feelings. In some ways I was pleased for him that he was going to start a new life and I knew that I was being fanciful imagining that we could ever have a meaningful relationship.

He arrived on a Saturday at 9am. He had as usual travelled from the Lake District in record time and I did not expect him until lunchtime. The porter knocked on my door and informed me that a gentleman was asking for me and that he was waiting outside. I rushed around to get ready and was with him within ten minutes. He was wearing his casual leather jacket and blue jeans that everyone wore in America.

He gave me one of his bear hugs whisking me off my feet.

'Come on Jo lets go, have you got an overnight bag.'

'Yes but.'

'No buts go get it we are going to the Highlands.'

I packed my bag and signed out and within half an hour we were leaving Edinburgh heading for the Forth Bridge. He was driving his Mazerati which he had left in England with Paulo.

He held my hand and said 'It is so good to see you. We will forget everything and have a great weekend. I am going to spoil you my little friend'.

It was the old Roberto back in action. We kept driving for about two hours and then stopped at Pitlochry for lunch. We found a hotel with a dining room overlooking the river. Each table had vases of spring flowers on them and he led me to one where there was a large bowl of primroses.

After we had ordered he produced a beautifully wrapped gift.

'A present for my Valentine', he said.

I was surprised as I had no idea it was Valentine's Day.

I smiled at him and opened it. It was a solid silver neckband and was it perfect. I never really liked expensive jewellery and loved simple things. He already knew my taste and what suited me.

I held it lovingly. "Should I wear it?" "You certainly should" he replied.

He fastened it around my neck.

Also inside on a card was a photograph of Bonny my horse cantering. On it he had hand-written in neat script.

TO MY BEAUTIFUL FRIEND JO. WHO I LOVE VERY MUCH.

I was overcome and thanked him tearfully.

We had fresh salmon and garden vegetables followed by Bread and butter pudding.

We took our coffee into the conservatory full of exotic plants and sank into a large sofa. Roberto put his arm around me and I let it stay there.

We sat like that for quite a long time contented and happy. I was joyful in fact I was overflowing with joy. I wanted to tell the world and the man next to me how I felt about him.

We then went walking in a bluebell wood and when he kissed me under a magnolia tree I knew instinctively that our fate was sealed whatever happened. We went back holding hands. He looked at me and said.

'I love being with you, we are going to enjoy this weekend. I have found a place you will like very much.'

'Where I said, tell me'.

'Wait and see' he said mysteriously.

We drove for another hour and then he left the track by a lake and followed a winding road up to a small house in the trees.

He stopped outside. 'This is it' he said.

He helped me out and we walked up to the entrance to what looked like a Swiss chalet overlooking a lake. The late sun was shining and it looked enchanting.

'How did you find it?' I asked.

'A friend of mine owns it, he comes fishing here.' he said smiling at me as he unloaded the car.

'It's wonderful'.

'It is and so are you.' he said and hugged me.

He opened the heavy oak door and went in. There was a large room with a gigantic fireplace with several baskets full of logs in the inglenook.

We put our things down and Roberto immediately lit the fire. Whilst he did so I inspected the rest of the house. There were three leather sofas and several sheepskin rugs on a natural oak floor. There were oil lamps everywhere but also some overhead lighting. The small kitchen had a gas stove and a pantry with plenty of provisions. Upstairs there was a tiny bathroom one bedroom with a carved oak bed that looked as if it would sleep six. There was lots of clean linen and several eiderdowns all neatly piled up in an airing cupboard.

When I joined him he had a massive fire.

'Smells good doesn't it.' he said

'I've put lots of pine cones on it. Come here give me a hug.'

'There's only one bed' I said,

'Yes and I will sleep on one of these great sofas by an all night fire.'

I made some tea and we sat side by side on the sheepskin getting warm.

'Would you like to go out to eat or should we go to the village and get some food to cook. Jim the owner said we can help ourselves but there is a little hotel up the road that serves dinner.'

I said 'Let's cook something that will be fun, after all we have eaten today already.'

He agreed and we sat and wrote a list. We needed bread butter and cheese and bacon and eggs mushrooms and salad having decided on an omelette. He said he would buy some fruit cake to have with our coffee. The simple act of choosing food together seemed quite magical.

'You stay where you are and keep putting logs on the fire and I will go to the village.' he said.

Whilst he was away I made up the bed and brought some linen down for the sofa and then prepared the kitchen for the meal. I also found some a gramophone and some records. There was lots of jazz and I knew Roberto would enjoy listening to it later. I was so happy I did not know or care what would happen in the evening it was enough to be there on our own at last.

He was quite a long time so I decided to have a bath as I had got chilled and knew in this way I could get warm and change into my new dress. I had just got out when he got back and had a towel wrapped round me. I called from the top of the stairs.

He shouted 'I will start cooking now and you can come downstairs looking like a princess when you are ready.'

I could not get over how happy he sounded. I put on my red woollen dress made of angora wool. It had a polo neck and I thought it looked quite pretty.

I combed my hair and let it hang in curls and wore a bright red lipstick the same colour of the dress.

As I came down Billy Holliday was singing 'Embraceable you' and two glasses of champagne were ready on a silver tray

Roberto had put a checked tablecloth and a vase of bluebells on the table.

He came through with beautifully cooked omelettes a tray with a salad.

He put them down and looked at me. He then held me tight.

'You are so lovely what have I done to deserve having you here and your dress looks amazing. Come on lets drink eat and be very merry'.

Then we drank lots of champagne.

I insisted on washing up as I explained that there was nothing worse than coming down to breakfast and having to wash dirty pots.

He tied an apron around me and kissed the back of my neck

I am going upstairs to have a shower and then we will finish the champagne and have a dance.

I loved tidying up and kept putting more logs on the fire and changing the music.

He finally came down wearing his black sweater and his blue jeans. He smiled at me and came over to hold me and dance.

'My Funny Valentine Sweet Comic Valentine' sang Dinah Washington and we danced for a long time.

Then we lay on the sofa watching the flames from the fire and the stars outside holding one another

He finally said. 'Do you think you are ready for a love affair?'

I said 'Are you'.

'From the moment I first saw you on your pony when you were sixteen.'

I said 'I think I do love you but you are going away and I may not see you again for a long time.'

'I know and I do not expect you to sleep with me .It was not planned, the cottage only came up at the last moment but I am glad it did.'

'So am I but I am still a ward of court, Dino would not like it and can you imagine what Gloria would say.'

'They need never know. In 18 months you will be twenty one and I will wait. You are worth waiting for. I am serious about you.'

'That's the nicest thing you have ever said to me. Will you give me until tomorrow to think about it? We both need time and you need to heal from your broken marriage.'

He pulled me up and kissed me.

'You just sound like Ruth full of good sense and you are right.

You go to bed it's too important a decision for you to make after several glasses of champagne. We are both mixed up emotionally and tired. Go upstairs and put a glamorous nightdress on and I will come and tuck you in and promise to be very honourable.'

That's exactly what he did.

'Think about what you want to do tomorrow and we will get up early and go and explore.' he said as he went downstairs to his sofa.

I was awake for a long time then I fell asleep. I woke up about 3 am. The moon was bright outside.

I kept thinking about Roberto downstairs and how much I loved him. I longed to hold him.   I went to the mirror brushed my hair and lit the oil lamp. I put on my silver necklace and bath robe. I watched the moon come out of a cloud and crept downstairs holding the lamp. I sat for half an hour on the rug keeping the fire going with more logs. I watched him sleeping and then did what I had always wanted to do push his unruly hair back off his forehead.

He stirred and opened his eyes. Smiling sleepily he pulled me to him.

Loving him was magical but making love was indescribable. Our sofa and later the four-poster became a universe only inhabited by us. We lay watching the stars and marvelling that we were together and so blissfully happy. At dawn we bathed together and he covered me with perfume and scented powder.

I kept my necklace on and he called me 'Cleopatra.'

'I told you I was going to spoil you' he said as put a matching silver bangle on my wrist and ankle, which he had taken out of a box, covered in rose petals.

We finally got up at 11 -30 am as the sun came shining through our window. He rushed down to the kitchen and made us some coffee. Then he sat next to me in a white towelling dressing gown smiling.

'I thought you were the most beautiful girl in the world yesterday but today you are more than that you have a new womanly look that is devastating. You take my breath away. I have thought about this moment for weeks now and never believed it would be possible. How could you want to be with someone like me? One day there will be hundreds of men out there for you?'

Roberto don't. I am not a fashion icon and never likely to be. I do not want men to look at me. I want you that's all. I will never change.

I will always love you. Maybe next year you will want another way of life that would not include me.'

"No that will never happen you will always be there in my head and in my heart.

I did love Rosa but this is different; perhaps this is what she feels for Will.'

We had some rolls and honey and lit the fire again whilst we lay on the sofa and talked. The sun went in and it started to snow.

'A perfect excuse not to go out'. He said.

'Yes we have our own universe to explore let's put on some music'. I replied.

That's what we did all day and went out to supper instead.

'Put on all the jewellery' he said as he brushed my hair.

He then produced another parcel which when I opened it contained a silver hair clip. He pulled my hair to one side and pinned it up making me look like a little girl in a school photograph. Now put a white silk blouse, your navy sweater and your ski pants and you will look sensational. My little School prefect.'

'Better leave off my anklet band then'. I said.

'Yes that is for later when you turn into my concubine'.

We drove about two miles to the pub, which was also a restaurant.

It was charming with lots of panelling, trophies on the walls and several log fires. We had a table by one of them and were fussed over by an Italian waiter.

Both he and Roberto acted like long lost friends after a few moments and I lost them to the language. It did mean however that we had the best of service and the added bonus of special wine from the cellar. It turned out that he was the owner's son and was over in Scotland helping out over the ski season. It made our evening more fun as he kept telling Roberto what a beautiful bride I was. Roberto could not stop grinning and loved the banter. The waiter was called Rudi and he said 'I am sure I have seen your face in a magazine, is she famous?' he said to Roberto.

'Infamous' said Roberto proudly.

'But I have seen her I know it -something to do with horses.'

We seemed to create a lot of interest from the other couples who were all much older, middle-aged and serious looking.

Rudi insisted we stay on when it became quiet and opened another bottle of expensive wine on the house. He then went into the hotel and came back with a fashion magazine from Italy belonging to his mother.

'There' he said 'It's you isn't it'.

It was the one Antonio had in his office. Roberto nodded and Rudi grinned.

'I knew it, I will tell my mother'.

We left soon afterwards. I was quiet when we arrived back.

'Are you ok Jo is it the photo'?

.'Did you know?'

'I knew that Antonio owned the rights. Dino sold it to him he can use it as much as he likes. Are you upset? In a way I am being exploited too. I should have the copyright.'

'I would have liked to have been consulted and now I realise why Dino gave me extra money this term, he was very generous.'

'Well if you have been signed up with Gloria's agency you should have been paid would you like me to discuss it with him'?

'No it's not your fault Roberto but from now on I will be careful in relation to money. I look forward to coming of age and becoming independent'.

'That will never happen because from now on I will take care of you. No one will ever exploit you again.'

He made us coffee and we sat at the table. He held my hand

'Jo tomorrow we have to go back can we talk about the summer. I want to meet you in Italy. I want to be there when you go for your portrait. There will be lots of activity and parties. I want to be by your side what do you think?'

I looked at him and smiled. 'Will you protect me from those wicked men?' I certainly will you are my everything. I love and adore you and want us to get married. Will you marry me when I am free?

"Yes" I said. "I will never marry anyone but you."

We talked a lot that evening about the future and my coming of age.

He explained that he would not be able to make any commitment until he knew how his commission went. However he was adamant about being with me whether it was in America or England. '

'I want you to start thinking of the sort of life we could have together. Where we would live etc and leave the rest to me.'

The second night was all the more precious in that I did not know for certain when I would see him again. I went to sleep in his arms feeling loved and cherished.

The next day we had to leave early as he had a plane to catch. He took me to my room on the pretext that he had to carry my luggage but we wanted a few moments together out of sight of the students coming and going.

'Remember me every night before you go to sleep my sweetheart' he said.

'I will think of you all day and every day Roberto.'

I pushed his hair back for him the last time and kissed him goodbye.

CHAPTER 14

MY NEWS

I did hear from Roberto regularly.

In his first letter he said how much he cared for me.

'I would never have assumed you would trust yourself to me and I want you to know what happened between us was not premeditated but I was captivated with you when I first met you. I had never met anyone so beautiful with such an engaging personality. I also felt that Dino and particularly Gloria were treating you appallingly and that is why Rosa and I asked you to come and stay. I was worried about you.

During that time I saw what a kind and loving young woman you were. I watched you with my children who seemed to adore you and particularly when you let them ride your pony and supervised their riding lessons. You seem to bring sunshine into our lives. I think the morning you shrunk my sweater in the washing machine and begged me to forgive you I started to fall in love with you. I laughed at you and gave you a cuddle and at that moment knew I wanted to hold you tight.

You are very much like your mother but you also have exceptional beauty and emotional intelligence. I am convinced that whatever you do you will be successful.

I was determined to look after you and watch over you at the time even though my feelings were strong and you were so young and inexperienced.

I knew that once we got to America Rosa would get involved with her family and get focused on her children's design project. I also knew it would be a matter of time before she left me for Will who she knew as a teenager and was supervising her project. They plan to run a vineyard in the Napa Valley.

I am of course still bereaved as I miss them all so much. However I hope when my life is more on track and I know what I am doing we can be together again.

You have only another year before you finish your degree and we can both decide if we can work out how it would be possible. I am serious about us getting married.

It is so frustrating not to be able to speak to you regularly but keep writing as I love your letters and promise to keep them always.

I have your fabulous photographs in my backpack. I am the envy of most of the men here so I have to guard them or they will be up on the mess wall.'

The letters were also full of his projects.

He declared that he would always do photojournalism in the future and was getting excellent feedback for his work. He said that they wanted him to go to Australia for the next assignment, which was anytime in July or August.

'But I am determined to be there for your painting.

You need me to protect you from the Monte Carlo lot as Antonio and Christo are ruthless in relation to women and you are definitely off limits my darling. I want you to be my wife. I love you and do miss you.'

We arranged to speak on the phone but it was difficult to take calls.

Twice there were calls from him I missed. On another occasion I found a note two weeks late saying he was in London for two nights and could I get to Kings Cross to meet him.

The porters in reception did not always take messages and were quite casual about it. Sometimes if they were listening to a football match on the radio they would ignore the phone. Urgent messages could be taken in the University offices but they were not always reliable either.

It took a while before I could come to terms with my weekend. I adored Roberto and would never regret that we had spent two nights together. I knew it that I was emotionally immature and inexperienced but I could not imagine loving anyone else.

I did want to marry him.

The male students at university were often very attentive and I was not short of offers but my heart was taken. However I knew that I should have waited until he was over his divorce. I started to feel uneasy for days and weeks and did not know why.

I called into the shop one day and bumped into Helen she insisted we go for a coffee. She was as usual doing her school trips and had brought some children to Edinburgh to a swimming gala. She wanted to know how I was enjoying university and I said I was looking forward to finishing the next year. I asked about the family, as I hadn't seen them for a few weeks. She said everything was going well.

Roberto is now in Africa I doubt if he will come back he seems happy to be traveling. There is a large team of them and Janey Joseph is with them you know the famous American author who sponsors an orphanage out there. I wonder if he is having an affair with her he told us a lot about her.

'Do you hear from him much'? I asked.

'He calls us a lot as we are buying his house now.

As you know it's bigger than ours. When we move in come and see us it will seem like home to you as you enjoyed your stay with Rosa, She was very fond of you.'

'Have you heard from her?' I asked.

'Yes she is very happy but feels bad about Roberto. I hope he will find someone else. Perhaps Janey will help him. He certainly seems to love photojournalism. I cannot imagine him working actively in the business again although he still has shares in it.'

My heart sank as she talked about him. I said I would see her at Easter, which was in late March. She asked me to stay and I said I would help out with the baby when they moved in.

I was upset when I got back particularly in relation to our conversation as I had not had a letter for ten days and felt quite depressed.

Added to that I had a strong feeling I was pregnant. I had been suffering from morning sickness for days and knew that I ought to visit a doctor. I realized that I would have to go privately as I was registered with the university Dr.

In the end I talked to Kathy. She hadn't been around since I had been away for my weekend as she had been on a placement. She listened as I told her about the weekend and how happy I had been. Then I told her about my insecurities around the situation and the fact that I was almost certain I was pregnant.

She was a quiet reflective girl with a gentle personality. At first she appeared quite shocked and amazed that it had happened so quickly but she was very understanding and said that she knew a Dr I could consult who worked in a private nursing home.

'Would you want to keep the baby if you are pregnant'? She asked.

I said 'Yes there is no doubt about it. Whatever happens I will love that child as I love Roberto. An alternative would be unthinkable.'

'What about your stepfather' she asked.

Of course I could predict exactly what Dino would say and he would certainly demand to know who the father was. He rang me a lot and when he could get to Edinburgh without Gloria he did. Sometimes he took me into the store and insisted on buying me new clothes. It seemed to give him a lot of pleasure. He would get very excited when new stock arrived and would call me. Once we were there for nearly two hours. He would keep coming into the changing room and adjusting the dresses. On the last occasion he bought me three cocktail dresses and a fox fur. I had no need for any of them Then he would take me out to lunch to places where he knew some of his business friends would be dining and introduce me. I almost began to dread these occasions. He would be devastated about my pregnancy and I am sure would want to do something drastic as I would have let him and the family down. He would also lose face especially as he was pinning a lot of hope on his relationship with Antonio and his agency. He would probably insist the baby be taken to Italy and adopted as I had heard discussions about other girls in the extended family. Mostly they were made to get married and nearly all were taken away somewhere to conceal their pregnancy. I think it was a nursing home in Naples.

I knew that I had enough money to live on and one idea was to just leave University in June and find a flat somewhere taking temporary work. I felt I could conceal my pregnancy until then giving me time to make plans.

Kathy suggested that whatever I did I must be where there was some support.

'When are you going to tell Roberto? He needs to know and from what you have told me loves you and wants to marry you.'

I explained that it was becoming increasingly difficult as he had various box numbers in Africa. I said I did not want to tell him by letter.I knew that I would see Helen and possibly the rest of the family over Easter. If he rang there I could ask to speak to him. I would tell Dino that I would not be around too much after that because of exams, which finished mid June. They were so busy they would not think it odd. Gloria had fashion shows every weekend and Dino was always in Italy. He did indicate that Antonio was pleased with the photo shoot and may come over around Easter to sort out some contracts. He said he expected me to be around to entertain him. As we were all due to fly to Italy on July 1st I would have to make all my arrangements before then.

Kathy true to her word arranged for me to see someone in Glasgow.

In fact Hugh was hoping to move there as a house officer January when he graduated. He was in the process of buying a house there which he intended to live in and let rooms to other students.

She came with me for the appointment. I took my birth certificate and was ready with a story in case the Dr asked me too much about my family. I talked it all over with Kathy on the train.

'What if Dino finds out' she said.

'He won't but if he does he will put me on the next plane to Italy somewhere in the mountains no doubt.'

'Would you tell him about Roberto?'

'No'.

'If you just disappear they will probably send the police looking for you as you are his ward after all.'

'I know I have to take that risk and cover my tracks.'

'At least term will be over and anyone who knows you will be long gone including me. I will not be there to help you. We shall be going to Australia for eight weeks.

If the house sale comes off before then I can ask Hugh if you can move in and supervise everything for us. There will be builders to see etc and I do want Hugh to come with me.'

'Well if Hugh would agree it would be a start and give me time to plan and make myself useful at the same time. I could pay rent. I do have money in the bank my mother made sure of that and I bank my allowance every month from Dino He is quite generous and I hardly touch it.' I explained that Ruth had built up a sizeable sum for me and with interest there would be enough to last a few years .I also knew that I was due a legacy when I came of age if it had not been swallowed up by the business.

The nursing home was an old converted mansion in extensive grounds. It was like a small hospital complete with operating theatres laboratory, x-ray and pharmacy.

There was a separate maternity wing where the patients had their own suites. The Drs were located in this wing and the whole unit self-contained with its own staff, nursery, and special care unit. We were seen straightaway by an older nurse who explained that she was the matron of the unit.

She was about 35yrs blonde and slim and with a ready smile. I liked her. Her name was Sister Katy Jolly. She took a history from me and I gave her as much information I felt she should need about my background. She was obviously used to dealing with single girls and was tactful and pleasant.

She showed me to a cubicle and asked me to undress and put on a robe.

Then I saw the consultant Dr Mary Reilly. She had red hair and looked fiery and temperamental but as I was later to find out very kind and resourceful.

She asked me a lot of routine health questions, took some blood and finally examined me. She confirmed that I was pregnant and that my baby would be due in November. She then asked me about the father. I explained that he was working abroad and had no idea yeti also told her that my mother had died and that my stepfather had married again and we were not close. I also explained that I did not want to tell them until I thought it appropriate.

She said that it could create a problem as I had to have a next of kin but we could deal with that issue later when I had more time to consider my future. She told me about the nursing home and if I had the means I could have the baby there and stay as long as it took to make arrangements. I explained that I did have my own bank account and could afford their fees and that within a year after the birth I would be independent and would be entitled to my legacy.

She was very reassuring saying that she would take care of me and that the staff were discreet and not allowed to break the confidentiality rules.

Afterwards Kathy and I went to lunch and discussed the events of the morning.

'You seem so calm and controlled about it all" she said.

'When I go away you will have no one but I will talk to Hugh and ask if you can stay in the house whilst we are away am sure the deal will be through any time now. I think he will be relieved to have someone to occupy it in fact I am sure he will he is a big softie. We are getting engaged this Easter when the family congregate. The Australia thing is a sort of early honeymoon so you see you are not the only one in love.' she said shyly.

'Well try not to get pregnant' I said.

'He is studying medicine that should mean something.' she replied.

I realised how lucky I was to have such a good friend and was so happy for her.

She was not beautiful girl but had a loving nature and carried radiance with her. In bed that night I was anything but controlled and allowed myself to cry but I held Ruth in my heart and knew that whatever happened I would instinctively do what she would have done. She had been through the war, blackouts, and bombs and had become widowed. She had looked after me and managed the business so I could be just as strong if I had to. Her weakness had been Dino but he had made her happy.

I was sure that if she had been around however disappointed she was in me she would have loved having a baby around and a grandchild to care for.

I fell asleep secure in the knowledge that whatever happened I would manage.

CHAPTER 15

EASTER.

Easter was early which suited me as I pregnancy would be concealed. I had not put on too much weight one dress size only but my bust was obviously enlarged so I tried to disguise this. Helen true to her word had invited me to stay for two weeks. During the break Antonio was due to visit the factory and a large dinner party was organised at Dino's house. I was expected to be around to escort Antonio everywhere. Dino had phoned me saying I had to give no excuses, as it was important to the business as Antonio wanted to buy shares in the company and have the factory enlarged to make silk. I was to stay at the house in one of the guesthouses by the pool.

'Listen Jo you are to buy some new dresses from our store. And go to the beauty salon and buy some make up. I want you smart and well groomed no preppy look. You know what chic means young lady don't you'. He then abruptly put the phone down. I guessed Gloria was beside him.

I called in to the Edinburgh shop and picked up a couple of two cocktail dresses. One was black velvet I which had a high neckline and a low cut back. The other was silver lame with a draped neckline and tightly fitting. I was happy with both. I left my books behind, as I knew I would be busy with Helens baby Jenny who was good-natured happy little soul. I spent the first week camping out in the old house whilst they prepared the one they had bought from Roberto. I felt sad as I did have some fond memories of us all having fun there. Flash backs of Roberto clowning around in the kitchen and playing guitar to the children. At least I was getting experience looking after a small baby learned to love her and walked miles with the pram. I did manage to walk to the farm several times and have long chats to Myra Lee. I also managed to ride Bonny several times. The other children by now had got used to riding him and seeing he was loved and cared for gave me comfort. I missed Roberto's children at such moments. Myra sat with me having coffee quite a lot and kept looking at me quizzically. I wondered if she had guessed about my pregnancy she was a canny woman. She said very little. I knew she liked Dino even if she was not so keen on Gloria. She was as blind to his faults as Ruth had been. However she was busy herself as the stables had expanded and she now kept four racehorses belonging to Paulo and Dino.It was early days and they were new to it all but it was slowly coming together with one or two favourable races. I was told that Antonio might want to see them so I warned Myra.

'Aye well however fancy he is he can have tea at my kitchen table and some fruitcake with the rest of you. And if you ever need anything Jo you come to me you must miss your mum and Rosa. I don't know what Roberto was thinking of letting his go off like that he is a strange lad and now he is gallivanting around Africa.'

105

Finally they were all moved in and Dino came over to announce that Antonio would be arriving the next day and staying in one of the guesthouses. He came to my room as I was dressing.

'Now Jo its time you matured a bit you are nearly of age. I want you to look after Antonio .I know he is interested in you and wants to help you with your career, so be nice to him. Wear your new clothes let him see that you are worth the money we are all spending on you. You have a gorgeous body. Flaunt it. Wear your low cut dresses and dazzle him you can do it.'

'I am not a race horse Dino but we got on well last time he is a nice man I am not in awe of him.'

'You don't understand he really wants to see you. He kept phoning when you left Italy and has been trying for weeks to get over here. Gloria seemed to think you had something going with him.'

'Well Gloria is wrong she seems to want to think the worst of me all the time'

'I know and I keep telling her to leave you alone- come here my darling don't get upset.'

He pulled me to him and held me touching my face.

'Jo look at me sweetheart you have to understand. Antonio is a powerful and a well-known playboy. He knows so many women but it is you he is interested in. I think he is serious about you.'

When is he coming?' I asked.

'Tonight, we shall dine here and tomorrow he will inspect the factory. He then wants to see the new horses and would like to go riding. He asked if you would accompany him. We will then have a meeting and afterwards fly to Edinburgh in his private plane. He will stay at the 'Grand Hotel' and we shall go to the flat. The next day we will all go to the races before he flies back to Italy. I want you to help entertain him, do you understand.'

'I am beginning to.'

'Remember one day you will be a director so start learning the game. I have great faith in you, you beautiful creature. My clients often ask about you. You could be our greatest asset. He put his arm around me, lifted my chin and kissed me. He held me for a few moments looking me up and down stroking me.

'Have you put on weight'? 'Yes" 'Well it suits you. Antonio is a very lucky man.'

Antonio was to arrive at seven pm. Dino asked me to be there at six and unpack. Paulo and Helen were to arrive later. The afternoon was busy Paulo stayed in his office. He very rarely engaged me in conversation. However he was always polite and seemed grateful for my help. He appeared to worship Helen and his baby. She was very outgoing and active and loved all sports. She never got involved in the business or with intrigues and gossip and rarely saw Gloria.

Mid afternoon Helen called me into the bedroom. 'Its Roberto calling from Nigeria .He wants a word about July. 'She handed me the phone and shut the door behind her.

'Dearest wonderful girl. I am longing to see you.'

'Hi Roberto, it's wonderful to hear your voice are you alright.'

'Yes but I am pining for you Go to the mirror tell me what you look like I miss you so much. Start with those gorgeous blue eyes. If your hair is tied up let it fall and tell me how long it is now. What are you wearing? 'My riding clothes I have just got in. But please Roberto I have to talk to you seriously as I missed you in London. I did not get the message.

''I was devastated I waited for four hours. I may have to go soon there is a queue for the phone. Be by this phone on May 1st.Helen has my new box number write darling write. It will soon be July.'

'I will- Roberto its serious I am having our baby.'

'Can't hear. I have to go love you darling.'

The line went dead.

CHAPTER 16

ANTONIO IN THE LAKE DISTRICT

Dino sent a car for me and I was dropped off at my room with my overnight case. I lay out my clothes and had a quick bath and started to get ready. The phone rang. It was Dino.

'I am coming over with Gloria she wants to make sure you are wearing the most appropriate outfit'.

This of course annoyed me but I knew I would have to carry on with the charade. I put on the black dress arranged my hair in a French pleat combed to one side and put on my pearls. They arrived in a hurry. Gloria was as usual over made up wearing bright red lipstick and lots of mascara. Her dress was very low cut. She said very little and let Dino do the talking.

He looked me up and down. 'Hmm what do you think Gloria will she do'.

'Yes but black is too old for her and she is not showing off her figure. Antonio likes sexy women and she needs high heels to show off her long legs'.

She talked as if she were discussing one of her models who were always superfluous and never to be talked to or allowed to join in a discussion. She went over to the blue one laid out on the bed.

'Try this one- come on hurry strip off we've seen it all before.'

I struggled into the blue one, which Dino had chosen in the Edinburgh store and presented to me late one night turning up at the University having had too much to drink. He would have insisted on staying longer had Kathy not turned up to rescue me.

He zipped me up and seemed pleased with the effect.

Gloria said. 'Your right Dino she has put on weight but that will certainly suit Antonio. He will not wander too far away from you tonight when he sees you in that frock. You can let your hair down he will like that too.'

She certainly knew her job her modelling agency was then number one in the North. I felt like a doll dressed up and ready to go to a party I didn't want to go to. They had it all organised. I was the sacrificial lamb going to slaughter. I struggled into my only pair of patent high heels, which were instantly uncomfortable.

I hadn't been in the house for a while and there had been new additions namely a painted portrait of Gloria on the stairs looking almost grotesque. Dino proudly showed it to me saying it had cost them a fortune and had been done by American artist whose work was valued in the art world. I did wonder whether she had it painted deliberately as there were plans for me to have mine done in the summer.

There were lots of gilt chairs around and large mirrors everywhere all from Milan. They looked out of place and tasteless somehow unlike the house in which Roberto had designed and lived in. That was a family country house with a large kitchen and a cast iron stove making it warm and enveloping .The dining room was laid out for a party of eight. We sat by the fire for a while in silence and Dino poured us drinks as we waited for Antonio.

Antonio arrived soon after by limousine having been picked up from the helicopter pad on the airfield. He flew everywhere.

Paulo and Helen arrived about the same time, as did the fourth couple a local businessman and golfer Gerry Brown. He was a local builder. His wife Jill was an attractive brunette looking smart in a green velvet dress. Helen greeted us all heartily and wore a simple blouse and skirt but had made an attempt with her hair which was cut in a bob and suited her. Everyone was introduced and all eyes were on Antonio and me.

He looked extremely sophisticated compared with the other men. His suit was literally 'a cut above the others' and he was slim and sun tanned. He kissed the ladies hands and gave me a quiet wink and then a hug saying

'I have met this beautiful creature before.'

I smiled and decided to be polite and play the business entertaining game to please Dino. We drank champagne and then went to eat. I sat next to Antonio who had Jill on his other side. He seemed pleased with this and gave her a lot of attention. She was a fashion journalist for the local paper so they had something to talk about. Dino and Paulo sat opposite and their wives sat together. Gloria seemed annoyed as I she wanted to sit next to Antonio but he had skilfully managed to avoid that.

He said very little to me but when he did he gave me his full attention.

He whispered as we sat down.

'That dress looks sensational you are more beautiful somehow than when I last saw you, you have a glow. I hope you have not fallen in love with a poor student.'

I smiled at him and said 'No'.

'That's a relief'.

I talked to Gerry on my other side who seemed to be looking at my low cut dress most of the time. Once he touched my leg lightly with his hand and suggested that perhaps I should go down to the golf club sometime. I asked him about his golf and his handicap and that seemed to please him so he gave me a running commentary about the last game he had with Dino and Paulo. They joined in and the conversation kept moving that way. He kept asking for more wine and pouring me some but I managed to hand it back to the maid without anyone noticing. Helen drank very little. She was able to join in the golfing stories also, as she was also a golfer with a low handicap, which left Gloria out of it looking uncomfortable.

Twice she demanded Antonio's attention especially when he was trying to engage Jill in a discussion about her articles on his new factory.

When we finished the meal we sat in the lounge for coffee and liqueurs. Gloria insisted we all danced to some new music she had brought in from America. The large bands were popular and she liked to play them loud on her new radiogram. The new style crooners like Frank Sinatra and Dean Martin were her favourites so we had to join in. The men were happy to do so all except Antonio, who sat in a corner talking to Helen.

Paulo danced with Gloria, Dino with Gill and Gerry claimed me. Gloria had dimmed the lights and I was at Gerry's mercy. He was very drunk. He held me close and made all sorts of suggestions.

'I have only ever seen you from a distance; Dino must have kept you under wraps. Don't be wasting your time with those Italians we can show you a good time right here. You are gorgeous .You would be a sensation at the golf club. Come down sometime I will buy you lunch. I know all the best hotels in the county. I will give you my card.'

I tried to excuse myself saying I felt a bit dizzy.

His attraction no doubt was his money .He was a well-known figure around the town in his Rolls Royce. Unlike Dino and his brothers he had no subtlety when it came to women and his exploits were common knowledge at the Rotary club and the council where he was a local councillor.

A very gallant Antonio interrupted him in full flow and saved me. He took me into a corner and we sat down.

'I have wanted to take you away from all of this all night Jo' he said.

'I think neither you nor I like this music, if I recall you prefer jazz.'

He sat and asked me in detail about my course and my grades, He seemed pleased that I was a serious student and remarked that I was sensible to doing the courses I was describing, as would need it if I intended joining the business. He told me that he had brought some of my photographs with him and if we had time later I could see them. He also had several artists' work to show me so we could choose together whom we would want to use in the summer. I had to go along with it and agree to everything knowing that I would not be there. When the party broke up and the others went home he suggested we went to his room near the pool and Dino could join us for the discussion.

Dino said that they were tired and that when we had decided he would look them over and give his opinion. He was pleased that we were getting on well and the fact that we were together suited him. He was very transparent.

The rooms were large and well designed like hotel rooms with drinks fridge's and bathrooms. Antonio poured us some wine and the proceeded to take out the pictures from the portfolio. They were only prints but they were high quality and it was obvious that Christo was the best in his field. I did not recognise myself and was pleased in a way because I knew whatever success they had with the project I would be almost incognito. I felt as if I was viewing another model.

'The Lady on the Horse' was very tasteful and only gave a hint of nudity the hair being the best feature.

'What do you think?' Antonio said.

'Well I am glad I am in disguise. Are you going to use it?'

'I most certainly am and I want to make sure that whatever revenue comes our way you get your fair share, I hope Dino understands that.'

'He will. He has never cheated me yet.'

'It is not him I am worried about it's that wife of his'.

He showed me some work of an American artist he knew. I had to show interest and indeed would have been if I had planned to be there. The project of course would be dropped and Dino would be furious.

When he put them away I said, 'Do you mind if I go to bed now Antonio I have had a long day and I am sure you have'.

'My dear girl of course. I think we are going riding tomorrow it is just what I need.

I look forward to it. I will see you to your room.'

He walked up the path with me and at the door gave me a kiss on the cheek.

The next day I was up early Dino and Gloria gave me strange looks as I told them about the photographs and the artists sketches which they would see later.

Antonio who had his breakfast in the room then came in dressed in riding clothes. He chatted to them as I went to get changed.

When I came back they said they had seen the proofs and Dino was particularly impressed with my pose on the horse. Gloria seemed proud of her connection with Christo saying he could make anyone look fantastic. We left them and Antonio grabbed my hand as we walked off leaving them wondering.

We did enjoy our ride. Antonio was an experienced rider and used one of the racehorses. We went miles up the fells and rested after an hour by a small stream. He said as he handed me his hip flask full of brandy.

'You would be very easy to fall in love with Jo'.

I replied 'I don't think I am ready yet I am too young for affairs'.

'Wise too I like that –I wasn't propositioning you but if I did it wouldn't be an affair, you are worth more than that'.

We ended up in Myra Lee's kitchen and she made us coffee.

Antonio in spite of his sophistication seemed to impress her as he explained his business interest with Dino. He also discussed the racehorses and said he intended taking us racing the next day. Once on that subject she expressed her opinion and he treated her with great respect. She told him about her long association with us and about my mother Ruth and my grandfather. He seemed pleased to hear about it and said so saying that he was sure my mother would have been proud of me had she survived.

As we went out she whispered 'A grand man you could do worse'.

I blushed and Antonio noticed. We walked back and Dino and Gloria were on their terrace having lunch. We joined them and when I changed they had a short business meeting.

The plan was for the four of us to fly to Edinburgh for the afternoons racing. I was looking forward to it as I had never been to the races so I was quite excited.

Afterwards Antonio was to stay in a hotel and they would stay in the flat I would go on to University and they would travel back by limousine.

Gloria and I put on smart dresses and for once I was allowed to choose my outfit. I wore a black suit and pearls and a white pillbox hat and Gloria wore a yellow fitted woollen dress, which made her look even plumper than she was. Dino liked her to show off her curves.

We landed very close to the racecourse and as I had never been in a helicopter before it was exciting seeing the Lake District from the air. The fells still looked majestic in the sunshine and when we went over the border the highlands were equally awe inspiring. We were able to pick out the lochs and when we approached Edinburgh and the bridges I held my breath in wonder as the sun glittered on the water beneath.

There were lots of photographers about as we landed, as it was an important race.

They took photographs of Antonio who was well known to the press and owned several horses in Europe. He was notorious for escorting starlets and models to premieres and fashion shows and featured a lot in the gossip columns. I hoped they had not caught me in their lens as I hung back a bit and let Gloria take the limelight. She enjoyed this of course and stayed close to Antonio. In the members enclosure it was all luxury and champagne and in spite of my misgivings I enjoyed myself.

Even Gloria appeared to be having a good time and stayed near the champagne waiter and Antonio.Dino was content with placing bets for us and chatting to owners and trainers. He was new to racing and needed to network.

We had a buffet and more wine but I as usual was careful not to drink too much. Antonio came over several times to put bets on for me and smiled at my joy when my horse 'Dandy' came first winning me £100.

He held my hand once and said. 'I have looked around today Jo and I can say now that not one woman here matches up to you in style and beauty. I think I am going to ask Dino if we can dine alone tonight as I do not think I could bear to have to converse with the two of them and make small talk when I have only a short time left with you. I will make sure you get back to University.'

He put it to Dino diplomatically and there was not a problem as Dino being an astute businessman knew that he had to keep Antonio happy as that was the point of the weekend. He seemed delighted that I had fulfilled my role.

Dino took me into a corner and talked to me seriously.

'I am giving you a cheque for the next couple of months and have included a commission for you as you are due some from the shoot. We are going away for a while to America and Italy. You can use the flat in Edinburgh. I know you will be doing your exams so if we do not see you I will send you your tickets for the Italy trip and details later. If you need anything contact Helen and Paulo. Be a good girl and behave well with Antonio. He has indicated to me that he is very smitten with you and has told me that he has great respect for you and will not treat you casually knowing that you are so young. He gave me the impression that he has been a bachelor too long and may be looking to get married so don't spoil your chances.'

I said nothing and smiled at him and thanked him for the cheque. As they left I thanked him for the weekend and said I would see them in July. They left us to go back to the flat and we proceeded to the hotel by car.

It was of a very high standard and set in rolling countryside. If I had been there with Roberto I would have been very excited and looked forward to spending the night there dining in their orangery and sitting out on the balcony under the stars.

Antonio suggested that we went to our rooms to rest and change for dinner. It was to be formal so I would finally wear my black evening dress which was sleek and elegant. I bathed and rested for an hour and tried to sort my head out and decide how I would manage the rest of the evening. I really liked Antonio and felt that the whole situation was impossible from every angle so I would have to face up to it and deal with it moment by moment. I was after all my mothers' daughter.

We were to dine in the orangey, which was warm and balmy full of exotic flowers.

He met me in the foyer and as I came down the grand staircase he smiled approvingly. My dress clung to my figure which I realised would soon be changing shape and in a month nothing I had would fit. He never took his eyes of me all night and was so charming I knew why he had such a reputation. I could have fallen in love with him like many before me but it was so unreal as if I was in a motion picture and he was the leading man, suave and sophisticated. I could never imagine him in kitchen cooking pasta and playing hide and seek with children like Roberto.

The meal was prepared by one of the top chefs in Scotland and was superb. There were game and home-grown vegetables followed by lemon soufflé. The wine was unbelievably expensive. Throughout the meal he kept asking me about my future and what I really wanted in life. I think he was surprised when I said that independence from the family was my main ambition. Then to create my own business.

He tried to take this further but I told him that I was unsure but was looking at options, one was property and one was in fashion with my own brand. I had touched on careers on my course and explored such things with my tutors. He looked at me searchingly.

'You could have about five years as a top line model and make a lot of money to enable you to do this and I could help you.'

I replied that I was unsure, as it seemed such a shallow life.

He nodded 'You are so wise young lady and I respect you for it.'

There was music playing in the ballroom and he suggested we danced. The lights were down and it was a slow waltz. He held me very loosely and we just enjoyed the music and continued chatting. He was attentive but at the same time appeared to be testing me. He however did keep saying how beautiful I was and how he had never met anyone quite like me. I felt extremely flattered and said

'But you are so experienced with women and must have lots of love affairs.'

'Ah you are right but I have had enough of the celebrity circuit I want to meet Cinderella and she is right here.'

'At midnight I may change back into a real person soon and lose my shoe'.

'Then I will come looking for you, you will not escape me'. he said seriously.

We sat down and listened to the music and watched the other dancers.

He then said 'I do not know anything about your love life have you ever been in love'?

I smiled. 'I am not sure- what is love'?

'You will know when it happens. It is what I am beginning to feel for you'.

He took a parcel out of his pocket.

I felt quite embarrassed and more so when I opened it. It was a diamond bracelet and it looked like the real thing.

'It's beautiful I don't know what to say, I hardly know you'.

'From now on I hope you will as I want to see you as much as I can. When you come over in the summer I really want us to get to know one another. Let me fasten it around your wrist, make me a happy man is it all right if I keep in touch with you?

I could come over here next month again'.

'I will have to get back to my kitchen'.

He laughed and held my hand leading me through the gardens.

I shivered and he took off his dinner jacket and put it round me.

We sat on a bench and he took out a cigarette and offered me one.

'I don't' I said.

'You are wonderful what beautiful children we would have with such a moral clean living mamma. Could you marry someone like me?'

'Antonio I am twenty years old. I have very little experience with men and would need to get to know someone really well. It is the most important decision one has to make in life.'

'I will ask you again in the summer.'

He held my hand 'Come on let's dance there's some jazz on.'

I went along with it and when he held me close I closed my eyes and tried to imagine it was Roberto.

'My Funny Valentine' sang Dinah Washington in my head.

He escorted me to my room and kissed me goodnight in the hallway.

'One day Jo I hope this will not be good night. This will be the beginning but it will not be in a hotel room. I will book a car for you in the morning and take you to university but we will breakfast together'.

That is what happened and when we got to university he insisted on taking my luggage in. The students could not help but notice us and groups of girls looked at

Antonio as if he were a film star they couldn't quite place.

Kathy came up to us and I introduced him.

'Is that Roberto' she whispered.

'No he is an Italian advertising mogul a friend of Dino's we were at the races together I will tell you later.'

Soon afterwards he left after having had a quiet conversation with the porter taking with him all of the contact numbers. I noticed him slipping him a large tip, which unnerved me slightly. He was certainly in a different league to Roberto and was not an international business tycoon for nothing. In Italy he was familiar with the Mafia who I knew very little about but it was well known that they took protection money from most businesses. As Dino once said that the reason they all liked being in England was that there was less corruption and no Mafia.

He called his car and gave me a kiss.

'Goodbye Cinderella sees you in July when we will sail to Monte Carlo and gamble our lives away'.

I went back to my room and Kathy was waiting.

'Wow' she said 'If that is Italian man hood I would like to see Roberto in the flesh'.

'So would I' I sobbed, 'Wrong man, wrong proposal?

'What he proposed'.

'As good as'

I looked in my pigeonhole it was empty.

CHAPTER 17

LAST VISIT TO THE LAKE DISTRICT

After Antonio left I decided to settle down and focus on my exams and to do some in depth planning with Kathy and Hugh.

However I received flowers every week from Antonio.

The porters now knew who I was and made sure I received my mail when it came. It was almost as if Ronnie one of them was on Antonio's payroll. It was disconcerting and I felt as if I was being spied upon.

Alas there was no mail from Roberto but Antonio wrote regularly. He used expensive embossed writing paper and wrote with green ink. His writing style was flamboyant and expressive but entertaining. He sent pictures of his yacht and an itinerary for a possible cruise in the summer. He begged me to reply so I sent little cards thanking him for everything. They were polite and to the point but he seemed delighted with my 'faultless good manners.' It seemed I could do no wrong.

I took another trip to the nursing home on my own and after an examination was taken to the office to discuss my stay and the fees. I agreed to stay three weeks prior to the birth and three weeks afterwards. Sister Jolly was exceptionally friendly we seemed to get on well together and we had lots of informal chats. I came to know her as Katie. I began to feel that I was not totally alone and it was a relief that I could finally make a few decisions in relation to my future life with my baby.

Hugh in the mean time had agreed to let me take charge of the house and use the basement flat, which was self-contained. I would organise and supervise the builders and when the tenants moved in would act as a housekeeper until Hugh and Kathy arrived back in October. Although I could afford to pay Hugh he would not accept my offer and said I could live there rent free until they came back. We had many discussions in relation to the period after the birth and they suggested I stayed until I decided I wanted to move somewhere else. Kathy encouraged this saying that we would all be like a family and everyone could help bring up the baby who would have lots of Rugby players as uncles.

All of this was reassuring and I began to feel heartened. It was not what I really wanted but it was a solid offer and I would feel safe amongst such nice people.

Kathy said that it was time I contacted Roberto. She said if it had been Hugh he would devastated if he thought there was a baby he did not know about. She thought Roberto should be told. I explained that I hoped to speak to him when I went to stay with Helen and promised to tell him. Three weeks later I joined them for the weekend.

I went by train and Paulo met me in Roberto's Mazerati. My heart jumped when I saw the car and for a second prayed that it was Roberto driving. He would jump out and pick me up and swing me round and laugh. But it was not to be. Paulo sober faced and serious gave me a faint smile and bundled my luggage in the back and drove to his new home without speaking. That was his way and he was like that with everyone. However he was utterly reliable and the business needed him.

Helen was pleased to see me and proudly showed me her baby's progress. She recognised me and laughed and I loved that as I was beginning to feel very maternal.

'Jo you look different somehow have you put on weight if so it suits you'. She said.

Although it was May they had a warm fire and the comfort of the room enveloped us. We settled down to have tea and cake.

I dare not ask her about Roberto and had to wait until she brought up the subject, which she did within minutes.

"I must tell you Roberto is in hospital in Mombasa. He had a car crash. He wasn't driving so it is not what you think. He is going to be all right but he has broken his leg and clavicle so it is going to be a while before he comes out.

We can write of course and maybe when Dino comes back one of them can fly out to see him or even bring him home. I think the party he was with will make sure he is all right. I know he promised to be around in July when you have your painting done he said as much as he was concerned that your interests should be protected. I spoke to him three weeks ago and he was going to call again this weekend.'

I did not know what to say and hoped my face did not give me away. I was bitterly disappointed. All I could say was 'I am so sorry- perhaps I could include a note when you write or you could give me the address of the hospital .We should all send cards to him regularly.'

'Of course we can do that you could write tonight.' she said

'I will buy a card tomorrow.'

I tried to sound so normal like the niece and friend I was.

'What about his friends.' I said.

'Oh they all go when they are backing off safari. I think that woman I was telling you about goes a lot. Well he has got no one else has he perhaps we should be grateful.'

We drank our tea and I played with Jenny on the carpet.

Helen said 'We can take her up and bath her then we can get ready for our meal I have asked Myra to come for supper. It will only be the three of us Paulo has to go out is that ok.'

I was relieved and it would be nice to see Myra.

I helped bath Jenny and put her to bed. Little did Helen know that one day for me it would be real?

She had prepared a casserole and we sat drinking sherry as we waited for Myra.

'She seems a good friend to you' I said speaking about Myra. 'Yes she is down to earth sometimes I have had it up to here with all the talk about fashion. Gloria has got a good business going with her agency and the stores and catalogues are really successful but it's not for me. We just about tolerate one another and since your mother died I have not heard her say anything nice to you. Dino seems oblivious to it all.' she said.

'I have to go along with it at least for another year'

'What do you want to do? I think Dino has you in mind for the business but Gloria will always get in your way' she replied.

'Well I don't waste my time at University I am learning a lot about finance. I talk to the tutors a lot. Property is always a good bet and I should be entitled to my inheritance next year.'

'What about a boyfriend Antonio seems very keen on you'.

'Well he is twice my age and an international playboy what sort of a life would he lead me if he were serious. I am not in love with him but it is hard to resist such a powerful man. I get roses from him every week and a three page letter. In some ways I wish this summer trip was not going to happen. It all started with Roberto and he is not here to pick up the pieces. I brought Roberto into the conversation quite naturally knowing that when and if the family found out about the baby they would not suspect him.

Antonio of course would be number one suspect but they would never challenge him and he probably would never know about the baby.'

It was all such a mess and I really would have to outwit them all if I wanted to hang on to our child.

Myra arrived and brought a large chocolate cake for our pudding. It was good to see her again and she looked at me as if she knew everything.

'You look very bonny lass, is it love, mind I was not expecting to like Antonio from what I read about him in the papers. He has been out with lots of film stars if we can believe what we read. He is very keen on you and he told me so. Will there be wedding bells in our valley next year?'

'Well I do hear from him regularly and I shall see him in the summer but I do not belong in his sort of world, I prefer it here. My home is around here one day if I am lucky I want to buy a cottage of my own in one of the villages so I can be near you all'.

'I can see he will be persistent he won't take no for an answer you mark my words'.

Helen served up our casserole and we settled down to have a pleasant evening. Myra told us about the racehorses. They had two wins recently. All in all her life had taken off since she met Dino all of those years ago. She had a happy family life with her adopted family and had made more money by investing with Dino than she ever would out of farming.

She asked about Roberto and was quite upset when she was told about the accident.

'I don't know he should never have gone away –they could have worked it all out and now what's going to happen to him. I loved that boy you know he reminded me of my late husband. He has such a cheeky smile and is such fun to be around. He was so unpredictable and he used to love my fruitcake. Remember that fancy dress he organised for the children on their ponies they all dressed up as cowboy's .He lit a fire and we all sat around and sang just like Roy Rogers.'

I wanted to cry when she said this, as I loved him so much.

The next day we went shopping and I bought a series of cards to send to him. They were by a famous newspaper cartoonist and had very witty slogans. I also bought him a book about a famous war photographer. If they ever arrived he would like them. Helen said that he may not be able to reply as his arm was in plaster so may have to get someone else to do it. I felt more cheerful in that I had made an effort to contact him and prayed I would have a reply.

As I said goodbye I gave Helen and Jenny a hug and thanked her not knowing if I would ever see them again.

CHAPTER 18

EXAMS

'I am wondering how you managed to keep your head down and study when all that was happening around you.' said Snowy.

'Well it kept me focussed. When I returned I had to prepare for my exams but I was confident that I had done enough work. There was a lot to think about and plan and I was grateful for Kathy and Hugh. They were to go away within the month and I would be on my own. We would only have a couple of weeks to sort out the house when they took it over.

They had found some tenants and knew that whatever happened to me I would at least have people around merit was all very stressful but I realised that my options were limited and this plan was the best on offer. Fortunately I kept well and took care of myself. I joined in one or two student activities and went on a few visits to local businesses with our tutors. I was always with different people so was pleasantly social with everyone but not too friendly. I had learnt a lot and was confident that even without the third year I knew enough to make a living for myself in the future. I had been taught about stocks and shares and the mechanics of the stock exchange and the markets. During my time alone I planned to make good use of it and buy some shares using a stockbroker.

The exams were spread out two a week for three weeks so I had time to go over to Glasgow regularly and meet Hugh. I had learned to like him. He was a giant of a man in every way. Kind, generous, gentle and compassionate he was the epitome of what was good about his profession. Coming from a medical background he was all set to follow in his father's footsteps.

On the first visit I accompanied them on an inspection of the house and met the builder Jim. He was in his thirties and a local man who set up a successful business after finishing his national service. He was pleasant and chatty. It was a tall Victorian house and pebbledashes against the elements. The situation was perfect as it was in a quiet street around the corner from the hospital. There was a garden back and front with many trees and lawns and a shed and a green house. It had four floors and a basement. Hugh planned to have his own flat on the first floor and let the rooms above. The basement flat was to be mine. Most of it was in good order. Jim agreed to start off with my designated flat, which needed painting and some new cupboards and bookshelves. Hugh explained the situation and we looked carefully over the plans and it all seemed fairly straightforward. He had a contact phone number and as there was a telephone already installed so there did not appear to be any communication problems. He was to call us once a week and I was free to make any decisions if absolutely necessary. Hugh tactfully explained the situation with Jim in that I would be given control whilst he was away but I also needed watching over as I was having a baby. I was glad he did this as I did not have to explain anything and he was going to be around most days with his two labourers.

On the next visit I met three of the new tenants to be who would be taking up residence before they got back. There was Kenny the artist who taught at the local Art College. His work was popular brightly coloured of the "Fauvist" school and very large He often had one-man shows. He was a redhead with wild curly hair and a beard.

He wanted to commandeer the garden shed to paint in. It was a perfect place as it was large and extended into an old unused conservatory. As he explained later he could leave his larger canvasses up to dry suspended on a washing line.

Then there was Karen another medical student in her 3rd year. She was practical pleasant and hardworking .She was very serious and wanted to be a heart surgeon. She loved cooking and hated fashion spending all her spare time in trousers and fishermen's sweaters. The other student was Danny who was a law student. He was Irish and had dark curly hair and loved Guinness, Rugby and Yeats, in that order. He and Hugh were good friends and played in the same team. He had a beautiful girl friend Eve who was from Finland. She was training to be a midwife, which pleased me rather. She lived at the hospital but wanted to stay sometimes at the flat. Hugh was very reasonable about that as it was still not acceptable in a lot of lodgings and rented accommodation.

We all went to the local pub on the corner afterwards and got to know one another. I agreed that they too should be told about my pregnancy to avoid gossip and to get them along side. They were all nice to me and did not ask me any awkward questions. Kenny and Danny gave me a lot attention. Kenny in particular decided to mentor me and always sat next to me when we were out together. I felt so lucky that they were going to be my new family in the next few weeks and months to come. I would need them all. Kenny would not be away for the holidays but Danny and Karen would be doing work experience in other places. They were told that I was in charge of the building and responsible for the rent and up keep. In a later business meeting with Hugh I suggested that we had cleaner come in once a week to clean the stairs bathrooms and toilets and keep the outside tidy and the brasses clean. He did not object to this and Jim soon found us someone .She was called Moira and in her mid fifties. She turned out to be very efficient and helpful and quietly kept order in what could have been a typical shambolic student household. So it was all set up and I had many nights in the pub with Hugh and Kathy fine tuning the details.

I also discussed with them how I was going to get away from university, explain my absence to Dino and get my mail. I decided to write a letter to him saying that I could not go through with the July plans. I would of course be in the flat preparing for the birth early November.At that point I would have hopefully a new plan and a new explanation. Hugh said he would ask his sister who was actually touring Europe to post some cards for me. I was grateful for this and hoped day I could repay Hugh and Kathy all of these kindnesses.

Meanwhile there was no new mail from Roberto but lots from Antonio He also managed through Ronnie to speak to me on the porter's phone.

'Did you get your flowers this week Jo what were they like'.

'Lovely thank you they were delicate pink roses.

'I have been to Monte Carlo and met Grace Kelly she is gorgeous. In the summer I shall be escorting you around all of these beautiful homes and introducing you to many stars. We shall enjoy life and I will teach you to sail'.

Even on the phone I felt uncomfortable with his plan for my future but of course it was out of the question. I decided to write to him at some point and send back the bracelet.

Every day I looked for mail from Africa and even wondered whether Ronnie was withholding it on Antonio's orders. I felt as if this could really happen and had paranoid fears about it. It turned out later to be true and it changed everything.

I rang Helen a couple of times .She said she had spoken to Roberto and he sent his love and told me to write. He was being moved to another hospital and later back to Italy to recuperate. I then realised that our communication would almost stop as he would be with them in July albeit in a wheelchair and have no explanation regarding my absence. I talked it over with Kathy and we both agreed there was little we could do short of writing and letting him know that the reason I was not joining them.

The time came for my last visit to the house before I moved in and Hugh had organised a party. Their flat was going to be locked. My flat was almost finished and Hugh allowed me to purchase my own furniture. I was very excited as it was my first real home of my own. It had two bedrooms a large sitting room and an even larger kitchen, as it had been the servant's quarters. There was even a tiny kitchen garden where my pram could go. The party was held in my kitchen and spilled into my sitting room. I had bought two very large sofas as I had admired the ones I had seen in Italy. I had a record player in a cabinet, a desk and lots of bookshelves and a piano.

We had a barrel of beer delivered and everyone bought wine. The rugby team arrived as did Kenny, Danny, and Karen. It was a good evening and I was happy in spite of myself. After years of being alone it was nice to be with a group of my own age with a similar outlook. Danny played some songs on the piano and we all drank a lot of beer and sang ourselves hoarse. The party went on until about 3 am when most people collapsed on a sofa or a bed or on the floor. I had a good feeling about them all and looked forward to being with in spite of my circumstances.

When everything was settled I concentrated on my exams and gradually started packing up to leave university.

It took me quite a while to compose my letter to Dino but I was satisfied with the result and sent it off. I kept a copy and still have it today.

Dear Dino

First of all I am writing to tell you that I am will not be coming to Italy for the painting and the rest of the photo shoots.

It is all too much for me and it is not what I want in life. I did not know how to explain it all to you. I do not want to be a model and I do not want to get involved with Antonio and the glitz and glitter of the summer season in Italy.

I will write to Antonio separately.

He has been writing to me and sending me flowers but I could never get involved with him. He is too sophisticated and worldly for me. I have to create my own life and have my own network of friends. I know you will be angry and I am sorry I cannot tell you in person. You have done your duty by me and I have appreciated it and respect you very much.

There was talk about me being involved in the business as Ruth had planned but there has been no discussion about it at all lately and I can only assume that Gloria is against this. If that is the case I have to make other plans utilising my degree when I finish the course. I am not ungrateful and I hope we can always be friends.

However it is my life and in a year I shall be able to make all of my own decisions.

I am travelling to France and Germany with friends. I will write and let you know where I am. In October perhaps we can talk seriously about my future.

Love as always
Jo.

The letter would be waiting for him when he returned from America and three days before he would be due in Milan.

So that was the end of my university life and as I left I did not leave a forwarding address. I would let the University office think I was going home and Ronnie was not around so my leaving was not noticed. I had hired a taxi to move my things to Glasgow and felt some regrets as we drove away. I would write to them in October and ask if I could defer my last year to give me breathing space in case I wanted to continue the course elsewhere.

CHAPTER 19

COUNTDOWN

Kathy and Hugh managed to spend one day with me before they left.

The renovations were going well and Jim and his men were reliable tradesmen.

Jim was courteous to me and within a couple of weeks the others would be moving in.

They discussed the financial side with me but there was very little for me to do as they had made private banking arrangements with Jim and the tenants.

I was there to hold things together and make contact with them if necessary. Fortunately they would be back a month before my confinement.

It felt strange at first with just me and the workmen rattling around in the large house especially at night when they had gone home.

I settled into a routine and I went upstairs to greet Jim and his men daily.

Every morning about 11 am I made them coffee and often made a few scones.

I went shopping and started in earnest looking for baby clothes, furniture and a pram. In the evenings I listened to the radio and read and occasionally wrote to Roberto using the last PO Box number. I started to get used to the idea that I was really independent at last. In some ways it was a powerful feeling being in charge of my own destiny. I knew I must stay on a positive course and not deviate, as that would keep me strong mentally. I tried to be honest with myself about Roberto and knew that I may have to plan a life without him for the time being. I still held him in my heart and believed that he loved me.

The first of the tenants to arrive was Danny who only stayed a couple of days as he was going to Finland to meet Eve's parents.

I asked him to supper and cooked him a spaghetti bolognaise Italian style. He brought a couple of bottles of Guinness.

'It's grand who taught you this Jo'

I explained about my Italian adopted family and he smiled and said.

'Is the little one Italian too.' I nodded and blushed.

'You shouldn't worry there's enough of us here to take care of you. Two Drs and a midwife. Think how many uncles he will have.' 'He' I said.

'Yes he' he replied 'It's a boy I know these things I'm Irish and have a bit of Gypsy in me. What is more it will all work out fine for you. Come on drink up give him his first drop of Guinness.'

I laughed and knew he was right. I was going to call him Toby.

I told him. 'It's a grand name' he retorted.

Karen came and went. I knew that even if she were at the house often we would not see much of her. She was a loner and was so focussed on her future career she had no time for friendships. At the weekends she often visited her elderly mother in a village in the highlands so was always exhausted when she got back.

Kenny the painter was the last to arrive but he was not going anywhere as he had an exhibition imminent. I saw him a few days after he moved in. He knocked on my door to discuss the conservatory.

'Come in and have some coffee' I said.

He had arrived in an old van and was unloading his paintings.

He obviously had his painting clothes on which were a mess like his paintings.

I had only experienced Renaissance art but knew about all the Impressionists and the new wave of American artists the Abstract Expressionists.

He was jolly and like Danny fun to be around.

I went into the garden with him and we told Jim what we were doing.

Jim always willing to be help offered Kenny a hand and said that if he needed any simple joinery done in the studio he would oblige.

He looked at the large canvases and shook his head not comprehending at all.

Kenny laughed and said 'There is a guy exhibits a pile of bricks in New York you would like that Jim.'

Each day I was so thankful for all the warmth around me.

Kenny started work early and took a break with myself and the builders and I gradually moved from scones to cakes and sandwiches.

I look on those days as very happy.

Even though I was facing an uncertain future and had no word from Roberto I kept cheerful and busy. July and August came and went and I could only guess what Dino would be thinking or planning. At least he would probably have accepted my explanation about my trip. He would have been furious about me changing my mind about going to Italy. He would have lost face and probably money too with the contract with Antonio. They may have only postponed it until my return to University, Which of course would not happen?

I kept all of my appointments with the Dr and Sister Jolly. I was told that everything appeared normal so I was relieved and gradually got used to my new shape and size and had fun buying clothes to disguise it. Sister Jolly whose Christian name was Katy asked if I would like to go coffee one day in the dining room of the nursing home. I agreed and we got on very well. She was a widow with a child of 5yrs who had just started school.

'I thought perhaps I could give you some advice as you are going to be a single mother like myself and when it comes to your birth you will at least know me.'

I was very touched and asked he if she would like to come to tea with her daughter Rebecca a few days later. It turned out to be another rewarding friendship.

I began to feel as if Ruth were somewhere around sending me warm and loving people to ease my loneliness. They came on the Sunday to tea. There was no builders and only Kenny in the conservatory listening to his favourite music and painting.

I showed Katy around the house and let Rebecca sort out all of my baby clothes and play with the few toys I had found.

Katy said. 'I love this house if there is ever a spare flat I would like one here ours is so cramped.'

I did ask her opinion on lots of issues and she in turn asked me how I would manage.

She apparently paid a girl to come and help her every day after the birth and then she kept her on when she started work. It worked until Rebecca started school and then she adapted her hours to suit. She was happy working at the nursing home as they let her choose her hours.

I told her that wherever I lived I intended working for myself. One idea was to open a shop. My background was in the retail business so it seemed sensible. She agreed and was very supportive. I was pleased she did not want to know about Roberto. It was painful to think about him and I think she knew that. I saw her every time I went for my check up and we ended up having a coffee in the dining room each time. She taught me about breathing in labour and gave me lots of books. There were relaxation classes but I felt too shy to attend so she taught me the basics at home.

She once came on a Saturday when Jim was still around. He hung around a lot longer than usual and they ended up chatting as I made them some coffee.

It appeared they were brought up quite near to one another.

In September Kenny had his show and I went to help. I met a lot of his artist friends and we all sat in the garden late at night drinking and singing as Kenny played his guitar. One day he asked me if I would sit for him. I did point to my size but he smiled sweetly. 'I want to paint you both.'

I agreed and each day for three weeks I posed for an hour in the nude with a robe around me .He wanted a modern mother but posed in a renaissance style. He wanted my hair arranged in tendrils over the pillow. He arranged me on a comfortable chaise lounge and had Indian scarves draping my body .I was not shy and trusted Kenny completely .He was very respectful but was delighted to use me as a subject, and sang as he painted. It was ironic that he was painting it at the same time as the other one was planned in Milan. When it was finished it looked quite surreal and strange as he used mostly an indigo blue with flashes of gold. In spite of its modernity it looked almost sacred. He called it 'The Seventh Month.' His artist's friends were in raptures and said it was his finest. It was destined for a large exhibition and I lost track as events took over.

October finally came and Hugh and Kathy came back followed by Karen and then Danny. We had a reunion party which was also a wedding celebration as they Hugh and Kathy decided to get married quietly in London on their return so it was yet another happy time for us all. They were thrilled with the work that had been done and asked Jim to the party. He came over and sat with me and I almost knew why and smiled when he asked me about Katy.

I decided to write another letter to Dino saying I was taking a year out of university as I had been offered a job in France. I said that I was well and happy and would let him know when I was settled.

This would see me through another few months until I was well and coping with the new life. I would then feel more in control as I approached my coming of age.

I arranged for it to be posted in France.

I also wrote one last letter to Roberto and sent it to Helen hoping she would send it on. It was simple letter guarded in case someone else opened it. I still have it.

> Dear Roberto
>
> I do not know if you will ever receive this letter. If you have no doubt there has been a lot of speculation regarding my disappearance. I am unable to speak frankly to you by post. Please try and read between the lines as you know me well and know that I would never lie to you. I could not come to Milan for personal reasons. If you were there I am so sorry I let you down but one day if we ever meet you will understand and forgive me I hope. I really wanted to see you as I needed your advice and help and still do. Whatever the family

say please trust me. It is vitally important that you do.

You have been one of my best friends and I still love you dearly so try and get in touch with me as soon as you are able. I have written several times but have not heard from you. I hope you have recovered from your accident.

All my love
JO.

I explained in a letter to Helen that I needed to apologise to Roberto for missing the shoot. I said I would contact her when I had sorted my life out and thanked her for her kindness to me. She knew that I had a difficult relationship with Dino and Gloria so maybe she would understand. I explained that I had good friends and that no one was to worry about me. I thought I had covered all eventualities but had not allowed for the unpredictability of childbirth.

CHAPTER 20

TOBY

Snowy listened patiently still and seemed keen to hear about the birth of Toby.

'I already feel involved with him after all I have fed him twice.' he said.

The other students and I all settled down into a routine and the months leading up to his birth were happy. Kathy had also left Edinburgh University so there was no one left in the faculty who knew my whereabouts. I requested my post to be sent to her but I never received any so I assume it was sent to Dino. I knew he would have contacted Ronnie.

Kathy and Hugh were very happy but he worked so hard we rarely saw him.

She worked for a stockbroker, which was helpful, as she was able to advise me through a minefield of investments. In the end because of my age it appeared that it was sensible to carry on using a high interest savings account where I could access money quickly.

However I planned eventually to buy property starting at first with a small shop.

I only saw Karen occasionally as she was so busy with her work and her mother. Danny and Eve came and went and we often met up in the pub. I saw Kenny nearly every day as we still had our coffee with Jim. He was almost finished and had managed to pluck up courage to ask about Katy. She duly turned up at the pub one night and they finally had a drink together. I gathered they made some progress after that. I didn't see her until I was in labour, which was soon afterwards. My labour pains started when I was in the conservatory with Kenny. It was three weeks early so I wasn't sure at first being aware of a backache only. Once my waters broke I knew it was surely happening and Kenny behaving like a real father went into panic mode and called the nursing home.

Luckily Katy was on duty and told him to put me in the van and move quickly. This he did and the smell of paint and turpentine made me vomit all over his canvas as by then the pain was unbearable and I was lying on the floor. When we arrived Dr O'Reilly was waiting for me and after a quick examination declared it was a breach and that I had to have a Caesarean Section. She wanted to go ahead as soon as possible but when it came for me to sign my consent form they realised I was under age. Because the baby was premature no one had got around to getting the papers signed.

Dr O'Reilly insisted I gave her Dino's phone number. She said that he could give his consent by phone, as it was an emergency but he would be expected to come to the hospital at some point and sign the appropriate papers. I was in too much pain to resist it all but I was devastated to think that he and Gloria would now get involved and worse still want to know who the father was.Dr Reilly was kindly but firm as she pointed out her reputation and that of the nursing home was at stake.

As the pains progressed the reality hit me at last that I was in a precarious position and at the mercy of other people. Whatever happened to me and this little baby I was about to give birth to depended on me being strong and courageous in the next few days? I would also have to act on impulse and make decisions quickly. I had no idea what my health would be like after the birth but I was already determined not to let it interfere with my possible plans as it seemed unlikely that Dino would allow me to stay with my friends in the flat.

Katy stayed with me and was calm and quietly spoken urging me to breathe deeply and relax. She also said that they would all be there to help when I came round so I was to calm down and let the baby come into the world. Then I was sedated at last. When the anaesthetist came Katy nodded when I asked if Dino had been contacted.

After that I knew nothing until I was in bed in a room of my own. Katy was holding my hand and told me that my little boy was well and beautiful but was in the special care baby unit being warmed up in an incubator. As I became fully conscious I was aware of abdominal discomfort a dry mouth and the knowledge that Dino may come in at any moment. However I had a great sense of relief that it was all over and that my new baby Toby was as well as could be expected under the circumstances. Katy took me to see him straight away. He weighed 4lbs 14 oz and looked so tiny and alone in the glass incubator. It was through tears of joy that I said 'Hello' to my little son for the first time. He was also jaundiced and fast asleep so I had to be content with holding his tiny hand for a few moments. Katy said that I would be allowed to take him out the next day and perhaps try to breast-feed him. Meanwhile I was exhausted and after a light snack was taken back to my room and given a sedative to help me sleep. As I drifted off I allowed myself to think about Roberto wishing he were there to make things right and fight my corner with me.

Katy was off the next day so another nurse took me up to see Toby. I was allowed to hold him and try to breast feed. When he finally opened his eyes he was Roberto trying to say hello. It was my second love affair. I brimmed with pride as he opened his eyes. Again I missed Roberto. I should have given him a chance and tried harder to contact him. I hoped and prayed that he would forgive me and one day would share this joy with me. In the evening the entire household descended on me. I sat in an armchair throughout as my stitches were uncomfortable. They brought flowers, champagne and glasses. It was wonderful to see them and I basked in their warmth and love. The room was full of hilarity. Danny and Kenny sang me a lullaby they had composed strumming along with their guitars. Katy took them quickly up to the baby unit where they were allowed to look in through the window. Jim told me quietly how proud he was of her and that he was so pleased she had been my midwife. They were seeing one another regularly.

I said 'She was wonderful and I shall never forget all of you ever for your kindness' They all gave me a kiss in turn. As they were about to leave Kenny lingered a bit and put a garland of flowers around my neck.

It was at that moment Dino walked in. He had put on weight since I saw him last and now looked like the rest of his friends a self-satisfied businessman. His black hair was slicked back with brylcream and no longer suited him.

He glowered at me as he came in and I knew that from that point onwards our relationship would never be the same. Gloria was there too but refused to see me.

My friends left quickly when they saw his face. He was clearly angry and lost his temper straight away which was something I had never witnessed before. Coming straight towards me he said.

'Now young lady what have you to say for yourself? I am appalled and disgusted that I have only just been informed about your pregnancy and birth. Gloria was right all along. You lied and deceived us and you have disgraced the name of Grimaldi.

I was beside myself with worry when you left with no forwarding address. You made a fool out of me and you have let us all down including your mother. Thank God she is not here to witness this. Who were those people? Is one of them the father of your child?

'No' they are my friends from university we have been sharing a house.

'Oh have you, well I know all about student lodgings,- wild parties, drinking, sleeping around .I thought you were better than that and you were once. Your mother and I were so proud of you.

I am now going to ask you once and for all who the baby's father is. Is it Antonio? Did it happen the night he stayed with us at our guest house? Gloria did see him leaving your suite in Milan.

'No it's not Antonio. I have never had a relationship with him. Gloria saw us standing outside my room New Years Eve. We were talking about Easter. I am sorry I did not tell you I was pregnant. I was frightened and knew you would be angry and disappointed in me.'

'Angry I am devastated. You were my precious little girl. I loved you so much I adopted you.'

He became more abusive and irrational like a jealous husband who had been betrayed. He grabbed me by the shoulders gripped me hard and started shaking me.

'Who is it.? I demand to know- it is my right.'

'I am sorry Dino I can't tell you.'

I was in tears. I was not only in great discomfort and pain but he frightened me.

'Its no use crying. I know now I have been too soft with you. I should have listened to Gloria. She must have known more than she said. You will tell me who the father is. I am warning you now if you don't tell me- when we get to Italy you will.'

I realised then what I had always been half aware of that he had an obsession with me and always had which accounted for a lot of things. He wanted absolute control of my life but did not know how to control his own feelings towards me.

'I am going arrange everything. I will speak to your consultant. I suppose there is a bill to pay have you thought of that.'

'Yes' I said. 'I had some money in the bank'.

He ignored this. 'As soon as you can leave you are coming with us and the baby will be going to Italy to the family. I made excuses to Antonio in July saying you were ill so there is a possibility we can pick up where we left off. The whole programme was ruined and the calendar delayed. Roberto wanted to stay involved and was to have come to Milan in July but could not make it either. He has to have more treatment on his leg and another operation.'

He looked me up and down. 'You're a mess pull your nightdress up and put on your dressing gown. I want to see the child, call the nurse.'

'I will take you, I would rather we went together.' I said 'From now on until you come of age next year will do as I say and that means everything.'

'If that includes separating me from Toby I am not going anywhere I said.'

He was furious. This time he slapped my face and pushed me back into the chair, glaring at me and clenching my wrists.

"You young lady will not speak to me like that again, you have run out of choices.

I will now spell it out to you Jo and tell you what the likely outcome will be if you continue in this manner. You will be taught a salutary lesson the Italian way. It has been tried and tested.

I will get you admitted to a private clinic near Naples. I know a psychiatrist who will commit you if I say you are unstable. Once I have signed the forms they can prescribe any treatment they like. They may try drugs. They usually get results one way or another. I will not question their methods.

Most of the Drs are retired and work out there a few days a week. They enjoy working with young girls especially pretty girls like you. You will be examined thoroughly and be given birth control. As long as I pay their exorbitant fees they will keep you there until I decide when you should be released.'

He started walking around the room gesturing the way Italians do when they want to make a point. He was also agitated and carried on telling me the sordid details of the 'nursing home'. almost relishing it.

If everything he told me was true it was a terrifying prospect. He certainly sounded as if he meant it.

'Of course you would have to work there and earn your keep. Your privileges would have to be earned. They do not employ servants. The girls do all the work, the cooking, the cleaning, laundry work and waiting on the staff.

Some of them go in during pregnancy. Their babies are often adopted privately.

They provide simple dresses for you to wear as your clothes will taken on admission.

Sometimes the Drs choose the pretty ones to entertain them when they stay overnight and have the odd party in which case you will be allowed your clothes and make up. They of course will like you especially if they find out you are the model in the photograph Roberto took when you were sixteen. It is now iconic and hanging up in most men's clubs and bars all over Italy. I can see you earning those privileges very quickly without getting your hands dirty. The downside of that is that the other girls would be jealous and make your life a misery. Some of them have been at the clinic for years and will never leave having developed real mental health problems.

They probably started off just like you, having a baby and then were gradually abandoned by their family.

Gloria thinks you should go anyway to be taught a lesson. I would of course visit you and if you do as I say, I may get you released. It's your choice - all I need is a name. Now I need to know when his birth certificate will be ready.

'It will be available a week today when the registrar visits. I shall also have my medical check on that day which is part of the discharge procedure.' I said quietly.

"I shall be here at midday to collect you and I will speak to the consultant before she examines you. I want more checks done before you leave. I need blood tests.

You will be living in the real world at last and as long as you conform and do exactly as I say we will put this behind us. I shall be going back today as I have to go to London on business. I will call the consultant on a daily basis. I shall request that you are not to be in contact with anyone including your student friends and arrange for two private nurses to be with you day and night. They can help you with the baby so you can rest. I shall expect you to spend the time making yourself presentable. I cannot be seen with you like this. You look terrible. I will organise a beautician to come and we will send you some new clothes. You will look smart and elegant when we travel. I shall be making arrangements to fly to Rome. I will try and rearrange things with Antonio whilst we are there. Now I know your true nature you can work for me too. You have two choices both will be under my control. You have had too much freedom. I take it you still have your passport.'

'Yes'

'Well I will take charge of that. If you have not given me a name before we leave England we shall fly straight to Naples from Rome. It only needs one phone call to book you in.'

I knew he meant it. He had everything to gain .He could get a committal order, claim my inheritance and leave me in the nursing home as long as he liked even after my coming of age.

We went upstairs to the baby unit. I was allowed to hold Toby at last. He was jaundiced still and looked very fair. He was not a little Italian at all apart from his curl on his forehead. The nurse asked me to breast feed him and Dino watched. He sat on a chair for a few moments staring and then abruptly got up and said that he was going and would be back the following Monday to collect us.

I decided then that I would have to leave with Toby before this happened. At fifteen days he should be thriving well and able to feed.

CHAPTER 21

MY ESCAPE

S nowy said   'Well Dino finally showed his true
colours what a dangerous man. The committal
plan must have been very frightening. It sounded
like something from a horror story or a gothic novel
but I can believe it still happens especially in that sort
of area around Naples which I believe is notorious for
Mafia control. Some of the girls would be no more than
children and would have ended up as prostitutes. Thank
goodness you are safe here Jo. I will help you all I can.
How did the escape go?'

'I had five days to plan and had no idea where to
go. That evening Toby was allowed to come to my room
at last and I started to care for him. Katy was on duty
until eleven that night. She was appalled when I told
her about Dino so when the patients were settled for the
night she came to my room. She stayed for two hours
and during that time we managed to find a solution.

I explained that Dino was about to hire two private
nurses to be with me day and night. He would also soon

find out where I lived. I told her about his plans to take me to Italy and the threat of the psychiatrist and the nursing home. He would certainly be planning to take Toby away from me. He would never treat me with respect again and had already inferred that I would be expected to entertain clients if I did stay in England. There seemed to be no choice but to leave as soon as possible. I told her that I had a distant cousin near London and I felt it was the only place I could go. I was distressed about leaving my friends whom I desperately needed as I had been so happy living in the flat amongst them all.

After I had finished she said.

'I think I can help. My sister Sarah is in New Zealand and her flat in East Sheen near Richmond is empty. She is also a nurse and is away for another six months maybe even longer. I am sure she would welcome a tenant. I could ring her for you; in fact when I get home tonight she is bound to be in as it will be midday there.'

'Perhaps she would consider even a temporary arrangement until I find somewhere else? It would be such a relief and much better than a hotel. The rent is not a problem.'

Katy also suggested taking over my flat if Sarah did agree until I decided whether to stay there or risk coming back. In which case I would not lose contact with my friends and we could all meet up when the dust settled. I explained about the birth certificate, which would be available on Thursday morning. If Dino did not come Friday then it would give me time to leave the evening before. There was the added problem of the nurses but Katy said she would sort that out. She knew a lot of agency nurses and as they often had breaks so we had to be one step ahead of them. We both realised that even our conversations were going to be difficult. There was so much to talk about but one thing was in our favour.Dr Reilly was going on leave on the Friday and she would examine me and check Toby before she left on Thursday afternoon. Katy said that she would be off that day so would not be implicated. She also said that Jim would almost certainly pick me up and take me to the railway station. We stayed up for another hour discussing the fine details. She promised to let me know the next day if Sarah had agreed to our plan. I had enough clothes with me and only needed a small case and a holdall, which I would use for Toby. I had my bankbook and enough money to buy my train fares and last two or three weeks until I found a new bank.

Dino would be furious. He would not like being outwitted and if he was planning on cheating me out of my inheritance he would not give up easily. Katy agreed not to tell the others immediately so they would not be implicated. As she left she said that if the nurses started in the morning we would have to communicate by letter or arrange a meeting time when they took a break. She said if necessary she would pass me a note through the librarian who was a friend of hers.

She gave me a hug. 'Go to sleep if you can and trust me, we will sort it all out and show this stepfather of yours that you too have powerful friends.'

The day nurse arrived the next day at 8 am. She was called Sheila and was in her fifties. She was quite large and her agency nurse uniform only just fitted. Her hair was in a bouffant style and she wore lots of makeup. She was quite friendly and kept asking me a lot of questions. She said that she had been told that I was not to have any visitors and it soon became clear that she was very curious.

She said early on 'You must tell me about Italy and those fantastic Italian men.' She was very transparent and of course must have been primed to find out who the father of Toby was. I told her as much as she needed to know and tried to chatty and friendly. She did let me sleep between feeds and gave Toby top up bottles when necessary. She made a great fuss over him did not mind taking over all his care.

There were several deliveries for me from our store in Edinburgh. She marvelled at the designer clothes, luggage and jewellery.

She said. 'Your stepfather is very generous he must have spent a fortune on you'.

'Yes he does not like me looking like a student. I prefer casual clothes but we are going to Milan and he wants me to look smart.'

She smoked so she often went outside or in the staff room. She spent a lot of time gossiping and talking to the porters and the young doctors who all smoked outside on the fire escape. I heard her saying to one of them.

"This case I have got is easy. She is supposed to have mental health problems but she seems alright to me, probably been spoilt by her rich daddy and ran off with some one her own age and got pregnant. Her father has asked me to watch her closely. He is Italian and super rich, you should see his car it's a red Ferrari.'

We began to have a routine and I had several opportunities to see Katy. Sheila enjoyed her food and male company and joined the porters and male nurses for lunch every day staying for more than an hour. I often said as she left that I would be in the library so that became a convenient meeting place.

Katy had contacted her sister and said she was delighted to have me as a tenant which meant that we could go ahead with the plans.

She had also seen Kathy who wanted to visit but I sent a letter asking her to write to me and meet me in London as soon as I was settled. I thought it appropriate that no one but Katy should know my whereabouts.

The librarian was friendly with Katy so she agreed to pass on notes if necessary and did not seem to think it unusual. The night nurse came on at eight and did not do much but did feed Toby for me enabling me to sleep. She was a friend of Sheila's but younger and more glamorous. She sat in the armchair, wrote copious notes and then read her many magazines sometimes falling asleep. Unlike Sheila she barely spoke to me. I was very relieved that Katy and I had made the Library arrangement as our final plans had to be made by letter.

I was to leave as the nurses changed shifts. They usually stayed in the office for about half an hour together comparing notes and chatting over coffee. I would take Toby in to see them and head for the nursery saying I was going to bed after taking a bath. The nursery had a fire escape and I would leave that way where Jim would be waiting for me in the van. Fortunately the fire escape was not very visible at the back of the boiler room. Katy would take most of my belongings the previous day in a laundry bag.

Two days before the hairdresser and the beautician arrived to give me a manicure and a facial. When the day finally arrived I was feeling well and refreshed. Sheila was still very chatty and continued her interrogation of me.

'Have you ever smoked' she asked 'I have heard that some students get stoned on dope.'

'No not at all. My friends are all serious about their studies as I am'. That put paid to that query.

Two more new outfits arrived by post from the Edinburgh store. One was a black suit and the other a cashmere camel overcoat. There was also a beauty case and some sun glasses. She marvelled at them. I had become quite fond of her so I gave her the glasses. She was thrilled as they were very expensive. I knew that I would have no need for them in London in November.

'There is a store catalogue around somewhere. I will give it to you later. Maybe we can get you a discount.' I said smiling at her. She was so transparent.

Dr Reilly had examined me the night before and said I was fit for discharge. She was very kind and wished me luck making a veiled comment about Dino and his attitude. She also checked Toby and said that he was well and at three weeks was fit enough to travel. I saw the registrar soon after and filled in the documents. I did not feel happy about putting Roberto's name on it in case Dino saw it but felt that if anything ever happened to me Toby should know who is father was and if we were ever reconciled it would be fitting.

Then all I had to do was to wait for the night shift and our escape. Katy had managed to get my luggage away. I had a rest in the afternoon and ate a full supper at six .A note from Katy said that Jim would be there at eight and have train tickets for me.

The moment finally arrived and I began to panic as the two nurses seemed in no hurry to go into the office as usual. They took their time hanging around the kitchen making coffee. I had to interrupt and think of something quickly. I remembered the catalogue. I went in the kitchen and gave it to them. I explained that all the designs were Italian and the very latest. Sheila grabbed it and took into the office.

'I am leaving Toby in the nursery whilst I have a bath and an early night. Can l take my sleeping tablet now' I asked them? They gave it to me and I pretended to swallow it. It was Phenobarbitone and it usually sent me straight to sleep. They would probably not bother to check on us for hours and if Toby did not cry the night nurse would go to sleep herself. I saw them close the office door and reach for their cigarettes eager to see the catalogue. I closed the nursery door inside, put a wedge under it and lifting up my sleeping son ran down the fire escape.

Jim was there waiting in the van as planned. I was shaking and tense knowing I was going into yet another new phase of my life but had the added responsibility of a little baby who would be utterly dependent on me. We picked up Katy who held Toby for me. His bed was in my holdall, which was cosy and warm.

They put me on a fast train to Glasgow where I was to connect with the London train. However there was to be a two-hour waiting time in Edinburgh that night as there had been signal problems. If anyone was looking for me they would assume I had already caught a train from Glasgow or was staying in the locality with my friends. I said a tearful goodbye as Katy hugged me tight saying that they would all come to see me as soon as possible.

'And Snowy you know the rest'.

He smiled 'Well done thank you for sharing it with me. Dino was not making light threats was he? I am glad for your sake you got away. I am sorry Roberto missed out on the birth of his son. I have a feeling that one day you will be together again.

You already had been under an enormous strain the night I met you and the last thing you needed was the episode in the waiting room.

All I can say is that the Staff Sgt will be disciplined. The Major will be as good as his word. He does not read the tabloids and will be off to Germany in two days so hopefully he will not hear about Dino and your narrow escape. Let's hope the lads do not get wind of it. They are all on leave anyway and will have dispersed. Some of them will be going to different units.'

'What about you' I asked.

'I will be at the MOD. I am to be detached to the legal department prior to my university placement. Now Jo try and think of this as a place of safety.

I will stay in contact and hopefully your friends will be down to support you.

Have you made contact yet?

'Yes briefly with Katy but I am calling again tonight for the full story. They did not find out I was missing until breakfast.Dino was furious of course and called the police. I am grateful for all your help Snowy but do not feel obliged to me.'

'Not at all it's a pleasure. My girlfriend Mimi may be useful to you. She is also studying law. She has lots of contacts and may be able to help advise you if you decide to set up a business or find yourself in a legal battle with Dino. When you are ready I will bring her over.'

'I would love to meet her.' I said and meant it. I did not want to lose contact with Snowy who was another one of Ruth's angels.

'Let's have another drink but I think young Toby wants one first' he said.

CHAPTER 22

PLANS

When Snowy left that day I had run one or two ideas by him.One was to enquire about the empty shop and how I could take a lease on it being under age. I was almost sure that I wanted to open a clothes shop. In that way I would become self-sufficient.

He seemed very impressed that I wanted to get on with it straight away.

I explained that I was my mother's daughter and she would have wasted no time.

He left smiling and said he would call and see me the following Sunday with Mimi his girlfriend.

Then I really was alone and spent the rest of the day shopping and taking Toby out. I had to buy a light inexpensive pram as all my baby things were in Glasgow. I started to explore further afield and studied the underground map taking one home with me. I planned to travel extensively on it familiarising myself with the names and locations. I needed to shop everywhere to look at prices and current fashions. I knew where a lot of the major wholesalers were already as I had accompanied Ruth down to London regularly. I also wanted to go to all the street markets around the Portobello Road. I lost no time in ordering a newspaper daily and several periodicals and trade magazines. I could see that Toby and I would be going places together. I already knew how to drive and sooner or later I knew I would need a van.

That evening I dyed my hair having had it cut short in the afternoon. The hairdresser was appalled and reluctantly attacked my golden locks. As I looked in the mirror I really did look like Ruth and decided to keep it in a bob as she had done on her birthday. She must have orchestrated it. She was there for me I knew.

Finally I was able to speak to Katy and Kathy who were getting to know one another as Katy had already made arrangements to move in. They gave me a commentary on what happened after I left.

'There was panic and all hell let loose. The nurses were sacked from the agency and Dino sent the police to our house questioning all of us. They drew a blank of course but I think we still have to be careful who we speak to.'

'I do not think Dino will give up in a hurry.' I replied.

'He will probably hire a private detective so if Jim comes down watch out. Tell him to leave at an unsocial hour and from his work address. I have seen the paper so let's hope the story does not run on. Any way I have had my hair cut and dyed.'

Kathy gasped 'No your beautiful hair was it upsetting'.

'A bit, but it's a small sacrifice to keep Toby.'

Katy asked me about the flat and Toby and if I got there safely.

'It's perfect and if I stay down here and your sister stays in New Zealand perhaps we can make it more permanent.'

I decided that it was not appropriate to tell them about the station incident until we met. I asked Katy about the shop and she said it used to be part of the bookshop next door so I needed to talk to the owner. She said that they planned to come down the following weekend and bring what they could. She would leave her daughter Rebecca with her parents.

Cathy was concerned about our health and well being.

'We are worried about you all alone and Xmas is just four weeks away. We are coming down to Hugh's parents who live in Hampstead so we will also come and see you. How can we contact you?'

'There is a phone box on the corner so I will call you most evenings. I promise.'

She also gave me her office number which was reassuring.

So altogether I still had my old friends and had a new one already.

As I breast fed Toby later I told him how lucky we were and what wonderful friends we had. I told him about his father and said one day we would find one another. I had read in a baby book that they loved the sound of their mother's voice so I talked and sang to him all the time.

I liked the flat and was determined to try and secure a lease on the shop downstairs. If I could stay there it would be an excellent location on the busy main road but adjacent to other thriving businesses in a square just behind our premises.

Apart from the book shop there was a modern coffee bar, which seemed to attract young people. They had skiffle and folk bands playing in the evenings. There was an art college in the area so the venue was very popular.

The next day I decided to find my savings bank and buy some books from next door and introduce myself to the owner. I was in luck the savings bank was only three blocks away. My account was in my old name so that also worked in my favour. I was still Jo Scott. Armed with cash I had a drink in the coffee bar and took stock.

It was quite a large café and had a lively atmosphere even at 11 am in the morning.

There was the buzz around the place. I was fascinated as most of the girls wore exotic and unusual clothes and make up. It was a mixture of the Existentialist look and what they called the Beatnik style. Black was the predominant colour. They wore long flowing skirts or tight narrow trousers. Most girls had long hair, pale faces and lots of black eye makeup. It was almost as if London had cocked a snoot at the 'Haute Couture' world I had experienced in Italy.

After three cups of coffee I had already started to say 'if'. If I could get a shop I would cater to that market. If I did I would try and get alongside some of them and visit their design dept at the college. It would be a project I could immerse myself in.

Whilst my prospective customers would be more up market I would have a small dept for the student. I could stock second hand model clothes and old stock the wholesalers wanted to get rid of. Excited I took Toby home for his sleep, had lunch and prepared to meet the owner of the bookshop.

Entering it was like stepping back in time. It had a Dickensian atmosphere with lots of lots of ancient wood panelling and bookshelves from the floor to the ceiling.

It was the sort of place one could stay in for hours with a cosy welcoming atmosphere. The counter was to one side and in the middle was an old leather sofa and small tables covered with newspapers and books. It appeared empty so I had to ring the bell on the desk several times.

The owner appeared covered in dust. He apologised for his appearance.

'I am so sorry but I have been up in the attic and several books shelves fell down on top of me, I suppose I ought to shut up shop whilst I clear up.

'How can I help?' he said brightly.

He was a tall sun tanned man with a shock of grey hair probably in his early fifties.

He had a well-modulated voice like an actor.

'Well I love books and I intend to come and browse often. I will certainly buy a few from you as I have been studying economics and there are several volumes I need to order. However I want to introduce myself.

I am Jo Scott and I am going to live in the flat next door. Did you know Mary, who is now in New Zealand?'

He smiled. 'It's like a village here we all know one another. Mary was a nice girl how is she.'

'I believe she is enjoying the life out there and has no fixed plans to come back so I am renting the flat for about a year.'

I felt that in the light of what I was going to ask him next it was sensible to talk about a long let.

'Well welcome I am Tony, book shop owner and resting actor. Unfortunately these days I seem to be doing more resting than acting. I am waiting for a break and I have a few auditions lined up. In fact I have one tomorrow for the radio.'

'That sounds interesting good luck with it This is Toby my baby. He can't quite smile yet or say 'Hello' though he tries.'

'Well I mustn't cover him with ancient dust. 'Hi Toby baby' he boomed as if he were talking to an audience a in the gallery.

'I think I will lock the door if you don't mind but do stay for a few minutes and have a brew, will tea be ok.'

I smiled. 'Thank you yes.' He pointed to the sofa.' There's room for you both'.

So far so good, I thought. 'About the shop next door, have you any plans for it'.

'Not really it needs a bit of work on it and my funds are low. I would rather rent it than sell it as one day I want to expand into there.'

So feeling bold and business like I used the skills Ruth had taught me.

'Well I have just left university and I want to open up a clothes shop.

I have had a lot of experience as my mother had her own business.

She taught me just about everything in relation to the retail fashion trade.

She died recently so I do have funds and if it is a success I would like to buy eventually.'

My new hair cut helped in a way as it made me look much older.

He looked at me quizzically and paused for a moment.

'Well I would be happy to show you around. Could you afford to have some work done as I have no cash flow'?

'Yes and I have a friend whose boyfriend is a builder. He would advise me. They are visiting me next week.'

He was quiet for a few moments.

'I have to work it all out perhaps we could talk again tomorrow. I more or less know the going rate. Would you be able to give me rent in advance'?

'Yes certainly and I know a solicitor who could draw up an agreement.'

I didn't of course but Snowy did. I knew it was vital to stay confident and say the right things.

He smiled. 'When I shut up the shop tonight perhaps you would like to look around. Of course it may not be suitable.'

'Well I do know one thing the location is good. I already like it here and the natives are friendly.'

We finished our tea and I left him to sort out his shop and clean up the mess.

I was very elated when I went back to the flat.

I looked up 'Ruth' I said. 'Please guide me'.

I couldn't wait until 6 pm. when Toby would be fast asleep.

Tony knocked on my door and I ran down to meet him.

'Sorry I am late I have been sorting that mess out for hours.'

'You must be exhausted perhaps I can make you a drink afterwards'. I replied.

He smiled. 'Thanks I would like that. Come on then let's go in.'

It turned out to be a massive building. I had prepared myself and had a clipboard making notes as I went around. I tried to sound as if I knew exactly what I doing which of course I did. I had been around for years when they had renovated the stores.

The window which was boarded up was like the one in the bookshop as it had been one building once. It was Georgian and had bowed windows. I knew it would look perfect painted in a pastel colour and could see two little bay trees outside.

It was an ideal back drop for a window display. I was already excited. The main room was large and I could see that it would hold a lot of stock there were four other good-sized rooms a kitchen and a little yard. More important there was a large cellar which looked as if it had never been used since 1820 when it was built. There was a brick in the wall with the date on it. The ground floor rooms were very dark and dingy being panelled like the book shop. I wondered if Tony would allow me to have the panels decorated in pastels as they did in that period. I could show him some books on the style I had in mind. There was quite 1 lot of work to be done but it was mainly cosmetic.

The fire place was huge and I could see it as a centre piece painted in white with a large Georgian mirror and fire dogs in the grate. I would go to the sales and buy period furniture to decorate it. It would look more like a classic drawing room than a shop.

At the back I could be more adventurous and have theme rooms. I also had an idea that I could stock a few children's clothes probably French.

Tony watched me. 'You seem to like it.'

'I do when I can move in'.

He laughed. 'I will take you up on the offer of a drink and we can talk. I will just run over to the off licence and get a beer, would you like one? I like Guinness'.

'So do I' I said.

Within ten minutes he was back and I made him a quick sandwich whilst we drank the Guinness and talked.

'Well it sounds as if you like it should we talk about rent.'?

'Yes name your price.'

'Well if you are prepared to pay for the renovations it would be such a load off my mind so I would be willing to charge you a minimal amount. Could you afford three months rent in advance?'

He suggested a realistic rental and I realised how much I had learnt up from Ruth and even Dino. I was amazed that he was charging me so little.

I pretended to deliberate as I had made extensive notes on immediate building work and shop fittings. It was of course a preliminary discussion but at the end he was very charming and gave me the impression that he really wanted me as a tenant.

'We can perhaps meet tomorrow lunchtime giving us time to collate our thoughts.'

He was obviously still had lots of work to do next door so I said good night went upstairs and poured myself another Guinness.

'Thank you Ruth' I said looking out of the window at the stars and the church steeple beyond.

CHAPTER 23

MIMI

For the next week I was in constant touch with Tony who seemed very enthusiastic about leasing his shop to me.

He was very flamboyant and I could see how he would fit into the acting scene.

Being self absorbed he showed no interest or curiosity about Toby. I was grateful as it could have been otherwise. We discussed drawing up a formal document by his solicitor and that was to be arranged. I wondered what would be involved and resolved to be ready with my answers.

As Snowy would be visiting I requested that I could have a copy to show to his girlfriend and if there were any problems with my status we could discuss them. If necessary she could find me a lawyer. The only problem I could see would be a referee and my addresses. I could use my old home address over the store and maybe ask Hugh to write a reference as I had taken care of his property. I could not see where my age would be mentioned.

Meanwhile I talked to him about the interior decorating and my ideas. He was used to seeing interiors being built in the theatre so he understood what I had in mind.

'In fact my dear I have the very book here for you.'

'Sold' I said when he presented me with the most wonderful book of Georgian interiors.

'About the panelling'   'Do it, it will look charming" he said as he looked at a room in the book decorated in a soft pastel shade of duck egg blue. It will make the fireplace stand out and the gold mirrors will reflect the light.'

I was so pleased he agreed and for the first time for a year I suddenly felt happy that it was all beginning to fall into place. Day and night my mind was scrambled with so many plans.

Toby was still a gurgling smiling bundle of fun and a delight to have around. His presence added to my life as if he had replaced my mother. I knew I would have to get help and decided to ask around about child minders.

When Saturday came Snowy arrived for tea with Mimi. They both looked so 'beautiful' as they walked in. He was already a tall handsome man but Mimi complimented him and added an exotic touch. She was exquisite.

Standing tall in a flowing robe of black with a large orange scarf and several onyx necklaces she looked like a princess. I wanted to sweep her up and transport her to Milan where Antonio would gasp at such beauty and style.

We greeted one another with a sisterly hug as if we both knew we would be firm friends. I found out later that they had known one another since they were sixteen when both were competing for the position of head prefect at their school in Jamaica.

She had heard all about Toby and I took her to his cot where he was fast asleep with his thumb in his mouth.

I explained how much Snowy had helped me and what a lucky woman she was to have such a wonderful partner.

She smiled. 'Yes he is now going to compete with me at law school where we are going to be together at last. We are also getting engaged at Xmas so we would like you to come to our party and experience a West Indian Xmas.'

'I am so touched that you are inviting me a complete stranger. I would love to come if it's alright to bring Toby.'

Snowy roared with laughter.

'Alright wait till the entire grandmas' get their hands on him you will lose him to some very experienced bosoms'.

I had made chocolate cake so over tea I told them about the shop. Snowy seemed so pleased for me.

'Wow that was quick work. Are you going to take it?'

'I think so if you will help me with the legal side. Tony the owner is going to draw up a document.'

'No problem you can give that your attention can't you Mimi.'

She nodded. 'Of course can we see it?'

'I will pop round and ask Tony if we can have the key, if you will stay with Toby'.

Tony was pleased to see me and was so anxious to get a move on with the agreement he gave me the key and said I could take as long as I liked.

Snowy picked up Toby for me and carried him whilst Mimi and I ran from room to room like two little girls going off to play in a dolls house.

I told her my plans and she agreed with everything I said.

'Why don't you make the cellar a trendy place for young people and have a few gimmicks like music and coloured lights.'

I thought it was a great idea and then she suggested a special room for ethnic products and materials saying she had lots of contacts.

I could see that whoever supplied her clothes knew what they were doing so I was really interested in her ideas. I also said that I intended having French and Italian children's clothes and would make that area parent friendly and have toys there for children to play with and a playpen.

She seemed as excited as I was and offered to help me when she had some free time.

Snowy grinned and followed us around talking non-stop to Toby as I myself did.

'Look at the two of them Toby crazy women with all their fashion talk we need to talk mans stuff how about a drink what do you fancy MILK,MILK OR MILK mines a beer come on lets go upstairs.'

Mimi laughed 'He loves children, he wants six and I want to be a lawyer.'

We eventually joined him and I took back the keys and told Tony that if he could let me have the document they could take it away with them to look at.

He was quick to respond and then I knew that it soon would become a reality.

Before they left Snowy said that they knew a builder who had done a lot of work for his parents who lived in Primrose Hill where the party was to be held?

Within a week the document was ready to sign and soon after I had paid my deposit and got the keys.

By the time Jim and Katy came down I was ready to go ahead.

CHAPTER 24

MY FRIENDS FROM GLASGOW

Katy and Jim were as good as their word left Glasgow at dawn on the following Saturday and arrived for coffee at about 10.30. They had stayed at Jim's house in case they were being watched.

After our reunion hugs they seemed so happy to see me and then told me that they had got engaged. It was wonderful news and seemed part of a new sort of collective joy around me. They had brought as much as they could cram into the van and we all unloaded it and found homes for everything. My pram was welcome as it was a big one and comfortable for a baby to sleep in.

We lost no time in looking at the shop as I was now the proud owner of the keys and the lease. Jim strode around with a clip board whilst we discussed Décor, colours, fashion etc.

'I think you are going to be happy here. It has a good feeling.' Katy said

I told her about Snowy and Mimi and how it all came about. She was appalled about the waiting room episode but pleased that I had some new friends.

Jim finally came in with his calculations and gave me a rough idea how much it would all cost. He did have his reservations about paying for the renovation of a rented property. He said the cellar if lined and heated would be very useful

I explained that Snowy had a builder in mind and they were due to arrive to see us about midday along with Tony.

When they all arrived all four men went to survey the building again. When they came back we all stood around having coffee and waited for the verdict.

Tony looked a bit anxious but the builder Jack Clark seemed very honest and straightforward and reassured him that the fabric of the building would not be spoilt. More important he knew about planning permission and building regulations. In the end they both agreed in principle about prices and shop fittings. Finally a sum was agreed and as they left I stayed on to talk to Tony. I explained that I did have the funds and if ever decided to sell to me would he take that into consideration.

He smiled. 'Your university taught you well young lady, it's a deal. I am pleased the property will be taken care of I will see that we add a clause to the agreement.'

Then Jim and Katy took me to a local restaurant for lunch with Toby.

'The shop will look splendid and with your ideas very tasteful. I was also impressed with your builder but I would get professional decorators in though as there is a lot of fancy Georgian plasterwork.' Jim said.

Meanwhile I explained exactly how I hoped to stock the shop and my plan regarding the recruitment of students. They were amazed that I was so focussed and that I had done so much in three weeks. Katy had seen Kathy and she said they were coming to see me Boxing Day. I told them about my West Indian Xmas. When they departed I felt a sense of well being that I did have loving friends I could trust and turn to. The shop alterations would make a hole in my savings but I knew I was making the right decisions. I also knew that somehow Ruth was guiding me.

I spent the next few days phoning suppliers. Tony allowed me to use his phone and I agreed to pay the next bill. We phoned the exchange and applied for a business phone in the shop. I knew there was a long waiting list for connections for home phones but I was lucky as I spoke to someone Tony knew and they arranged for me to get it done straight away and an extension to the flat. It was such a relief and it was done before Xmas.

Jack had said that he could put a team in mid January so I was happy that my new life would really begin after the New Year. It would be all down to me my mother's daughter.

With peace of mind at last I decided to go Xmas shopping. On Xmas eve I had transformed the flat with a Xmas tree and fairy lights. I had a small TV which in a strange sort of way was company. Toby seemed to like the lights. I was invited for a drink with Tony when he had finished for the day. He introduced me to his mother Alice and his sister Jill who were both charming and educated. They both told me stories about his acting ability and the parts he had.

'I can imagine he is very good actor, he has a lovely voice'. I said.

'He is a very good Shakespearian actor and had some small parts for The Royal Shakespeare Company in Stratford.' said his sister. We are not supposed to tell anyone but you know that serial they have on the radio every evening he has got an audition for the Squire who buys the old manor house.'

I smiled at the news.' He would be perfect.' He did eventually get the job.

They were very keen to know about my shop. They both held Toby and did not ask any searching questions. They did however suggest that I might need a child minder or a nanny.

'I know, much as I value my independence I think I would like someone to live in.

Jill said 'I think I can help you there, my brother has had an Italian student staying with him. It's a new idea. They are called AU PAIRS. There is a special magazine you can buy where they advertise. In return for lodgings and food they help with the family. It might be just right for you and good company. I will ask him if she has any friends that want work'. 'An Italian girl would be wonderful as I speak Italian and would like Toby to be brought up with the language.' I said.

I excused myself and took Toby off to bed. As they said goodnight they said they would not forget about the Au Pair and they were as good as their word.

CHAPTER 25

OUR FIRST CHRISTMAS

C hristmas was not the quiet one I had imagined.
I had bought Toby a Stieff Teddy as it would
hopefully stay with us forever and not only be
well loved but become an antique one day.

Jill and her mother left me some perfume and
chocolates. They obviously felt sorry for me and were
going out to lunch.

I decided to go to church in the morning. I found one
on the green further down the road. It was full of people
and everyone was shaking hands and being friendly.
The candles were lit and when the choir came in singing
'Once in Royal David's City' I allowed myself to cry and
think of Ruth and Roberto and how much they both
would have loved seeing my baby infant boy on Xmas
Day. The mood did not last long as the Sunday school
class performed a simple nativity play. They forgot all
their lines and Joseph dropped the baby as he was
putting him in the crib. Mary gave him a piece of
her mind in exactly the same way as her own mother

would have done. The Shepherds came on late because they could not find their sheep. The vicar's wife was in despair as she brought them in with their mouths full of chocolate they had found on the Xmas tree in the waiting area.

It was fun, jolly and joyful.

I knew then that one day everything would come right that sometimes joy happened when one least expects it.

Afterwards I caught the bus to Primrose Hill to the house belonging to Snowy's parents where the whole family were celebrating a West Indian Xmas.

It was a Georgian three story house and as I stood at the bottom of the garden admiring the elegant façade I thought 'one day I want to live in a house like this'.

I was greeted at the door by Mimi and there was music and laughter coming from every room. After my first Rum Punch I remembered very little of the day but wonderful food and marvellous company. Toby was taken off me straight away and handed around by various smiling relatives all who seemed experts in childcare.

Mimi introduced me to some of the other guests and then showed me her beautiful Ruby ring.' He must have spent a year's pay on this' she said

'Come and meet his parents they are by the piano, he is playing carols.'

They gave me a warm welcome and no one seemed a bit curious on how I came to be there.

His father Gil a successful Barrister was tall and distinguished. His mother Mabel was only about Ruth's age and looked charming in a white silk dress. She welcomed me as we stood and listened to her son playing 'Hark the Herald Angels sing'.

I wanted to say 'Yes Angels came in many disguises. Sometimes they were 6ft tall and were rewarded for their good deeds by the Queen'.

He jumped up and kissed me on the cheek wishing me a 'Merry Xmas'.

I smiled at him.' Thank you it already is- thanks to you.'

We had more punch and then Gil asked everyone to gather around for a toast.

'To my son Albert and Mimi' he said.

'I thought I was proud last year when he was given an OBE but I am just as proud today as he presents his lovely fiancée Mimi who we have known and loved as long as we have known him. Inseparable at school but competing with one another for every prize apart from 'Prom queen'. Please raise you glasses to Albert and Mimi.'

I was surprised to hear his real name as I was used to Snowy and continued doing

He was used to it, it amused him.

Gil continued.' As a wedding present we are going to hand him the key to this our lovely home we have now owned for eight years. We are going back to Jamaica where I have been offered a post as a High Court Judge and we shall live in our family home once again. All I ask of them is that when we return in a few years time to visit there will be the sound of children's voices playing in the shrubbery'.

Everyone clapped and cheered as it became obvious that even Snowy and Mimi did not know about their new home or indeed his father's appointment. I was so happy for them and pleased I was there to witness their joy.

Afterwards we ate a traditional West Indian Xmas meal. We were seated on ten tables in their long dining room, which in Georgian times would have been a ballroom. Mimi insisted I sat with them. Toby had been put to bed upstairs in the nursery which was equipped for grandchildren as they already had two.

West Indian waiters were hired for the occasion and served the meal to us. I shall always remember the meal it was traditional yet exotic.

THE MENU. (Which I kept.)
Pumpkin Soup
Lobster Bisque with foaming cognac
Roast Turkey with Apricot thyme and cornbread stuffing.
Rum soaked Xmas pudding and brandy sauce.
A medley of West Indian fruits.

The wines were the very best French wines from their extensive cellar.

Throughout the meal someone played Jazz piano as well as traditional carols.

I asked Mimi if Snowy would play for us later and she said that she was sure he would. She proudly said 'He is a great jazz musician'.

I enjoyed this loving happy family atmosphere with so much to celebrate.

It was a great privilege to be invited. Their warmth kept me going and I tried not of think of Ruth and Roberto and how things might have turned out.

I got home about nine in the evening. One of the family dropped me off in his car. Toby was asleep and once in his cot slept until morning.

I fell asleep very quickly as the rum and wine had been very potent.

I dreamed of Roberto standing by the lake. He was calling me and pointing to the house.

I awoke at 8am to a snowy Boxing Day. I looked outside and cars were stuck in the snow. Everywhere looked sterile and clean and quiet. It gave me a sense of peace. I knew then that I must not waste a minute and that I should use my spare time writing down all I wanted to achieve and how I would do it. I had been to business school and now it was time to get businesslike. Katy had brought my typewriter, which had been a gift from Ruth when I matriculated. I bought a folder and labelled it 'Toby ¬Jo' the name of my new store. I made lists of stockists of antique paints and wallpapers. I drew rough sketches of the rooms and each time Toby had a sleep went downstairs to explore and make sketches of the layout.

Even when he was awake I wheeled him around in his pram from room to room wrapping him and myself up well as it was below zero. There was an old grate in the grand fireplace so I started to collect sticks in the park and by the canal on our walks. Once I started the ideas came thick and fast. I felt the presence of Ruth very often and didn't care if it was my imagination playing tricks with me. I felt surges of energy and creativity at those times. During the time between New Year and Xmas I made great progress. I kept my first folder and years later I marvelled at it as it was packed full of meaningful notes to myself.

I also had a visit from Jill and Tony. He was so shocked that it was so cold that he rushed next door and brought a couple of ancient looking paraffin heaters. Jill brought something just as valuable the phone number of the Au Pair contact.

'When your business gets started I would love to come and help you if would have me'. She said.

I appreciated this as she had a quiet sensible way with her and a delightful sense of humour. I could picture her in a smart black dress greeting my up market clients.

At the end of the day I had a Manageress. 'Wonderful!' I thought thank you Ruth' One of the first things on my list said 'van' so after much consideration I decided to discuss it with Snowy who I would be seeing after the New Year. They were so keen on my business idea they wanted to visit as much as possible.

I did however call about the aupair and had an appt to meet a girl when college started on January 5th.

By the time Kathy and Hugh arrived on New Year's Day they found me in high spirits looking healthy and well and more like my old self but with my dark hair cut short. They poured out the car and unloaded yet more of my belongings from the old flat. They looked so well and happy. Hugh bounded up stairs lifted up Toby and swung him around and gave him to Kathy who cuddled him looking distinctly broody.

I laughed at her and teased her 'You want a baby don't you.' she smiled and nodded. We went to Hampstead and I had tea and supper with her parents Peter and Mary.

They obviously knew my story and were warm and welcoming.

They adored their giant of a son in law Hugh as we all did.

We all played Scrabble and I won a game.

It completed what was to me a wonderful Christmas surrounded by loving people with generous hearts.

CHAPTER 26

FIVE YEARS LATER

When Toby was five he started our local church school.

He was a happy go lucky healthy and according to our au pair Remy 'So handsome'. She spoke Italian to him all the time and he could read simple books in both languages before he entered the reception class.

My business exceeded all my expectations so when the house next door to Snowy came up for sale in Primrose Hill I bought it.

We were very happy there. Toby was never lonely because they now had two children Bruno aged four and Emily three. We were almost like one family.

Snowy was by now a lawyer and still in the Army.

Mimi however preferred being a housewife although she did lots of voluntary work through her church helping immigrants and advising them on legal matters.

When I finally came of age I wrote to the lawyers in Edinburgh to enquire about my legacy. They replied saying that there was no legacy and that at Ruth's request the money had stayed invested in the business. I wrote back to them with Mimi's help and said I was there when she died and that I had seen the will. I also told them that on no account were they to declare my whereabouts to my stepfather. It appeared that they had evidence of a further will in favour of Dino and the business.

I let it go at that point as I was already successful myself and felt emotionally healthier because of this. In a way I finally felt liberated. I did not want any connection with Dino or his company. This detachment had to include Roberto also.

I persuaded myself that I had to give up any sentimental ideas about seeing him again. I had to allow my mind to close him down.

The sizeable amount in my savings book had given me a good start and through Kathy and my tutors at the L.S.E where I was a part time student I acquired enough knowledge to manage my own shares and buy and sell small properties making a profit each time.

My business expanded year by year and two years after the opening Tony sold me his shop and I was able to own the whole building, which looked magnificent when, restored. It became well known in the area and gradually other shops started to copy my ideas. I was congratulated by the local council and asked to speak at lots of functions as a local entrepreneur.

There was a Regency arcade near and that was refurbished housing lots of unique specialist shops. There was an antique shop, a bookbinder, a delicatessen, a specialist wines shop, herbalist and an art gallery.

Tony had got the job in the long running radio serial and bought a little bookshop in a place called Hay on Wye in Herefordshire. His mother still lived over the shop with Jill who was my manager. Occasionally Tony would call in and see us and we would all go out to eat.

On a personal level my social life revolved around children's activities.

I was always looking for new opportunities to expand and constantly looking for new talent. We went through mini skirt revolution, which seem to tie in with the phenomenal rise of English pop groups like the Beatles and the Rolling stones.

I also let my hair go back to its original colour although it was never quite so curly. Occasionally Snowy and Mimi and I would have a night out at a jazz club and they often asked Snowy to jam with them which we encouraged.

They often had dinner parties and asked me along sometimes with a spare man.

We also had a television and Toby and I used to watch the children's programmes together. I had an old Morris Minor estate car which I used for visiting my suppliers. However as a luxury, I bought myself a sports car which Toby loved. It was of course a Mazerati. It was a fantasy of course but sometimes I allowed myself to see Roberto driving it one day. I often picked Toby up from school in it and drove down to Brighton where after four years of searching I had found my cousin.

She was called Frances and was a schoolteacher specialising in English and drama. I found her through the army with Snowys' help. It was official and by writing her a letter he was able to look up her records and post it on to her without divulging her address. She was in her early forty's and had served as a WAAC in Germany in the headquarters in Berlin. She had a mane of red hair and porcelain like skin.

Her boyfriend had been killed in action so she had never married and I was her only relative. She lived in a flat overlooking the sea in Hove and we formed a friendship that would last and she became a real

Auntie to my son. She had a lot of family photographs of my father and mother and grandparents, which was very important to me. She was light hearted and loved playing games with Toby and Snowy's children. She was passionate about the theatre so when she came to see me she dragged me out to wonderful plays in the West End. Her favourite was the 'Old Vic' and it became mine too. We often took Toby with us. He enjoyed the 'Midsummer Night's Dream' and 'Twelfth Night.' and would strut around in the garden making the children pretend to be actors in his plays he had written.

At some point in our friendship I told her about Roberto and she knew without asking that it was painful to talk about as was her own doomed love affair.

Everyone teased me about my lack of interest in men. Snowy tried very hard to introduce me to various acquaintances but I drew back always and retreated into myself. I told myself that I was content with life as it was.

Once Major Sandy Taylor called into the shop as I had spoken to him at Snowy's wedding. He was visiting MOD but had been posted to Singapore.

I did allow him to take me to dinner. He turned out to be very interesting and told me that he was never at ease in a home as he had spent most of his army life camping out and living rough. He spoke eight languages and was already learning Chinese.

He was posted to Malaya where there was terrorist activity.

I had no secrets anymore so I told him how I had come to be on the train and how I had managed on my own. He seemed very impressed and asked about Toby.

I sensed loneliness about him and asked him about his family life.

He had none really. He had been married once and had a son who he never saw.

The army was his family as it was to many ex public school boys, orphans and boys from broken homes. He saw me home and asked if he could write to me and I said yes feeling sorry for him knowing that the next day he would snap into action.

Later in Malaya he would certainly be leaving his gentler side in the barracks.

So life went on but around about my 28th birthday things changed and at an extraordinary pace.

CHAPTER 27

ROBERTO

By the time Toby was eight years old I had a very successful business and a lovely home in Primrose Hill.

We lived next door to Snowy and Mimi who had two children, Bruno aged seven and Emily aged three. Bruno attended Toby's school and we were almost like one family. Although I had Remy my Italian au pair to help me Mimi often had Toby to stay with them after school. Remy sometimes stayed at the flat as she was studying at the local college. She had been with me eight years and was indispensable. She taught Toby Italian and he was more fluent than me. He was a wonderful child bright intelligent, tall and good-looking like his father. He was very well mannered as were Snowy's children.

It was the month before his eighth birthday that I had news that would change our lives forever.

I had a letter from a firm of solicitors in Edinburgh saying that they had managed to trace me through my previous solicitor who had handled Ruth's affairs.

The letter stated that my stepfather and mother Dino and Gloria had both been killed in a car accident in four months previously.

They explained that the will and the estate were so complicated that although I was entitled to some sort of legacy it was still in the process of being   finalised.

It disturbed me and I was shaken for a while as it brought back a past I had been trying to forget. Much as the two of them created a lot of unhappiness for me it was tragic and memories of the early days came flooding back. Dino had loved my mother and in his strange way loved me too.

I made contact and they wrote back suggesting I go up and see them and speak personally to Mr Paulo Grimaldi. I assumed he had taken over and was probably staying at the flat as the main offices were Edinburgh.

There was no mention of Roberto.

I decided to go up immediately and see Paulo and the solicitors on the same day.

Hopefully I could then write to Helen at some point. She had always been concerned   about my welfare and I liked her.

I took a flight to Edinburgh and planned to be away two days as I had to be back for Toby's birthday party which Snowy had organised.   He had built a pirate ship in his garden and the children liked it so much that they were having a pirate party and   going to wear fancy dress.

I caught the plane to Edinburgh and stayed in a hotel over night. It was strange being there again and memories of Ruth's death came flooding back. It was painful revisiting that particular time. The next day I visited the solicitor at about 10 am. His name was David Black. He was new to the case and seemed confused.

He explained that for some reason there had been a second will when my mother died and I did not have the inheritance I expected. He also said that I would be entitled to a few thousand pounds but most of the inheritance was tied up in the businesses. Paulo would be at the head office if I called and that it appeared that he was taking over the stores. He said that his dealings were with Paulo and that he had never met Roberto as the senior partner usually dealt with the case and was away.

I was extremely nervous when I arrived at the very large extensive offices in the same block as the store.

On the ground floor there was a desk which was manned by a smart young receptionist in wearing black. Ruth had always insisted that all the store and office staff should wear smart black suits and it appeared they had still kept up the tradition.

I said that I wished to see Mr Grimaldi and that we were related.

The receptionist stared at me and said.

'I am afraid he is not here today would you give me your name and I will call his secretary.'

'Yes it's Miss Grimaldi'

'Are you- are you Miss Jo Grimaldi' she said inquisitively.

'Yes' I said. 'I am.'

'There is a large photograph of you in Mr Grimaldi's office.

It's beautiful'.

'Is he coming in today at all'?

'No he is away but I can take you to see his secretary I am sure she will help you.'

She spoke to her on the phone and then took me up to the first floor offices.

Mrs Tyler was a pleasant smart lady in her 50's.

'Hello I am so pleased to meet you come into the office I will make you a coffee.

We have been trying to contact you for weeks. I think the family will be relieved that the solicitors have finally located you. If I may say so you are just like your portrait.

You weren't at the funeral were you?'

'No I didn't know I had lost touch.'

'It was so sad Mrs Grimaldi had no relatives so we all sat on her side of the church. We couldn't move for Italians.'

I smiled to myself imagining them all there with their noisy children. Funerals were less sedate in Italy and Dino had been popular.

We went up in the lift and I stepped into the office which had 'Managing Director' written on the door.

As I went in there was a very large framed picture of me on the wall the one Roberto had taken for Ruth's birthday.

'That was one of the first things he did when he came in here from Africa he must be very fond of you', she said.

I was unable to grasp what she was saying.

'You mean Roberto is the new managing director I thought Mr Black said it was Paolo.'

'Oh he is new, the partner is away and he gets the brothers' mixed up.

I keep telling him we have the good looking one. I don't expect you have seen him for a long time as he is a free lance wildlife and news photographer. He is wonderful, did you know that he supports three orphanages.'

'No I had no idea.'

'He was so shocked by the thousands of displaced families in Nigeria and Biafra and their suffering that he spends his spare time fund raising.

He has no home and evidently lived in tents in the bush with the other journalists most of the time although of course they did use the hotels in the cities sometimes.

He is staying at the flat at the moment. We hope he will stay here as we all like him very much. He has the girls in a flutter I might tell you.'

I held my breath as I half expected him to walk through the door.

'When is he due in?' I said casually.

'He said he had to fly to London on urgent business. He is flying back later today or tomorrow morning.'

'Oh' I mumbled which was all I could say as I was nearly in tears.

'Can you not stay, I am sure he would like to see you.'

'Unfortunately I can't. I will have to call him and arrange another meeting.

I have a special birthday party to go to.'

'Well here's his card and here is Paulo's I am sure he would like to see you too.'

'How is Paulo?'

'They have just had their fourth child though I expect you know that.'

'No I didn't'.

'They have two boys and a girl and are moving into Dino's house.'

I thought about Roberto's house- 'Beside the lake beneath the trees' like the Wordsworth poem. I had been so happy there.

'What's happening to the other house?'

'We think Roberto might buy it back.'

'Does he have his family with him?'

'No he is on his own but I believe he wants his daughters to come and visit.'

I looked at my watch.

'Well if I hurry I may just catch an earlier plane. I will have to get a taxi to the airport. I really do have to be at this birthday party. Could you please give this Roberto?'

I gave her my business card.

She looked at it 'Goodness me do you own the 'Tobyjo' Company.'

I nodded.

'You have lovely clothes they are very different.

When the girls here go down to London they always bring something back from your store. I am sure Mr Grimaldi will be sorry he missed you.'

She saw me out and I caught a taxi to the Airport.

My mind was in such chaos. I was shivering. I almost had a panic attack.

I allowed myself to fantasise about meeting him.

Would he even want to meet me and would he still care?

Perhaps he never received any of my letters. I certainly hadn't received his if he had written any at all. Then there was Toby how would I handle that. There was so much to think about.

I had a comfortable first class seat on the plane and covered myself with a blanket shivering all the way back to Heathrow. We disembarked quickly as there were only ten of us on board.

There was a queue of passengers waiting to go to Edinburgh on the next flight.

Then I saw him before he saw me. He was reading a magazine. There was stillness about him. I panicked and paused for a moment unsure of what to do. I looked for the exit and watched the other passengers vanish almost wishing I was one of them.

My heart really did miss a beat. He was wearing his leather jacket and jeans and he looked exactly the same as he did nine years ago but thinner. His hair was still falling over his forehead. He looked up to check the board but by this time I was next to him.

'Roberto'? I said gently as if asking him his name.

He paused and looked at me in complete bewilderment then his expression changed as he shouted my name out loud and lifted me up in the air.

'Jo what are you doing here. I have been all around London looking for you, where have been for the last eight years.'

'In hiding but I have just been to Scotland looking for you.'

He put his hands on my shoulders and looked at me.

'You look wonderful. I cannot believe it. It's like a dream, and I have missed you so much. Come on let's get out of here. I am not getting on that plane.'

He held my hand and pulled me into the first class lounge which had just emptied and held me in his arms for a long time.

'Where are you going now' he said.

'Home are you coming'.

'Oh yes I am definitely coming let's get a taxi'. he said tearing up his boarding pass

In the taxi he stroked my hair.

"It still shimmers in the light and so do you. Where have you been and what happened to you? Please don't tell me you are married. I don't think I could bear it.'

'No' I said 'and you.'

'No I kept my word I love only you but I have been so involved with various projects in Africa I've had no time for a social life.'

'Your secretary told me about the orphanages.'

'Yes they are my priority and seem to swallow up all of my money.

I raise money through my business connections. I was heading up a team attached to a relief organisation. Once I started I couldn't stop. There are thousands and thousands of displaced people in the Congo and Biafra many of them children. I knew lots of pilots flying in with supplies. They gave us lifts. Once we were there we had no time to do our real jobs. They needed our muscle and put us to work. I was only one among hundreds of relief workers.'

'What will you do now?'

'I live on very little so I will try and make the business work to my advantage. My salary will go to the orphanages. First of all I am going to fight for your legacy. I was determined to do that even if we hadn't met. I am afraid Dino was responsible for a lot of shady deals. Never mind that now. You and I have eight years to catch up I want to know everything.'

'You will soon.' I said smiling inside thinking about our little son.

'I cannot believe you are here'. He said.

He called through to the taxi driver.

'It's very important I get this lady home as soon as possible. I will give you double the fare if you can find a short cut I haven't seen her for eight years do you understand.'

The driver chuckled. 'I think I do Ok! Hang on to your seat straps.'

He swung around and found his way through a myriad of little streets and then we were there.

I was very proud of my three story Georgian house.

Roberto looked amazed as we walked up to the pretty blue front door with its shining brass door knocker and the bay trees in the porch.

'Is it all yours?'

'Yes' I said proudly.

'Welcome home Roberto.'

'Do you mean it?'

'Yes I do you are not the only one who has waited eight years.'

We threw our luggage down and just hugged one another for what seemed like forever.

I put the kettle and made some tea then briefly showed him round missing out Toby's bedroom. He looked out of the window.

'There's quite a party going on next door, are they your friends. They have a large bonfire.'

I held his hand. 'Yes it's a special one I have to go - no we have to go.'

He looked apprehensive. 'No Jo please stay here with me for a few more minutes.'

'It's important come on, come with me, don't resist me. Do as I say and don't ask questions.' I literally dragged him next door.

Mimi met us in the hall. She kissed me on the cheek.

'My word who have we got here. Who is this handsome stranger? You didn't pick him up off the streets.'

I smiled at her and quietly said.

'This is Roberto! And Roberto this is my wonderful friend Mimi and just striding in with an arm full of balloons is her hero and mine Snowy.'

Snowy seemed to know who he was.

He shook hands. He said later that he knew as soon as he saw him because he was the image of Toby.

For a second no one said a word. Then Snowy took the initiative.

'Come on Mimi go and sort out the cake and I will give out the balloons.

Let's leave Jo here to talk to Roberto.'

'What lovely people' he said. 'But I think you brought me here for a reason.'

'I did, hold my hand Roberto and don't say anything.'

I took him over to the window.

Toby was standing on the ship holding the wheel and shouting.

'This is Toby your Captain speaking.'

His black curly hair had fallen over his forehead.

I put my arm round Roberto.

'That little boy is eight today and he is your son Toby.'

Roberto didn't move a muscle. I could feel him stiffen. I squeezed his hand and looked at him. He was crying.

'Why didn't you find me and tell me. You must have been so brave.'

'I thought you didn't care, you stopped writing.'

'I wrote every week for a year but I now know where my letters went. Dino had a pile of them in his office. He got them from the hall porter at the university. Did he know?'

'Not about you but he threatened to take Toby to Italy to be adopted. Because I refused to tell him who his father was he planned to commit me to a private clinic near Naples on the grounds of instability I left the Maternity home before that happened.

'How could he do that to you of all people, my own brother?'

'Let's talk about that another time I want to take you to meet Toby now.'

I held his hand ignoring the assembled crowd of parents.

I led him down past the bonfire towards the large pirate ship which had taken Snowy six months to build.

I called. 'Toby I have just arrived from Scotland.'

'Hi mummy did you bring me some Scottish soldiers for my fort'.

'I did darling but get down I want you to meet my friend Roberto.

I knew him a long time ago and he is coming to stay with us.'

Roberto helped him down and shook hands.

'Hi Toby I have just come back from Africa'.

'Hello. Did they have elephants where you were? I love elephants.' he said looking up curiously at Roberto who was tall and suntanned and smiling his big generous smile that I had missed so much.

'Big ones I rode on one once.'

'And tigers.'

'Enormous ones and very tall Giraffes.'

'You didn't shoot them did you?'

'No I would never ever shoot an animal. I take their photographs. I have a magazine in my case which contains a lot of my very best ones. Would you like to see them later?'

'Yes but I would also like to go one day - to Africa.'

'I could take you as to the zoo and see the animals there if mummy agrees.'

Toby looked at him expectantly.

'Can we really'.

'Yes there is one outside of London in the country where the animals roam wild. It's called Whipsnade. They don't have to stay in cages there.'

I held my breath they were so alike.

'We can talk about it later but I think the children want you to blow out the candles now.'

He ran off to where Mimi was cutting a big chocolate cake.

Roberto held on to me and through his tears smiled as the children sang 'Happy Birthday'.

'Its incredible -I am speechless. Is there an angel around here somewhere or am I having the most wonderful dream of my life?'

'Yes she is called Ruth' I said squeezing his hand.

He looked at me. 'I missed eight years of our little boy's life and abandoned you when you needed me .Will you ever forgive me.'

I smiled 'I already have.'

Toby blew out the candles and brought us some cake.

"You really will promise to take me to the zoo Roberto."

'I never break a promise Toby I will take you to the Zoo on Saturday if mummy will allow me to and one day we shall go to Africa all of us.'

Toby looked at me.

'I like Roberto mummy you can marry him if you like'.

He skipped off his face covered in chocolate cake and jumped on the boat again.

Roberto looked at me and took me into his arms saying.

'I do like'.

Snowy came up to us with some warm punch and we sat by the bonfire until all the parents collected their children.

Later as we helped clear up Snowy had a chat to Roberto. I knew they would get well and they did. Snowy had served six years as an Army lawyer and then became a Human Rights Lawyer. They had an intense conversation about Africa.

Mimi and I washed up.

'You look so happy Jo who would believe it. It's like a fairy tale.'

'I always knew it would happen one day but I was getting tired of waiting. I love him so much.'

'And he loves you, I can tell and so can Snowy. We are so happy for you. He is a good man.'

'He is more serious now but he is also such fun and full of surprises just wait.'

'We will leave you alone tomorrow and take Toby to school for you so you can have some time with him. You have a lot of catching up to do so take your time. Let's all dine together Saturday night if Roberto would like to that is.'

We carried a happy grubby little boy home and he insisted that his new friend Roberto should help bath him and read him a story,

Roberto said. 'Sorry Toby I do not read stories I tell them and they are all true is that ok. And I have some real pictures. Should we start with the elephant that lost his daddy?'

I left them to it and had a bath. I cried and cried and cried with joy and excitement as I covered myself with soap bubbles. As I dressed myself I looked in the mirror and said.

'Thank you Ruth I know you are there'.

Toby fell asleep holding the picture of the elephant.

I made a drink for Roberto as he had a shower.

He came out in his towel and looked at me smiling.

I went over to him and pushed his hair back.

That was it really, that night our second child Rosy was conceived.

Next morning. I woke up after 9am and wondered if it had all been a dream.

There was no sign of Roberto. My heart sank. Had he gone again had it all been too much-? Then I saw the note.

> Dear Jo Grimaldi
>
> We guys were up at six and left 'mummy asleep.'
>
> Got a lift with Mimi, had to take Toby to school.
>
> Rob.

I cried again into the pillow beside me where he had lay and cuddled me all night. It was all so overwhelming.

He arrived back at about 10-30 with an arm full of shopping and three bunches of pink roses. He gave me a big bear hug and sat me down.

He said 'Do not move. I am afraid there was not a lot of choice at Woolworth's' this morning but I hope this will do for the time being.'

He knelt down by me and produced a curtain ring out of a paper bag.

'Will you Josephine Grimaldi marry me Roberto Grimaldi next Friday at twelve midday at the registry office Caxton Hall London?

Will you love me forever till death us do part.'

'I will' I said.

He covered me in kisses and we sealed the proposal in the way lovers do when they are happy.

'How did you do it' I said later 'The wedding arrangements.'

'I rang them and they had a space so I said we would be there at 2pm today with our documents to fill in the forms. I will have to pay some vast sum for a special licence. Its normally 7s 6 pence so I expect a reward.

Shall we ask Snowy and Mimi to be our witnesses?'

'We shall 1 see them tomorrow night I am sure they will say yes.' I replied joyfully.

'Come on let's get a taxi we are eating at the Savoy.'

He had a word with the taxi driver as we got in about a detour. I knew he was planning something else. We arrived at the jewellers twenty minutes later. The doorman ushered us in and one of the senior assistants served us.

'Engagement rings' said Roberto.

'What would madam like? I will bring over a selection.'

Whilst he was gone I said.

'Roberto just something simple please. Think of the orphanages I would rather the money went there.'

'That is why I love you, you are not only the most gorgeous woman I have ever met and the mother of my son but you have a loving and caring heart. This ring will be a symbol of my love and hopefully will be passed down to our children so I want it to be special. You do want some more children don't you?

I nodded amazed at his sense of fun which I had missed over the years.

'I do a blond curly haired little girl just like you. I have already chosen a name for her so we have to have a lot of ' love ins.'

'And what is this name am I allowed to know.'

'Rose after my English Rose but we shall call her Rosy.'

'Well that was a long speech I love 'Rosy' already. Very well I shall choose a ring I like and not look at the price.'

I came out with a single sapphire.

Roberto had already told me that my mother's sapphire necklace was in his safe and was to have come back to me whatever happened.

'Put it on now next to the curtain ring.' he said.

'Then I know that we are officially betrothed and you are nearly mine.'

The assistant smiled when we did this. I explained in the taxi that I wanted to use Ruth's wedding ring on the wedding day.

We had lunch at the Savoy and Roberto and I talked all the way through it.

He wanted to know everything.

'I never thought this day would happen. I used to dream about you when I was in the bush in Africa. The pain was unbearable but it was nothing compared with what you must have gone through being abandoned by your lover to give birth on your own.

Tell me some of it and I want to know how you met Snowy and Mimi.

I told him about the train and the house and Kathy and Hugh and the other Students.

I also told him more about Dino having threatened me to send me to Naples and have me committed.

He was shocked. 'My God my own brother would have done that. That place did exist and it was a notorious breeding ground for prostitutes. It was financed by the Mafia. They too had daughters. Thank God you escaped and would I have been told probably not.'

He was furious about the waiting room.

'I owe Snowy a lot don't I?'

I told him about his OBE and his bravery in Korea.

'Was one of your friends a painter called Kenny'?

'Yes why'

'Well I thought I saw a picture of his in an exhibition of a model so like you lying on a couch. It was called the 'Seventh Month.' It was very well done and you looked ravishing. It was painted so well in the pre-Raphaelite style so it was hard to date. Even with my experience in Art I would have quite believed it if it was dated around 1910.

'Yes it was me Kenny was one of the lodgers he also helped me.'

'That's not all Jo.Dino bought it and had it in a room by his dressing room.

It had a combination lock and when we opened it the whole room was covered in photographs of you including the Milan ones and the one Antonio used for the Calendar and half the men in the world drool over. There was also a lot of memorabilia including letters you sent from school. There were also photographs of you as a child some in the bath. That's when I found my letters.

I had a feeling about the 'Seventh Month' but then I put it out of my mind, as there was so much to do. There was no date on it and I was so mixed up at the time. I seemed to see you all the time on buses on trains I thought I was going mad.'

I shivered as the realisation came to me finally of something I had always suspected which was also played out in the maternity home. Dino did have an obsession with me. Everything fell into place. The hair washing, the clothes, hanging around when I bathed. His visits to the University and the fury about my pregnancy and his cruelty afterwards. And earlier when I was eight. He would lie in bed with me and read stories and tickle me. Sometimes they would be about princesses and he would sit me down comb my hair out and dress me up in a beautiful dress and say 'You are my special princess'.

Once he took photos of me lying on a couch with only a nightdress on when I was eleven. He then sat me on his knee and cuddled me. Ruth came in and told me to get dressed. It stopped after that as she must have explained to him how inappropriate it was.

Roberto said. 'Jo I am really sorry I brought this up its probably upset you and this is meant to be a happy day'.

'It is Roberto the happiest day of my life and he can't hurt me anymore. And it's best to resolve these issues.'

'Let's finish this champagne and go to the registry office and we will just be in time to pick Toby up.' he said

He stood up 'Come on mummy get your coat on your getting married next week.'

'When should we tell him' I said.

I was gradually getting to know my future husband again. He was creative with his ideas.

'Well with your permission I would like to take him to the zoo early tomorrow on my own. I have already told him that we have to get up early and make a picnic. So try to imagine, we are eating our hot dogs and he is playing with some toy animals I have bought him. I will say. 'Toby- did you mean it on your birthday when you said 'Mummy you can marry him if you like' because if so I would like.'

'I hope he says yes what if he doesn't.'

'He will. I am his father I know about boy's stuff he will definitely say yes. By the way he speaks very good Italian, you have thought of everything.'

'That was Remy my au pair and good friend. She is in Venice at the moment. I chose an Italian girl because I knew his father would approve. Yes take him Roberto it's a lovely idea.'

'Why don't you go to your shop and we will meet you there.

Tell them you are getting married. Close the shop for a half day on Friday and invite them all to the reception.'
What reception.'

'Oh yes I have the phone number of caterers who will come and do it all.'

I smiled. I didn't mind it was a good idea and I had to get used to my new action man taking over my life.

'Anyway I haven't seen the shop properly. I only saw the entrance .I spoke to someone called Jill.'

'Yes she is the sister of the bookseller who sold me the shops.'

' She was the one who told me you were still single. I just told her I was in love with you and had come to whisk you off to darkest Africa.' he said happily.

We walked out holding hands and caught a taxi to Caxton Hall.

CHAPTER 28

DINING NEXT DOOR

I was amazed that it was possible to get married at such short notice.

We had our birth certificates and passports and were duly registered.

I felt as if it was a dream and that I would wake up at the railway station or in Italy without my baby.

In the taxi to the school Roberto said.

'Think in a five days time you will be Mrs Grimaldi and I will have the only baggage I want in life.

'Don't be rude calling me a baggage.'

'Well after last night I should be calling you something stronger Miss Grimaldi its time I made an honest woman out of you.'

That was definitely the old Roberto talking.

I pushed his hair back and the taxi driver laughed.

'Have you two just got married'? I like decorum in my taxi.

'Next week' said Roberto 'she has kept me waiting eight years'.

'Oh that long, go ahead enjoy yourselves.'

He said 'I will close the hatch.'

'Don't bother' said Roberto 'we have to pick our son up from school turn right at the next junction. Can you wait for us?'

'Certainly you're paying.'

They had already started to come out of St Martin's School. We saw Mimi who already had Toby. I jumped out.' Mummy has Roberto come.'

'He has darling look in the car, say goodbye to Mimi and thank her we will see her tonight .You can sleep there if you like.'

He ran to the taxi to a bemused taxi driver.

'Hello Roberto. Are we still going to the zoo tomorrow.'?

'We are you have to get up very early as we are taking a picnic. We will have to make lots of sandwiches and buy bottles of lemonade.'

He got in and showed Roberto his reading book.

'It's my homework can you help me when we get home.'

I sat in the front and left them alone.

I was choked full of emotion. The taxi driver took my address and we were on our way.

'You have a lovely boy there he looks Italian.'

'He is they both are.'

I wondered what he was thinking as I sobbed quietly next to him.

They must see and hear lots of strange things, London taxi drivers I thought.

When we got in we had tea and cakes and after going through Roberts portfolio and seeing his amazing wild life photography in typical child like manner Toby said.

'Can I go and play next door now'.

I called Mimi who said it was ok and said she would expect us at about 7pm and she would feed all the children first.

I gave my store a quick ring but as they weren't expecting me back until Monday there were no great problems. I said I would call in the next day.

'Come here baggage' said Roberto we have to go and change but it may take some time. Do not remove the rock or the curtain ring but you have my permission to remove everything else.'

Two hours later we were dressed and ready for our dinner party.

Roberto went through my clothes and insisted on choosing my outfit.

He chose a white clingy midi dress.

He combed my hair just the way he had done when I was sixteen.

I went to my jewellery case and brought out my silver necklace and bangle.

He came over and rummaged around in the box. 'And the ankle band' he said

'You are still my concubine not my wife yet.'

When I was ready he said.

'You look just like a white angelic virgin. I shall look at you all night and pretend we are going back to our cabin in the mountains.'

We dashed next door laughing like a couple of teenagers.

The children were all fast asleep and we were ready to enjoy ourselves.

Mimi and Snowy had laid a lovely table had lit candles and were playing jazz.

'Mimi was the first to see the sapphire. And what is that on your finger'.

'Oh my engagement ring you mean, my sapphire' I replied.

She gasped 'We are getting married next Friday. Will you be our witnesses' said Roberto? 'We have waited eight years and that's too long.'

'Wow' said Snowy 'you are fast worker of course we will that's absolutely fantastic well done you two that little boy in there is going to love it. He talked non-stop about you Roberto all through tea.'

'Well don't say anything when he gets up. I am taking him to the zoo and then I am going to ask his permission to marry his mother.'

Everyone laughed.

I could tell that they really enjoyed Roberto's company and his quirky sense of humour. He was on form and so happy.

They asked him about his work. He spent about an hour going into detail about his almost rootless life. I listened intently too as it was all new to me.

All he seemed to carry was his camera and few clothes.

He said things were so cheap he bought new shirts, as he needed them.

However he still managed to get back to Nairobi and Mombasa to get his copy and photographs sent in. He had a network of friends mostly journalists, pilots and aid workers. They had land rovers and light aircraft at their disposal.

Finally they did ask what his future plans were.

'Well in the last 48 hours thing have changed I seem to have acquired some baggage. They will no doubt need some consideration. I will of course have to return to Scotland. It will take at least six months to sort that mess out.

Jo wants me to buy our old house in the Lake District so that is very much on the cards. Any way I want to thank you for all the support and love you have given them both.'

'It's nothing she is like a magnet everyone loves her she has good friends to go back to if she goes back north.'

'What do you think of her shop? We were there when it was boarded up and she spent her first Xmas with us. Two years ago it was two shops but the owner moved his bookshop to a place called Hay on Wye. He is an actor and is in long running serial and is based in the West Country.'

'Well it looks fabulous I am so proud of her. She is a smart cookie like her mother Ruth.' said Roberto.' I guess she must have looked like her when she dyed her hair. I can't imagine her without her glorious curls'.

I sat taking it all in glowing with love and pride and joy

I could not take my eyes off Roberto and longed to take him away again and just love him.

He was very curious about their lives too, as he knew too well how in many circles black people were treated. He had lived in America and had always been appalled by the way the black population were treated. He took Time magazine and knew all about Martin Luther King and the peaceful demonstrations. He said he was banking on Kennedy to make a difference. He was a great advocate of mixed education and hated the idea of children being sent to school on buses with armed guards.

He declared that he could never live permanently in America again when its own people were suppressed and murdered. He worked for two major magazines and film companies but managed to avoid going back there always being on location.

Later we talked about the wedding arrangements and what we would do afterwards.

We thought we could get caterers in and have a small party. In this way we could have the children with us. We then told them that we planned to have a white wedding in the church in the Lake District in the summer. In this way we could invite absolutely everyone we knew and liked.

Mimi was intrigued.

'Oh I love weddings' it will be so exciting.

'Can we come?'

'Of course Snowy will you be my best man. Paulo won't mind. I want you not because you have the OBE and are a special person but because you have watched over Jo and Toby like a brother.'

'Yes and you can see where I was born and visit our old shop.' I said.

I could see Snowy was very happy to be asked. He beamed.

Then we finished the champagne by the fire listening to jazz.

When it was time to go we hugged one another.

Snowy said 'You have the second best woman in the world Roberto hold on to her and don't go to Africa without her.'

'You are absolutely right I will never go anywhere without her come on 'baggage' let's go home.'

'The end of a perfect evening' I said as we undressed.

'Not quite' said my handsome lover.

'I have to talk to Rosy'

CHAPTER 29

THE ZOO

True to his word Roberto was up and making the picnic at seven am.

He had a rucksack with his camera in it and was all packed and ready to collect Toby at 8.30.

We arranged to meet at one o'clock but I decided to go to the shop earlier to tell them about my wedding and honeymoon plans.

We had decided to fly up to Edinburgh and then go to the Lake District.

Roberto had bought a new car which had plenty of room. It was a convertible with four seats as Toby was coming with us.

At eight he came up with a cup of tea for me and gave me a kiss.

'Wish me luck with our son.' he said.

He ruffled my hair as he sat on the bed.

'I should have been more organised so we could have had some 'Rosy time'.

I said 'I think the log cabin business wore us out.'

I smiled at him 'Fancy making a log fire and going to sleep on the sofa and expecting me to come down wearing only my silver jewellery.'

'Well it worked- wasn't it fantastic.'

He leaned over me put his head on my stomach and said.

'Rosy if you are in there darling tell her to behave herself and not be so wanton'.

'Well off you go you have a boy probably sitting on the doorstep waiting for you. and he was.

I washed and dressed and put lots of loud jazz on the radiogram dancing and singing for joy. I rang the caterers and was to meet with them Monday. Then I went to the store.

It looked lovely as I approached.

The first bow window was showing the latest models and that week as it was approaching the Xmas season it was ball gowns.

The second had glorious array of children's party clothes from Italy and France.

This was lucrative as rich mothers came from all over London to buy unusual outfits for their children. Toby had served me well.

I had a very large section of American white wicker nursery furniture down in the showroom which looked attractive in the show room a perfect back ground for patchwork bedspreads and exotic dolls and Stieff teddies.

I had kept the colour lavender blue inside and outside and always had bay trees or hydrangeas outside in large blue and white ceramic pots.

My staff was eight in all with three extra part time students.

I always used design students as they chose clothes suitable for the bargain basement and designed some of them. Like my mother I paid excellent wages but demanded loyalty, respect and responsibility.

I was rarely let down and we were a happy crowd like a family really, my only family.

The students enjoyed being downstairs as I let them play the music they liked as long as they looked after the customers. The latest was rock and roll replacing skiffle. The café up the road was still a thriving club with regular musicians and we were popular with their clientele.

I could see Roberto going in to check it out.

As I went in Jill was already there. She was an excellent manageress.

She was totally involved with the shop and so was her mother Alice as she still lived in the flat above the old bookshop. I let her stay for a low rent. She would often come in and help out and on the odd occasion look after Toby.

I hid my hand with my ring on it.

'Hi Jill how's things' I said calmly.

She smiled. 'Well' she said obviously ready for a good gossip.'

'When I opened on Thursday there was this gorgeous man standing outside.

He was hovering and I didn't know wither he wanted to come in or not. You know the way men behave when they are buying underwear for their girlfriends.'

'Did you ask him in'?

'Well he was so good looking I succumbed as I was curious. He looked lost.

I asked him if he needed any help.

I was smiling to myself. I knew exactly what she was talking about - who could resist him.

'So what happened next.'?

'He said that he wondered if TOBYJO meant Jo Grimaldi and I said no it was Jo Scott.

'He paused for a moment and said 'I think I know her was her mother called Ruth'. 'Yes'. I said.

'Is she here or is she coming in.'

'No' I said 'She is not in today'.

He seemed disappointed and said.

"Thank you for your help, would you give her my card please. By the way is she married yet? She was going out with an Italian eight years ago when I knew her?'

'And what did you say.'

I said 'No you had such a busy life but you were not short of men asking you out and that I couldn't understand it because you were so lovely.'

'Did you say anything about Toby?'

'No of course not.'

I walked over to the window put the closed sign up and took out a bottle of champagne.

'Jill thank you for that get the girls down stairs I have an announcement to make.'

When they were assembled I gave her the champagne to open as I wanted to hide my ring. She poured it out and seemed confused. She was obviously wondering what it was all about.

I then lifted my glass and showed them my sapphire.

'I got engaged yesterday drink up.' I said to my incredulous staff.

'Who is it' they said in unison.

Jill said 'it's him isn't it.'

I laughed 'Yes. Its Roberto Toby's father.'

They all cheered.

'And we are getting married on Friday at Caxton Hall at one o'clock. I am closing the shop at midday and you are all invited and to the reception afterwards at our house. If you want meet him he is coming here today around three with Toby.' I said wryly.

'Try and be subtle all of you, he does look like an Italian film star' said Jill. 'Remember me telling you about him the other day standing outside the shop at opening time.'

'Oh I saw him when I came in' said Jenny a very pretty redhead.

'I rushed in the dressing room to put on my lipstick hoping to serve him but he had gone.'

'Ok champagne break over' I said. 'We have to have to work hard today if we are closing early Friday.'

I could hear them all excited about my news as they left my office.

I should think during the lunch break they would be trying outfits on for the wedding.

I managed to do a lot of office work before Roberto arrived.

At precisely three pm their taxi drew up. I heard the girls saying hello downstairs,

as they had deserted their posts in a rush to see Toby.

Finally he came running up stairs. I had taken my ring off in case he noticed.

'Mummy, mummy where are you.'

'Here Toby have you had a good time.'

He ran in with a big bag of goodies.' Look mummy Roberto bought me a camera'

Roberto came in winked at me and said.' It's only a Brownie but it's a good one to start with.'

'Did you take pictures?'

'Yes'

'What of'

'The daddy elephant in the story that lost his baby and the mummy. They were left in the jungle.'

I raised my eyebrows...

'What else.'

'A tiger he was scary. He came right up to our car.

'Did you see monkeys?'

'Yes they were swinging in the trees .One sat on the roof of the keeper's car eating a banana.

'And did you have your picnic.'?

'Yes we had hot dogs and ice cream and a funny drink called COCO COLA. It's American. Roberto lived in America.

'And guess what I spoke Italian and Roberto said I got it right.'

I moved over to Roberto who indicated that he wanted to speak to me.

He held my hand behind his back and took my ring.

'Well you sounded as if you had a great time. Anything else.'

'Yes'

'What'

'Roberto asked me if I meant it when I said he could marry you.'

'What did you say?'

'I said 'yes' but he has to ask you properly.'

'And how is he going to do that.'

'Well - with a ring of course'

Roberto said something to him in Italian.

Toby answered back slowly

'Yes you can ask her now'

Roberto took his jacket off took the ring out of his pocket and knelt down.

'Will you marry me JO?'

Toby smiled and gave a little wiggle.

'ER I said ER'

Toby said 'Say yes mummy please say yes'

'OK' I said 'We could get married next Friday if you like.'

Roberto cuddled us both and Toby ran off to tell the girls.

'You did it well done, and we do not even have to change his name or birth certificate.'

'You mean I am on it' he said.

'Of course you are his father'.

'There is a glass of champagne left for us I opened one for the girls.'

I handed it to him and he said. 'To you Jo Grimaldi'

Now I have to see the results of your eight years hard labour and then we are all going out.

'Where'

'Wait and see, give me my tour first.'

He liked the cellar. I explained that some of the ideas were Mimi's, the music and the murals. I then showed him my baby dept.

'That was a good idea Jo as you already had a baby. The clothes are very stylish.

'Italian and French I said.

He picked up a gorgeous frilly girl's dress.

'We will have this for Rosy'.

'You really mean it don't you'

'I do but I still have to work on it.

'It's a wonderful building. How did you get your decorating ideas?

'Well I liked Jane Austen and I have a book of the interiors of that period which is when this place was built. Snowy found me a West Indian builder called Jack who as you can see did a perfect job.'

I showed him the flat.

'This is where I came the night I escaped from the nursing home.'

He put his arms around me. 'I am so sorry all that happened but look what you did Ruth would have loved all of this.'

'She orchestrated it, she liked you Roberto.'

'Well it's time Toby had his next treat. Come on let's find him.'

He was in the cellar telling the girls all about Roberto in Africa. They were intrigued.

'Come on Roberto is taking us on another adventure I said.'

We got in the taxi and Roberto stood outside talking to the driver.

'Where are we going' said Toby.

'Secret' said Roberto.

The taxi drove us towards the river quite a long way. Finally we stopped outside a riverboat.

'Come on hop out' said Roberto.

'That's where we are going for a trip up the Thames.'

We climbed up helped by a member of the crew and then Snowy, Mimi, and the children came out of the cabin to greet us.

'We are going to have dinner at an inn by the river. On the way back we are having fireworks because its 'Guy Fawkes Night' tonight and we will be able to watch everyone else's all over London as we sail.' he said.

'Roberto did you hire it just for us.'

'Of course I wanted to give Snowy and Mimi and the children a good time.

We have drinks and food on board if anyone is hungry.'

We ate in the ancient inn once frequented by pirates. The children looked in wonder at pictures on the walls of them. Some were quite gory, lots of hangings but they didn't mind. We had fun Roberto style and the children had a ringside seat as they watched the river fireworks as the sun set. We drank champagne all the way back and then took a taxi to Primrose Hill with three exhausted children

After his bath Toby cuddled in between us both.

'He said to Roberto'

'You can kiss mummy now she has her ring'

'You mean like this' he said'

He carried him to bed and the elephant saga continued.

CHAPTER 30

WEDDING

There was a lot to organise for our wedding day and every minute was taken up with planning not only the occasion but the rest of our lives.

After much discussion Roberto felt it was his duty to tell Paulo although we wanted to keep it a surprise for everyone else we knew.

He needed to make sure that Paulo could negotiate cover for him at the company as daily there were important decisions to make and papers to sign.

He also needed to talk to him about the house.

We agreed to spend two weeks together and travel north to see my friends

Roberto would then have to go back to Edinburgh travelling home at weekends until we had made the arrangements to be together permanently.

Toby had a half term holiday and Snowy and Mimi offered to let him stay with them but we both wanted to take him.

We compromised by saying he could stay with them on our wedding night.

Roberto continued to enthral Toby and was determined to make up for the lost eight years. He had the photographs developed and taught him how to fix them into an album. He asked him to write his thoughts on each photograph. He has it still and I cry when I look at it. Underneath the elephant one he had written. "This baby elephant had lost his daddy but like me he found him. Mine is called Roberto.'

He took him to school every morning and picked him up. I introduced him to the teachers and Toby announced to his friends that he had a new Daddy.

Hr never called him Roberto again it was always Daddy. He wanted to be like the other boys. One day we would tell him when the time felt right but we felt that he had guessed already.

Roberto was used to playing with children and did not need anything but his imagination as the African children devised their own toys and games.

They also loved singing and Roberto played the guitar to accompany them.

He said it was wonderful to hear the African children singing their own tribal songs.

The played a lot of football and built dens in the garden with Snowy and his children for whom he had developed a great respect.

They all had such fun. It added a new dimension to my life and both Mimi and I delighted in watching them. I also felt that all of these years Roberto he had been compensating for the loss of his own children. We had never got around to seriously discussing his girls.

He saw them when he went to America usually for a month at a time when he combined business with pleasure. He was excited about the prospect of living in his old house again so that Poppy and Posy could come over and revisit old memories too.

Rosa and he were on good terms. She already had two sons by Will her second husband and was a successful designer. I could never understand why they parted but Will was her childhood sweetheart and an artist who helped her in her work. They had a good life and had a beautiful home in the Napa Valley in California.

By Wednesday of that week we had seen the caterers and the florist.

I had been over to one of our Italian stockist to look for a dress on the Monday.

I took Mimi. I usually went everywhere by underground but on this occasion I took my Mazerati which of course Roberto approved of. For years I had only ever had a van so that I could go to markets and wholesalers and replaced it as necessary.

We had a happy two hours and left Roberto talking to Paulo.

They got on well and never had any major disagreements. It was Dino and particularly Gloria who seemed to create the problems.Paulo was very serious and even tempered. He quietly stayed at the helm. I wondered how he coped with a house full of children.

When we arrived back we were all secretive and absolutely refused to show Roberto my dress. It was my favourite colour indigo silk with a low neckline and a fitted waist with a very tight skirt. I intended wearing my sapphires and a strand of pearls in my hair which would be looped up in the fall in ringlets. I also bought some blue satin shoes in the same shade as the dress. Mimi had chosen it all and also bought herself a paler blue chiffon one which draped in folds to the floor.

When she left I sat on the sofa with Roberto with a glass of champagne whilst he told me about his conversation with Paulo.

'Well I would have loved to have seen his face' he said.

I first explained that I could not come back straight away and he was concerned and asked me if I had a problem because he would get one of his managers to go over and cover for me.

No I said 'I am getting married.'

'Getting married? Who to'.

'You will have to wait and see. You will meet her when we arrive on Saturday night. We will be staying at the 'Cedars' in the village. Don't be offended Paulo about not being asked I will explain - please trust me. We are having a second ceremony in the spring in the church with all of our friends and Helen can be matron of honour.

There is a reason why I had to get a special licence. And - I do want my old house back.'

'So you are staying then not living on a campsite for the rest of your life. She must be some gal to stop you doing that. Anyway you have my blessing. I care about you my brother and want you to be happy. Can I tell Helen?'

'Of course and give her a hug from me but don't tell anyone else. I want to go over to Myra's with her.'

'Well alright he said but I need details of the event when and where'.

'OK' get a pen.'

'Did he seem pleased?' I asked.

'Yes he has changed a lot now he is a family man. He actually smiles and drinks wine. You know he became a Catholic when he married Helen. They are seriously religious.

'Oh I see.' I said that's why they keep adding to their family.'

'Yes' he said 'Which reminds me I have to have a long talk to Rosy'.

On our Wedding day we had to get up early as the caterers were arriving at 9am.

As usual Roberto was up at six. He had decided to camp in Toby's room in his sleeping bag to the delight of his little son who now had his walls covered in wild animals.

They both brought me breakfast and I allowed them to have a cuddle with me in my four poster bed. Toby was very excited about the wedding. He and Snowy's son Bruno had new suits. I had to have long talk to him and told him not to rush around and annoy the caterers.

Roberto said 'It's all sorted he is going over to get ready at Snow's house and they are going to play first. They are learning to play Monopoly. Its time they learnt about Real Estate. They enjoy it you should see them piling up their money.

We were on our own for half an hour.

Roberto said. 'I never dreamed this day would happen, it's weird getting used to happiness again. I keep expecting you to disappear as if it is a fantasy I love you.'

I love you too.' I said as I pushed his hair back.

Then he gave me a present wrapped in a satin Indigo bag covered in white flowers.

In it was a large antique silver locket engraved.

'To Jo my darling wife on her wedding day Roberto.'

In side there was a picture of him and one of Toby looking so alike with their hair all over their forehead'

On the card was line from one of Yeats poems.

'Tread softly you tread on my dreams.'

On the chain he had put the curtain ring.

My hairdresser arrived and Roberto went next door.

'See you later my darling.'

At midday Mimi arrived to have some girl talk as we both got dressed.

We had a glass of champagne and giggled as we put on our beautiful dresses.

She gave me an exotic West Indian garter to put on as something 'old.'

She laughed 'It looks like it's from a bordello but Roberto will love it' she said

'Well' she said 'those boys will be so proud, all of them I think we look rather gorgeous don't you.'

For once I believed it.

We went down my stair case which was decked with white flowers.

Even more stunning were my two boys both in immaculate grey suits and holding their cameras.

'She's coming' shouted Toby 'Mummy you look very pretty.'

'Yes' said Roberto as he flashed away 'very pretty indeed.'

He whispered in my ear 'A yummy mummy for Rosy'

The catering staff all lined up and clapped and Mimi and Snowy looking equally regal walked out with us to our cars.

We all sat very quietly during the journey and even Toby was lost for words.

Roberto held our hands.

We were the first wedding in the afternoon and were ushered into an elegant room decked with white lilies. The registrar was already waiting for us as were our other guests. We hardly had time to see who was there as they suddenly arrived in mass having waited in another room

The children all settled down and were a little overawed by the occasion.

We were ushered to the front followed by Mimi and Snowy. The registrar had a beautifully modulated voice and began.

The words that were so simple were moving and poetic. They were taken from the King James Version of the Bible.

I tried not to cry as we repeated the responses.

It seemed to be over so quickly and as Roberto put Ruth's ring on me I was overcome.

'Forsaking all others' was so true for both of us. We had both done that for eight long years.

We looked at one another and as our eyes met we were both in tears. Toby could not contain himself any longer and decided to join us.

Everyone laughed as he looked up at Roberto and said

'It's ok you can kiss mummy now'

Everyone turned out to be quite a crowd.

When we turned round there was all the staff from my shop wearing half the stock.

Remy my au pair was there. She had been told by Jill and had flown in from Venice.

Jill and Alice and Tony were there also and my cousin Frances.

Then I saw Paulo and Helen standing behind them all. They had driven up in the night. It was wonderful to see them. I was so touched. They hugged us both.

Helen had burst into tears as she realised that Toby was the reason I had disappeared eight years ago without a word to anyone.

'It's alright now Helen we eventually found one another. Say Hello Toby this is your Auntie Helen and this is Uncle Paulo. They have three children and we will see them next week.'

Paulo hugged and hugged his brother and for the first time I saw the real Italian in him full of emotion and crying like his wife. He knelt down and gravely shook hands with Toby.

'You are one of us now Toby a real Grimaldi'

He then said to Roberto

'This young wife of yours suits you very well Rob where did you find her. Come on Jo it's my turn for a kiss. You two must have quite a story to tell us.'

I was surprised and touched as he had always been so quiet and reserved.

I realised then that he too was quite handsome and distinguished looking.

As the father of three children he had matured and there was a special 'goodness' about him. Of course Helen knew this all the time, as I knew instinctively about Roberto. He had always been overshadowed by Dino's powerful personality and Roberto's Joy De Vivre and energy for life. He had always been the brains behind the organisation and the one everyone trusted.

I was so pleased we were reunited.

Our party was fun and the jazz band Roberto had hired helped make it a lively happy atmosphere. There was no formality but Paolo insisted on making a speech which again was new for him as Dino always took charge even at parties.

'What can anyone say? It is difficult to put into words how happy we all are today that my beloved brother has been reunited with our beautiful Jo and their son Toby.

We want to give them all our love and support as they start a life together and rejoice in their happiness.'

It was followed up by an emotional Roberto thanking Snowy and Mimi and my few friends for their support during the last eight years and inviting everyone to the big wedding in the spring by our lake.

We finally danced to my favourite song as everyone cheered.

'Embrace me oh my embraceable you'.

Then we all danced all night.

CHAPTER 31

HONEYMOON

The next morning we all sat around the kitchen table discussing the party and drinking champagne with orange juice

What with our many guests some of whom who had decided to stay the night it was impossible to have a quiet time with Roberto.

The memories of the 'Wedding night' even were vague.

I seem to remember lots of rose petals and lavender and a jazz band playing

'Sweet Rosie O'Grady under my window and endless bottles of expensive champagne. Roberto had soon found my garter and said it was his most prized possession and wore it in the shower.

By 10 o'clock Toby and Snowy and the children had arrived and were in deep conversation with Paulo and Helen. I gathered Snowy had told them how he met me.

Remy had taken over the house keeping role and was very happy to be speaking Italian to the two men. Roberto was highly impressed and thanked her profusely for teaching Toby Italian and taking care of me. He gave her an envelope with a large bonus in it and some flowers.

Like the rest of the girls she duly paid homage to his looks and personality and was soon treating him as one of the family. She was as moved as I was when she saw the interaction between father and son and as excited about his return and our marriage. She agreed to stay on and clear up and deal with all the domestic issues whilst we were away. Having met a young American when she was staying in Naples with her grandmother she was also in love. He was to stay in her life. She was incredulous when she arrived back to such excitement. As she lived in the flat over the shop when she was at University she knew the girls and they had told her everything.

Roberto had again been up at 6am.I had started to get used to this as it was a habit of his when he was in Africa getting chores done before the heat set in. He used the time to sort out his photos write letters and reports on my typewriter before I even stirred. Sorting Toby out was a pleasure for him and I loved to see them having breakfast together. He had the car packed already and he said to me as he leaned over my bath making cheeky remarks.

'Come on wife it's time to start our honeymoon. I hope you understand that we have to be celibate tonight as we will have Toby in bed with us. So don't get too cuddly. He produced a large warm snowy white towel and enveloped me in it and then around us both.

Finally we headed out waving to our friends and neighbours.

Paulo followed soon after arranging to meet us half way for lunch.

Toby fell asleep within an hour so we did not have to entertain him.

We had about six hours to talk and by the time we got to our meeting place we had made a lot of decisions about our future life.

Occasionally I pushed his hair back for him and gave him his sun glasses.

He smiled at me and said. 'The first time you did that I nearly crashed the car.'

We had lunch at a coaching Inn meeting up with Paulo and Helen.

Toby was wide awake and asked Paulo about their children.

'Did they have a boy" he asked

'Yes' they said 'Two one was seven and was called John and the other one Mario was four'. Jenny their daughter who I had looked after was nine.

Helen said 'Would you like to play with them whilst you are here we have a tree house and we live by a lake.'

Toby was very excited about that. 'When' he said

Paulo looked at us.' How about Sunday afternoon you can all come and have supper with us .We will be going to church in morning. Is that alright Jo?'

I looked at Rob. 'Of course we could go to the village church ourselves.

At some point we have to organise a spring wedding and we need to meet the vicar. Do you want to do that Jo and then we could call on Myra.' he said.

'Perfect 'I want to sit there in peace and thank God and Ruth for my blessings, for my wonderful husband and child and all the friends that have been sent over the years to love and guide me. I have also brought my bouquet for Ruth's grave.'

'Well we shall do that and I will join you to give thanks too especially for our little boy Toby.'

Toby gave a wiggle and smiled.

Paulo said 'If you buy the house Rob it will be just like old times.'

'I am working on the idea. Jo didn't want a wedding present just a house in the Lake district and that one in particular.'

Helen joined in. 'Do it, it will be marvellous having you there.'

Roberto ever the diplomat said. 'We will have to consult Toby first.'

CHAPTER 32

SUNDAY AT CHURCH

We arrived at the Cedars at about 7pm and Toby travelled very well.

Being a city boy he loved seeing the mountains and the sheep.

The sun had shone all day so even in cold November the landscape looked stunning.

I had forgotten how much it all meant to me.

The fells were snow capped and Toby kept saying 'Can we go climbing one day.'?

My man of action said straight away.

'Of course we can. We men can go the women don't really like it.

They like wearing their high heels with little bows on don't they.'

Toby chortled 'Mummy does she wears them every day for work.'

'You will have to tell me more of mummy's secrets'.

'When can we go?'

'Well maybe Wednesday but we have to go to Scotland one day to Glasgow and Edinburgh. I suppose we could go there at the weekend let mummy decide it's her honeymoon.'

'What's a honey moon do you have to eat honey and kiss.'?

'Yes' said Roberto we have to have honey and kisses every morning for breakfast and every night before we go to sleep when the moon comes out.'

'Doesn't it make you feel sick?'

'Never' said my mad husband 'It's very yummy.'

The hotel was very smart and had a recent change of owners so I was glad that no one recognised us. Our room was the biggest they had and looked out on to the lake. We could just see the light in the garden of the old house from the windows.

Roberto saw my face when I spotted it. 'You do want it don't you'.

I put my arms around him 'Yes' I said. 'For Toby and Rosy'.

Toby heard me. 'Who's Rosy' he said.

I smiled 'We made her up but if ever I have a baby girl we want to call her Rosy.'

There was a large four poster and a tiny child's bed in the corner exactly what I had asked for.

'Should we wash and get ready for dinner' said Roberto. 'You will have to wear your smart jacket.'

'Are you going to Roberto?' said Toby.

'Yes mummy says it's an order and you know mummy's' they get very bossy at times. I love my leather jacket and she never lets me wear it.'

'I like it mummy it's nice, when I am big I am going to buy one just like it' he said

And so the infatuation with his father continued.

They did look pretty good when they were scrubbed up and for fun I put my high heels on with bows.

I left my hair down and they both said.

'We like you in that especially your shoes'.

We enjoyed our meal, which was Roast lamb and fresh vegetables. Toby had two helpings of ice cream.

It was about nine when we put him to sleep on our big bed.

I went down to read the papers whilst Roberto went on with his elephant saga.

I joined him about ten and they had both fallen asleep.

So I spent the night on the child's bed with freezing feet.

The elder Grimaldi shook himself at 5 am and surveyed the scene.

He came into my little bed and we had kisses and the honey.

'This is cosy he said can we do this again.' He said as we snuggled down.

We stayed like that until nine and then Toby woke up and came over to us saying

'You are in my bed'.

'Ok Goldilocks get out this moment and get dressed and ready for your porridge and honey'. said the funny man.

There was no problem that night getting him into it.

That was the way our wonderful honeymoon went 'very sweet moments' interspersed with Roberto's constant and endearing entertainment of his son.

After breakfast we went to church and dressed up again.

Whilst Roberto loved his casual clothes he always liked to obey conventions and insisted we were dressed smartly.

The organ was playing and I felt very tearful knowing that I would be visiting Ruth's grave with the two loves of my life.

Somehow every hymn we sang seemed meaningful and touched my soul.

My favourite one was 'Dear Lord and Father of mankind forgive our foolish ways.'

The majestic organ seemed to reflect the awesome scenery outside the fells and the lakes I had grown up with.

The vicar had a fine delivery and his lesson 'In beginning was the Word' he seemed to pick up the power of the moment and the depth of our feelings.

Toby was used to church as he went a church school so he behaved appropriately following the service. Roberto seemed quiet for once but as we prayed he held my hand.

Afterwards losing no time he went off in search of the vicar to make an appt about wedding number two.

I took Toby into the churchyard and showed him where Grandma Ruth was buried beside my father. As he put my bouquet on the grave he said.

'You didn't have a daddy either did you mummy.'

"No I was only five when he died.'

'That was sad I am glad I have a daddy now.'

Roberto heard him and stood with us for a long time.

'We will bring your grandma some flowers from the hills when we go climbing should we Toby.' 'Now let's go and see Myra.'

'Who is Myra' said Toby.

So I told him all about Myra and my horse Bonny.

'Can we see Bonny?'

'I hope so if she is still alive. She will be about ten now which is old for a horse.'

We drove down to Myra's which was about two miles but only half a mile from Roberto's house which we intended seeing the next day.

At first it seemed as if there was no one at home.

It all looked well kept. The outhouses were in excellent condition and freshly painted. The yards were swept and I could see lots of stables. 'Of course she had a stud and racehorses now' I said.

Roberto was impressed and for once very quiet.

'I see a pretty 16 year old girl with golden hair riding on a pony followed by two more little girls riding out for the first time. You all looked so beautiful. Get in the car quickly I can see Myra coming across the field'.

He ran over to her so that she did not come in the direction of the car.

I watched them hug and I could see she was delighted to see him.

He told me later that the conversation went like this. He shouted something in Italian when he approached her and she ran over to him and put her arms round him saying

'Hey Roberto lad where have you been all of these years we have missed you. It was sad about Dino I am so sorry. Although I have to say it we won't miss his wife she never could fill Ruth's shoes and my did he change when she married him.

Still we all paid our respects like village people do.

You didn't come to the funeral.'

'No I was still in Africa I couldn't get back in time.'

'What about Rosa, and the girls.'

They are twelve now and have long dark hair. They want to be ballet dancers.

Rosa has a decent husband who is very good to all of them.'

'And what about you lad I heard you were an international photographer working for big American magazines and such like. Don't you run an orphanage out in Africa'?

'I support three I will tell you about them some time.'

'Helen told me about you. I always liked to know, we missed you- they have their horses here so I see a lot of her. It took me a long time to take to Paulo but he is a good man. He was always so quiet. Not like you we had some good times when you were here.

I still have my adopted family the children are 10, 11, and 12 yrs now.

'Yes I know they must keep you on your toes are they here'.

'No they are away with their other grandma this week;

By the way do you know what happened to Jo, Ruth's daughter she was a lovely girl. We still have Bonny. I am sure the poor thing is staying alive waiting for her to come back. No one says a word about her not even Helen.

Dino was very keen for her to marry that playboy Antonio you know.

He came over to see them and they brought him to see my horses. He was smitten with her. She refused to marry him and we have never heard from her since.

I think Dino was furious with her. He wouldn't talk about her and Helen knows nothing or won't say. Can't you find her? Why surely she must have a legacy or something from Ruth.Oh here I am rambling on come inside and have some cake. Please tell me you are coming back and not going back to Africa.'

I think by that time Roberto had kept the surprise long enough and said.

'Just before you pour the tea I have to get something from the car.'

He left her taking her cake out of the tin.

Then in I walked.

She stood still in absolute shock.

'Jo is it really you come here where have you been all these years.' She said putting her arms round me.

I had no time to say anything before Roberto walked in with Toby.

'Oh my - oh my and what's your name sweetheart'

'Toby'

'Hello Toby is this mummy.'

'Yes and my daddy'

'Well aren't you just like him.'

She touched his hair.

'You have his curls' she laughed out loud.

'Come here I am your Auntie Myra from now on. Do you like cake, look I have some little gingerbread men here. I make cakes everyday for my grandchildren when they come home from school.

'Yes please I would like a cake. Where are the children?'

'Gone to Newcastle today to see their other Granny.'

'I have to sit down' she said 'This is just like Xmas for me.' she said wiping her eyes on her pinny.Come here let me cuddle all of you again.'

We sat down and talked but we were unable to hide anything.

Within five minutes Toby had spilled the beans.

'We are on honeymoon' he said.

'Daddy says we have to have honey and kisses every night and in the morning.'

'That sounds like daddy he is very naughty' said Myra'

Later Toby said 'Can I see your horse mummy'

Yes darling I am longing to see her.' I said.

I walked in front whilst Roberto followed trying to explain the saga in as few words as possible. Myra was very keen to hear the details but when Roberto said they were going to be around for a few days and that we may be moving back she said.

'Well Jo can tell me herself one day. I would have helped her you know she must have struggled. Your break up with Rosa had nothing to do with it did it.

'No we were thrown together a lot after that and I fell in love with her. I wanted to get married but she insisted on finishing her degree. I got the job on the magazine expecting to fly home to see her often. Then I broke my leg and I had to stay in Nigeria.

The Biafra war started and the airlift. I got involved in all sorts of work with news agencies covering the stories particularly the genocide in Biafra. In the end the horrors I saw and had to photograph made me grow up. I began to see life very differently. There were thousands of displaced children and orphans. It was like living in a massive concentration camp. Several of us were interested in setting up orphanages in areas the refugees fled to. I was only one among many thousands doing relief work. There were hundreds of Missionaries, Peace Corp worker, Pilots, nurses, and aid agencies. It was all about oil of course that part of Africa had it all. Every one of those people had a story to tell and I have hundreds of undeveloped pictures still. I hope to stay involved in some way and raise money to support the project and hopefully encourage people to do voluntary work out there.

Meanwhile Jo told no one she was pregnant and all of our letters were mislaid. The porter at the university sent them straight to Dino.He had a pile of them in his case when he died.'

'More like Gloria found them.' said Myra.

'Jo never received her legacy and has managed on her own all of these years.

When we were left to sort out the estate I was determined to seek her out and provide her with some sort of funding from her mother's estate. Little did I know that she had my son?

'And now she has you and you both deserve to be happy. Roberto don't ever leave them again.'

'Don't worry they are far too precious to me. I have been searching for her for eight years and did not know Toby existed until two weeks ago.'

We were married at Caxton Hall on Friday and we are having a large wedding here at Easter. I hope you will come.'

'Of course I will I wouldn't miss it for anything, it like a fairy tale. When you get to my age you like happy endings.'

Meanwhile I heard Bonny whinny as I approached her.

She nuzzled into me and to Toby's delight nuzzled him too.

Roberto came up and said 'She knows you all right Jo and she knows that Toby is your child. Am I right Myra'?

'You are Roberto'

'Do you like her Toby?'

He nodded and wiggled.

'We can ask Myra if we can come back and you can sit on her if you like and I might ride her tomorrow.' I said.

Roberto always thoughtful took out some sugar lumps.

'There Toby hold one on your palm like this and she will love you too. Look she is giving me a nuzzle perhaps I smell of honey.'

We went back to Myra's kitchen and she asked us to come back the next afternoon and have a farm house high tea.

'You can help me Jo send those two boys off for a walk up the fell tomorrow. I want know everything'.

Later you can take Toby out for a ride if you like. I will let you have some horses.

'Can we take lots of pictures tomorrow daddy?' said Toby.

'Lots and we will go and buy some more film and I have to get you some walking boots and socks and a really good water proof. We will take a picnic just like we did at the zoo.'

'Yes and you can take some of my cakes if you like' said Myra tearfully.

'Yes we do like' said Toby imitating Roberto.

'You have done a good job there Jo. Your mother would have been proud of you and that little boy wouldn't she Roberto.' She said as he ran to the car.

He nodded and smiled 'Very Very' he said as he put his arm around us both.

'Right he said let's get to my brothers house and you can meet their children.'

CHAPTER 33

HELEN AND PAULO AT HOME

Toby lost no time in getting to know the boys.

We had no sooner arrived when ten year old Jenny no longer the two year old I knew and loved took charge and took them all off to play in the tree house near the lake.

The house looked happier and more homely. Gone were the ostentatious mirrors large china animals and gold brocade sofas and in their place 'Comfort.'

Large sofas. A big log fire, warm carpets and sheepskin rugs.

Instead of paintings all the family photographs covered the walls including some Roberto had taken.

The kitchen now had an Aga in it and the largest dining table I had ever seen.

They still had the guest cottages where Antonio and I had stayed but one was used by their au pair and the other a studio and playhouse for the children in the bad weather. There was a stove in it and they could paint their models there. Jenny had an easel as she liked art.

It finally felt a happy house as it had never seen much joy. We relaxed and had some wine and pasta in the formal dining room whilst their Italian au pair fed the children in the kitchen.

Helen seemed so pleased to be with me.

'Please can I have some time with you' she begged 'I have so much to ask you missed you when you had gone.'

'And I missed you and it think it's wonderful to see you both with your gorgeous children. I bet they will be fell runners'.

'Well its funny you should say that' laughed Helen.

When the men disappeared into Paulo's office to find some malt whisky she said.

'Paulo wants us to all to have a family 'Pow Wow.' before you leave for Scotland on Friday. Paulo adores Roberto you know. He thinks we four should re-evaluate our lives and rethink the company's future. You know how good Paulo is he never really had too much conflict with Dino not until Gloria came along anyway. As they more or less share the company now he wants us to all sit down and brainstorm about the future.

Now you are part of the family he wants to find out what you both want to do.

He is in full agreement that you have been treated very shabbily by Dino and that you are entitled to a legacy. He also admires Roberto and the work he has done in Africa. We are involved in the local Catholic Church and I think they will sponsor one of the orphanages.

He is all in favour of the company leading the way in supporting charities so much so he wants to talk to Roberto about a foundation encouraging students and post graduates to consider volunteering in their holidays like they do in America.

He already has been in touch with an Oxford company who do similar work.

So you see there is a lot to talk about. We could have a preliminary talk and you two can go away and think as I expect you have to sort out your own logistics out. I do not expect Roberto want to be separated from you both for a minute. He said as much. He is like a little boy with a new Teddy he wants to hold you all the time in case you disappear. He will be back in a minute checking on you. He is so sweet with Toby and very funny. They look so alike, its heart warming to see them together.' she said.

'Don't set me off again I have been in tears all the week.'

'Anyway should we all meet again on Friday?'

'Yes I think we will like that.' I said.

'Toby can stay tonight if he likes you can't have had much time on your own,'

'Well if you mean on my own in the little bed I have had plenty'.

I explained about our sleeping arrangements and our early morning trysts,

'I can just imagine Roberto's comments –and he is so good with Toby.' she said.

'Yes' I said   'Some of it is due to him missing the girls growing up and some of it is linked to the pitiful children in Biafra.'

'I don't like to use the term 'grown up' in relation to Roberto because we love his boyish nature but I think what I mean he has grown in stature, he has become a fine man.' said Helen.

With that they all descended on us men, whisky and children.

'Mummy, mummy can I stay here tonight they have a lot of soldiers and a fort and a train set and racing cars.'

Roberto looked at Helen smiling as she muttered to him and pushed his hair back.

'Of course he can its time you had your honeymoon.'

I heard him whisper back 'Thanks dear Helen I was hoping you would say that.'

'That all right with us isn't it Roberto – I said leaning over him on the sofa and
giving him a kiss. He actually blushed'.

'Yes but I shall be here at nine am to go shopping for your gear for our climbing.'
he said to Toby as he left.
They all scrambled off again.
Toby shouted as he left.' Don't forget the honey.'

'What was that all about' said Helen'

'Just Roberto telling tall tales again'.

We spent an evening relaxing and getting to know one another.
They had changed a lot and Paulo even allowed Robert to tease him about being a daddy himself and gave him space to tell us about his love for his wife and children and their little idiosyncrasies.
Paulo had talked to Roberto about the 'Pow Wow' and we agreed to have it early Friday morning before we left. Our time not Roberto's but he would no doubt have got Toby up and packed the car before we all stirred.
Having peeped in at our sleeping son holding a very grubby picture of an elephant we said goodnight and walked back to the hotel in the village.
We had warm coats and the cold air woke us up. We walked hand in hand to our new heaven that was

the four poster bed. The moon came out from behind a cloud and as we looked at the distant chimney of our house in the moonlight Roberto said.

'Now Honey and Rosy'

CHAPTER 34

TOBY ON BONNY, RIDING OUT

The next day we slept late until 8am. There was another empty champagne bottle
On the floor and I only seemed to be wearing my silver ankle band.

'Roberto showered and sat next to me as room service arrived with breakfast.'

He buttered my toast and said 'Anything else madam.'

I looked at him and smiled. 'Mrs Grimaldi I do have a son to pick up.'

'I know off you go'

'Let's just take a trip to that little bed I like it there' he said

He looked at his watch. 'We have just twenty minutes'

'No go'

'Just for Rosy'

I never did finish my toast.' Later I met them in the town for coffee where they both Informed me they had

had a second breakfast. Toby couldn't wait to show me his walking boots and his new thick woollen sweater and a waterproof jacket.' My sweater is made from the wool of the sheep here it is the same as daddy's'.

It was black. Roberto always wore black sweaters they suited him especially when he wore a coloured cashmere scarf. He also had some riding boots and a hat.

'Daddy has got some new ones too. He left his others in Africa but he used to ride elephants there.'

As one does, I thought. I laughed 'Well I haven't got any either I don't ride at home.

'No' said Toby 'You just wear high heels.'

'Women' said Roberto to Toby.

'Come on we have to buy you a blue tweed jacket and some white jodhpurs. You need some anyway if we are going to live here. I want to take some photos when we go to see Paulo in the office. He came into my cubicle as I was trying on the jodhpurs and zipped me up.

'You are going to look just like that little sixteen year old I fell in love with.' he said patting me on the bottom.

We took the clothes to the car and then visited the shop and my childhood memories.

Toby of course had never been there.

I felt a twinge of sadness as we went in expecting to see Ruth walking down the central staircase. Roberto held my hand for a minute.

'Do they have toys here mummy' Toby said'

'Yes Toby we sell everything'

With the mail order company being so successful they had just started the American system of ordering from the in store catalogue and being able to pick the items up at the warehouse at the back of the shop the next day. It had been one of Roberto's ideas and people came from all over the county to use the service.

I looked around all the floors and could see Gloria's influence. There was a lot of cheap tacky merchandise badly displayed. I knew if I had any say in its future just about everything would be have to be updated. In London I had learned to compete with the very best stores.

Roberto said 'I see your little brain working overtime you want make changes don't you 'TobyJo' here we come am I right.'

'How did you know?'

'You are my other half. I know what you think now.'

''Yes' I said 'let's pretend we are shoppers come on Toby get in the lift let's go to the Toy dept on the fourth floor. As we entered it was empty and soulless.

'This should be down stairs in the basement and not just a toy dept but a wonderland with electric trains rushing round and Austrian musical boxes playing etc. In a month it will be nearly Xmas. They need a grotto, a Santa and tasteful decorations. It could look like any ones dream of Xmas with the tree covering two floors. We have a period building and it's a perfect setting for a 'Dickens Xmas'.

As I was talking Toby had dashed off to see a bicycle.' I held onto Roberto.

'Do not do it Roberto, no more today. Just get him a few soldiers.' 'Sorry you are right, all he needs is our love but I can't help it I have missed eight years.'

Toby reluctantly left but in seconds was quite cheerful as Roberto gave him the soldiers he had been wanting for his fort.

'You can write a letter to father Xmas and if you are very good this week and next week and the week after that and the week after you may get some surprises on Xmas day'. 'OK' said Toby.

I smiled thinking about all the other Xmas's days I had spent wanting Roberto to be with us sharing a special time.

We toured the rest of the shop, which was busy and crowded, but I knew we could do a hundred times better.

I sensed Ruth around me urging me to do it.

We headed towards the airfield which housed the mail order Company and Paolo's office. It had changed out of all recognition. There were new roads, car parks, a sports building and a large cafeteria. There were acres of warehouses and garages housing delivery trucks all with our company name on them. We parked outside the photographic studio, which was the only building I recognised. '

I want to have some pictures taken today in your new riding clothes.' Roberto said.

We parked outside Paulo's office and went inside. His office was quite modest but had a lovely view of the lake. His secretary Joyce welcomed us and already knew Roberto who then introduced me has his new bride. I knew I would have to get used to the delivery of this news within this large organisation and the fact that I was Dino's stepdaughter. Later they decided to inform the staff officially by publishing it in the in house Magazine. Meanwhile Joyce brought us in some coffee whilst Paulo finished signing documents.

He got up and came over and kissed me.' It's not often I get to kiss a pretty woman at 11.30 in the morning.' he said.

He moved over to a chair and invited us to sit down.

'Hi Toby the boys missed you this morning go and have a swing on my new chair.'

Toby spent the next few minutes spinning on the revolving chair. Joyce then took him to the staff cafeteria for some ice cream.'

'Have you seen the store already Jo' he enquired.

'I have and of course I would love to see it updated.'

'I had already heard about your amazing success in London not knowing who you were of course so maybe you might consider as an option taking over your own Mother's store. When we meet on Friday this is one of the options I wanted you both to consider. I also want you to know that both Roberto and I were going to honour our debt to you anyway. The fact that you are with us again and part of our family is such wonderful news and it makes it much easier to go ahead with our plan. Roberto is so proud of you both.

'Thank you I have already been thinking independently of my husband.

I am looking forward to Friday.' I said smiling at him.

He really had such charm now. Gone was the faceless grey man I had always known.

'Meanwhile we are going for a photo shoot as a family and then we are all going for a ride.' I said.

As we left I gave him a kiss on the cheek. I decided that next to Roberto, Snowy, Hugh, Jim, Kenny, and Danny he could join my A list of wonderful men in my life.

Paulo walked to the door with us all as the rest of the staff looked amazed.

I could almost hear them gather around Joyce to hear the gossip.

We went into the studio, which had hundreds of photographs and magazine stills covering the walls.

'Mummy mummy that's you.' said Toby as we saw the famous one of me that had launched Roberto's career. It was the one I hated but was still sold by the thousands.' I like the one better' he said pointing to the one of me on Bonny.

Roberto joined us and introduced us to Karl a new talented photographer from Germany. He smiled at me and shook hands.' Hello' he said warmly.

'Well you are the he mystery lady Jo. I would be honoured to take a family portrait.' 'We are going riding so Roberto has insisted we wear our outfits for the shoot.'

That's fine with me you all look so happy, I want to capture your 'joy'.

Roberto and Toby were soon ready but Karl like Roberto and Christo insisted on getting my hair just right. I had to sit next to the wind machine several times as my hair was very long.

Then he took several of us all dancing to music.

Finally of course the two of us posed casually sitting on the floor leaning against one another which looked perfect when developed Roberto then took over and persuaded Toby to pose for some action pictures.

We had such fun as he got him to make faces, jump up and down and kick a football. Then holding the big camera he wanted Toby to pose as a cameraman taking one of me with my hair flowing. That photograph was developed in black and white and could have been Roberto himself at 8 yrs of age. It hangs in the Study today. Finally he insisted on taking some more informal ones of me 'His Honeymoon Girl.' which he framed and kept by his bed always.

After our tour we said goodbye to Karl and set off to see Myra She was thrilled to see us again.

'Look at you all dressed up. I have a very quiet Pony lined up for Toby and Roberto can ride one of Dino's racehorses. I expect you can't wait to ride Bonny Jo. Bonny will be the word when you all go off together. The little pony is called 'Eddy.'

Whilst you go and get Bonny sorted Jo, Roberto and I will get Toby walking around the paddock on him. Come on Toby come with your auntie Myra.'

She was clearly delighted and so was Toby. He was so happy and loved the pony. He had never had an animal before. I had always wanted to get him a dog.

Then Roberto took his leading rein and led him out into the field taking him around several times until he felt secure. I stood next to Myra who put her arm round me as she saw my tears.

'It's all right Jo you can be happy at last. They are a wonderful sight.'

We went for a gentle ride up the fell taking it in turns to lead Tony. Bonny never seemed to stop whinnying as if he too loved my family.

Roberto went ahead of us occasionally and galloped away on the racehorse.

'Would you like to live here' I said to Toby.

'Yes I would very much' he said. 'Would Daddy be here, he's not going back to Africa is he'

'No   not without us and yes we are talking about living here in a house. He lived in once just around the bend of the lake near to Paulo's house.'

'Can we go see it?'

'Tomorrow after your expedition with Roberto'

Two hours later we took the horses back. The grooms appeared but Roberto said

'No thank you girls, we rode them and we take care of them. Come on Toby let me show you how it is done. Let's send mummy in to get her high heels on and look pretty and we will do the men's work.'

Toby even enjoyed the process. Roberto gave him a bucket and spade and said'

'Toby this is the fun bit we have to fill that bucket and carry it over to that big pile over there. Do you know what happens next? Well Myra spreads it all over her garden and it makes her vegetables very tasty?'

Toby went 'Ugh' and laughed.

I left them to it and had a shower and changed.

'My you still look beautiful Jo you're not going back modelling are you my dear' Myra asked.

'Not at all have we to sort our lives out and we want some more children'

'Oh that would be lovely come on I want to hug you for Ruth's sake. Now let's lay the table. I have some homemade wine.

Has anyone said anything about the accident yet?'

'Roberto won't tell me he says it's our honeymoon and he doesn't want to spoil it. I think Helen will tell me tomorrow we are meeting up for a chat.'

Well that's a good idea you need to know and close that door well and truly shut.'

The boys turned up and Roberto said.

'Let's ask Myra where the cowboys have a shower.'

'That way boys' she pointed towards the outhouses.

'They look so good together; he is a very happy man.'

We had one of her farmhouse teas then she took Toby out and let him feed the   chickens bringing back some eggs for Helen. She gave him a riding whip she in had in her store.

'We don't believe in cruelty to animals but it is customary to carry a whip. Mummy will show you when she teaches you next time.'

When they went out Roberto pulled me on his knee and said.

'Now the house shall we do it do you want to live here and have hordes of children and leave the city behind. If so we have some more serious talking to do.'

'Well I want Rosy and maybe another so yes I think I can already see a way.'

He looked at me. 'I have to keep reminding myself that not only have I married Lady Godiva and Helen of Troy but a financial genius as well. Let's go back immediately and make two more babies before you change your mind. Now rearrange yourself we are about to be discovered.'

'Mummy, Daddy, Auntie Myra says her Labrador Milly is having puppies'

Said an excited Toby.

'Oh' said Roberto 'Is she, that's wonderful news.'

CHAPTER 35

HELEN REVELATIONS

Toby woke up before us and had got himself dressed apart from his climbing boots.

He and Roberto were away by daylight. They were to come straight back to Helens when we would visit the house and show Toby his future home.

I bathed slowly luxuriating in the warmth and comfort of the hotel bathroom thinking about the past two weeks which still seemed like a wonderful dream.

I now had everything I ever wanted and everything Ruth would have wanted for me.

I arrived at Helens around 11am and we sat down to coffee. The children were at school.

'I am glad that we have this time on our own. I have been wanting to talk to you as we have so much to cover after eight years.' she said.

'Tell me all about your life after I saw you last.'

I told her about the students, Kathy and Hugh and Katy and Jim and the house we all lived in. Then I told her about my birth and Dino's attitude and rage.

I also tried to explain how Roberto and I met after Milan and how we spent the weekend together in Scotland.

'Remember when I last stayed when he spoke to us both. I wanted to tell him I was pregnant but we were cut off.

'But you should have told me. You should have trusted me I would have helped you' she said.

'I did expect him to come home but then there was the accident. After that he stopped writing or so I thought'

'Well that is another story I believe Roberto has already told you how Dino had bribed the porter at the University to send him all your personal mail. I think Antonio was in league with him originally. He was very serious about you and needed to know if he had any rivals. Then I think Dino got obsessed with the idea himself.

When they opened up his room all the mail was there and lots of other things he had managed to keep to himself. There were private detectives reports and finally an address. It had a recent date on it so I am sure he was about to follow it up and visit you.'

'Roberto did tell me about the room, did you see it.'

'No I am glad I didn't. Roberto and Paulo spent a week sorting it out and clearing it

There were documents that Paulo never knew about relating to the early days of the business. There was lots of illegal stuff relating to land deals and bribes and importing goods illegally from Italy. He spent sleepless nights worrying about all of that.

There were scores of photographs of you as a child and all the ones Roberto had taken. They covered the walls and some of them had been enlarged to six and eight foot. The one that Antonio had bought was framed in a large gilt frame alongside the one he had done for Ruth's birthday. The painting covered another wall. Gloria would never have known about that or how much he had paid for it. It also had a very large expensive frame on it. The frames alone would have cost about 300 pounds each.

There were letters from you from boarding school and university.

There was also a diary with detailing his life with you and Ruth and his special relationship with you. He mentioned drying your hair and cuddling you in your nightdress and reading you stories.

'She loved being tickled and I loved doing the tickling.'

He wrote that sometimes he would go into your bedroom when you were asleep and just look at you. Some entries were about his love for you as you grew older.

Then when you were sixteen and taking you to boarding school in his open top car. He said your golden hair was blowing in the wind. That day he stayed to watch you play hockey. 'I loved to see my darling in her short skirt running down the wing chasing the ball.'

He detailed the last day he took you shopping and how he bought you clothes and helped you try them on. He said how beautiful you were and how jealous his friends were when they saw him with you in the restaurant.

He wrote that he was planning to take you to Italy on your birthday on his own without Gloria. He was going to charter a Yacht for the weekend.

That was the last entry. You must have left by then.

I felt quite shivery and disturbed as she told me all of this.

His attitude when he came to the hospital completed the picture.

It was more disturbing especially as he married Gloria who was opposite in every way.

It was as if her overt sexuality had to compensate for the feelings he had for me.

She was always aware of it and I believe that her jealousy of Ruth and myself was as strong and as obsessive as his feelings for me.

In the end it destroyed them both.

'Will you tell me what happened' I said.

'Well I will but are you sure; you are on your honey moon.'

'Nothing will spoil my happiness and I need to know everything so that we can live our lives without the shadow of Dino any longer. I need to deal with it and face it.

I have you and Paulo, Roberto and Toby in my life now'.

'Well Gloria never knew about the room. It was part of the closet under the eaves.

It was had a combination lock and only Dino had the numbers.

They had their own dressing rooms so I doubt that she ever went in there much and the entrance was hidden.

He was in there one night when she was supposed to be staying at the flat over the shop as she wanted to catch an early train to Carlisle. She arrived back at midnight as the trains were cancelled due to bad weather.

The housekeeper was at the other end of the house in her room asleep. We can only surmise what happened.

She must have disturbed him. He had an armchair in there, a desk and a safe. There was a half open bottle of whisky still when the police went in. I think she had a lot to drink because she was seen in the cocktail bar at the Grand Hotel near the shop at about 11. 30. It was mentioned in her post mortem that she had consumed a vast amount that night. Can you imagine what must have gone through her mind as she saw it all? She must have been shocked surprised and appalled as she saw the life size pictures on the walls. Some of the room was smashed up and there were broken picture frames and bottles about. It would have been a culmination of years of having to deal with her own feelings of jealousy and insecurity.

According to the housekeeper she heard lots of shouting shrieking and abusive language from both of them. It went on for about half an hour. She then heard her running down the stairs and smashing glasses on the drinks cabinet as she helped herself to some whisky Dino had left out. Then she heard going out to her sports car and revving the engine. She was shouting at him and swearing.

Out of the window she saw Dino jumping into the car with her, still in his dressing gown. He was trying to get her to come back indoors and wanted to stop her driving. She hit out at him and pulled away nearly running him over. He got in again and tried to hold the steering wheel but she pushed him again and drove out of the drive onto the main road straight into a large articulated lorry. They were both killed outright.

The housekeeper heard the crash and rang the police.

They eventually rang us and Paulo had to identify the bodies the next day.

'It must have been hard for you and distressing. I expect the papers had a field day with it all.'

'They did. Paulo took it very badly and wired Roberto who arrived as soon as he could.

We had the funerals to organise, the house to sort out and afterwards the business. I don't know which was worse for Paulo.

He uncovered a lot. He was shocked at some of Dino's activities and the illegal deals he had made. You never knew Paulo very well Jo but he has great integrity and is honest and hardworking. He had a handle on everything or so he thought.

However he is a very competent businessman so I get the impression that he has managed to unravel the mess Dino left behind.

As you know Roberto has a very serious side and is extremely decisive. He has been a tremendous help to Paulo who incidentally adores him as we all do.

He is delighted that you are both back. I have never seen him smile so much as in the last few days. It as if the cavalry had arrived to a doomed fort.' She said.

'Thank you for telling me.' I hugged her.

'It was a terrible thing to happen. They were part of our lives we must acknowledge that. I feel better for knowing so don't worry about me anymore. It must have been a strain for you too with your young family'.

'Well I would do anything to help Paulo I love him very much. I am so pleased you are both now in our lives. I am looking forward to Friday to see how we can most effectively plan the future.'

We went for a walk with the baby and discussed the houses and our lives.

She said they had made the main bedroom into a children's room. It was all freshly painted. Dino's room was all opened up and now housed the electric train set.

The walls were covered in colourful posters.

We had lunch and waited for Roberto and Toby to return so that we could revisit the house at last. I couldn't wait.

It was about 3-30 when they got back looking tired, damp and grubby but happy.

Toby shouted 'Mummy we cooked sausages on a campfire up on the mountain it was great fun. We saw a golden eagle. 'Oh yes' I said. Roberto grinned.

'Well I think it was and winked but we will check it out in the encyclopaedia of birds tomorrow. We took a photo didn't we Toby with the Brownie.'

We all had a drink and walked over to the house before it got dark.

It had not changed. It was a large Edwardian house with windows overlooking the lake. Ivy and Wisteria covered the walls and the large welcoming blue front door with its brass doorknocker opened out to a pretty cottage garden full of apple trees leading to a boat house and landing. There were two long sitting rooms a small breakfast room and a very large kitchen, which doubled up as a dining room.

Toby raced around the rooms and up into the attic and then back to us breathless with excitement.

'Mummy mummy can we live here with Daddy please. And can we have one Auntie Myra's puppies please and can we go riding again PLEASE.'?

YES, YES, AND YES, I said wondering where the puppy would fit into it all.

As Toby disappeared off with Helen to tell the children we lit some candles threw some logs on the fire and made ourselves comfortable for the rest of the night.

CHAPTER 36

DECISIONS

I glad that we took the time to be with Myra and when we took Toby back to our hotel he fell asleep on his little bed soon after his elephant story.We had the evening to our self and enjoyed a romantic dinner in the conservatory looking at the lights from the houses overlooking the lakes'.

'Tell me what you would really like to do Jo' Roberto said seriously.' We really ought to have a list of suggestions when we see Paulo on Friday. As you can see we get on really well and there is no reason why we cannot come up with a formula to suit us all. I hate saying it but now there is no Dino it makes life easier. Can you imagine what it could have been like? Now tell me which direction that pretty head of yours is leading you.'

'Well this is what I would like you both to consider.

We could buy his shares of the two stores and sell your shares in the mail order business to him. It would mean that we would be independent of one another and give you both a sharper focus. Paulo may like that .On paper he would fare better but as I already have a business we could run the three stores as one group and one company and make them all the best that they can be. We both can do this using my formula with 'TobyJo' and your experience. Whatever he is planning in relation to my inheritance it could be dealt with when we trade shares.

We could use the house as our base and yes I do want us to live there. and we will keep the flat in Edinburgh. I think we could convert my lovely house in Primrose Hill into three flats. We could rent two and keep the one downstairs which also has the basement and the garden. Then we could have the choice and reverse the process any time we choose. I want to stay there sometimes as Snowy and Mimi are like my family and we would have to go to meetings at the store about once a month .I have good staff and trust them all but I cannot let standards drop and we have to continue to be innovative and be trend setters not followers .I would expect the other stores to be exactly the same. With the rent we can buy more properties.

Roberto looked at me.' You amaze me with your grip on things you are really a wonder woman.'

'I know it is your project but I have also had ideas about the charity.

We could extend the barn and have it as base and offices where you could establish the charitable organisation you have in mind for the African orphanages.

Roberto said. 'Well my mind has been working that way too but I was unsure wether you wanted to leave London. I can see us all being happy here and I think it is possible that Paulo may want the same thing to run his own company at last.

We could all discuss our involvement with the charity which we could be a sort of family led project. Two independent Grimaldi companies coming together to form a charitable organisation. We finally agreed to put it to Paulo the next day.

We had a good evening with Paulo and Helen and slept in their spare room. Toby disappeared into the boy's bedroom sleeping on the floor in a sleeping bag.

Roberto was up at dawn typing a draft of our plan in Paulo's office. We were to leave after the meeting.

I had contacted Kathy and Katy the day before to tell them that I was coming to see them. I asked them if we could meet up at our hotel at 4pm with the children suggesting that the others might like to join us if they were free. She promised to tell them. I said as I had some important news for them and I wanted to take them all out for a meal. We packed the car and Toby went off with the children whilst we finally had our family meeting.

Paulo was a natural chairman and no longer had to play second fiddle to Dino.

He explained to us all that it would be a while to get the business on track again after Dino's death but he was used to handling the many crises with or without Dino.

The company was very sound and prospering particularly the mail order side.

He felt it could be expanded even more. He said that during the next few weeks he and Roberto would be looking at every aspect of the company to plan for the future.

He realised it was early days for us as a couple to make major decisions but we should all look at the big picture and decide where we wanted to channel our energies.

He felt that he and Rob would be acting as caretakers for the next few weeks but we needed to think which direction we all wanted to go in. He addressed me and said that he was aware that there was a debt to me but as my status had changed this needed be taken into consideration.

Roberto was quiet and attentive listening carefully to his brother. When he finally spoke he was serious and businesslike. We only had a preliminary discussion ourselves about my ideas regarding the division of the company but he had really thought about it and had already translated it into a working plan spending three hours that morning.

He explained that the two of us had discussed the merits of dividing the company and trading shares and that the idea had been mine. He mentioned our strengths and said that it seemed logical to do this as I was experienced in the retail trade and already had my own store. He thought we could run the three stores as a group led by myself. He suggested that Paulo would find great satisfaction in taking over the mail order company completely. We were already the market leaders in the country.

Then he talked about the charity he would like to set up and run himself under the umbrella of both companies. He went even further and talked about a Foundation, which incorporated the charity that would raise money for the orphanages. More could be set up in parts of the world where they were desperately needed and would be independent of religion and race. He went on to say that we could sponsor individual children and offer funding to create scholarships and sponsorships both in education and sport not only in the developing countries but in our own.

Finally he looked at me and said. "If this happens I would like us to consider naming it *'THE RUTH SCOTT FOUNDATION.'*

I was of course very touched by this and very happy that he had thought so deeply about it and not said anything. When he had finished Paulo looked at Helen and laughed.

'What a way to spend a honeymoon reorganising the company.'

She also smiled. 'Well it's certainly interesting and I for one love the idea of heading up a charity of our own .The sports idea is very near to my heart and I would want to be part of it. I also think it's a lovely idea to name it after Ruth.'

Paulo leaned back and became very thoughtful.

'Well Jo you seem to be the expert on fashion now. I gather your business credentials are quite impressive too. We also are indebted to you and your late mother.

I also think Roberto's idea to name the charity after Ruth is very appropriate.

I am thinking as I speak here but in principle it all seems like an interesting plan and could possibly be the answer.

He smiled at me 'I am sure you would like the family shop back.'

I said 'Yes I would love that thank you Paulo it is very generous of you.'

He continued. 'I think I like the idea of taking control of the mail order business on my own. Of course you and I will have to discuss this in more detail Helen'

She nodded approvingly. He could do no wrong in her eyes.

He went on to say. 'Both companies are almost equal in their profitability.

Financially I think Roberto and I could work out something workable to the advantage of us all. It will take months to look into it and a few more to finalise it.

If we do divide but unite as a charity I think I could see a way of making an even greater impact in this area. We could work as a team without being competitive.

I love the idea of supporting overseas charities and orphanages for displaced children. If we go ahead I agree I think it is important to look at where there is a need in our own country too and our own area. We perhaps could look at education here and offer bursaries. We could have a general fund where people doing valuable voluntary work in the community could request grants from us.

I personally would like to start incentive schemes with the staff and offer bonuses and shares for high achievers and even sabbaticals for staff who would like to volunteer with some of the projects. I would also be looking at training and some form of apprenticeships working with local technical schools.

I cannot tell you how pleased I am that we appear to all be thinking along the same lines. It will be a test of all of our combined skills if we go ahead.

I realised that he meant every word and I could see it all happening.

He was impressive.Dino had never really run the company Paulo had.

So that's how we left it in the capable hands of Paulo for the time being.

Roberto would be back at work within a week and slowly between them they would look at the big plan and hopefully enforce it.

It would mean that I would be the managing director of a company owning three stores and maybe more.

I wondered where I would fit a new baby into all of this. I knew Roberto would get great satisfaction developing the foundation.

With his background and talent I could see the reality.

I could picture the barn and further buildings and offices near our home. The walls would be full of stunning photographs of Africa and the children in the orphanages and their new schools. I could see the publicity machine as his photography would come into play creating glossy brochures and catalogues advertising our foundation.

And Ruth would always be there among us following my own father's dream of creating educational opportunities for children. Their name would live on.

Perhaps we could even rename the two shops again and call them J. R. SCOTT.

J was James my father and R of course was Ruth but now it would be Jo and Roberto.

The mail order company would continue as Grimaldis'.

After a relaxing lunch we prised Toby away from the tree house, said our goodbyes and headed off to Glasgow.

CHAPTER 37

GLASGOW

We arrived in Glasgow and were booked into a country house hotel in acres of grounds. We had booked a large suite and it was very luxurious. It had a child's room attached. Roberto joked as we explored our palatial accommodation. 'Well at least we have our own little room to hide in if we are invaded by Toby.'

The weather had been kind to us all the week and as we watched the sun setting over the mountains we marvelled at our views.

He left me to unpack, as we were to spend two nights there and took Toby down with him to see the manager to check on the reception we had booked. We were to have a Regency room usually used for weddings. It was to be laid out for dining for twelve plus the children. We were to have lots of floral displays and champagne served to the guests as they arrived. I had asked for bouquets of roses for each of my female friends to be placed on the table. There was plenty of room for the children and toys available plus a special menu.

I had spoken to Kathy earlier and she said that they were all coming including Karen. She asked me why it was all so mysterious and why Toby and I we were in a large country hotel and not staying with them. I told her that it was a surprise.

We all had an early night and Toby was delighted with his little bed so we enjoyed the luxury of ours a four poster with curtains.

The next day Roberto was up early and took Toby to breakfast followed by a walk around the grounds where he knew there was a large play area for children.

I went down to the reception room several times and hand wrote the cards for the table. I also took down some photographs of our wedding they had rushed through for me at the mail order studio. Roberto had organised a case of Italian wine for each couple which was stored at Paulo's. Dino had always had it imported.

They arrived back about two pm so we all had lunch and a rest as our guests were due at four to allow the children to be included. The two of them made me so proud as they changed into their smart suits. Toby wore his school tie and Roberto his university one.

'Now what do you think I should wear' I said to them.

'You can wear your high heels with bows if you like' said Toby.

I laughed and put on my red angora dress I had carefully stored for eight years.

'Mm' said my husband 'That is more like it I remember it well, what do you think Toby, that's her Valentines dress should we smother her with kisses.'

'Later' said Toby 'On the honeymoon'.

We went down early to inspect our room and it did look charming. We instructed the Manager to call us when our party arrived and then have them escorted to the reception where we would be waiting with the champagne waiter.

Toby investigated the toys and rearranged them whilst we waited.

Eventually we took the phone call and our party appeared to arrive together as they had come in a convoy of three cars.

Roberto stood behind me as Toby rushed forward to see the children he already knew.

There was Henry aged 7yrs, Simon aged 6yrs who were the sons of Hugh and Kathy.

Both were dark haired boys with serious natures. Then Jake also tall and dark but more gregarious. Born a few days after Henry he was also 7yrs and the son of Katy and Jim. They were so alike they could have been twins and were already firm friends spending a lot of time together. They all ran off to inspect the rocking horse and a pile of cars stacked in a large toy garage in the corner of the room.

As Toby went with them he shouted 'That's my Daddy Roberto we are on our honey moon.'

We all hugged one another as they came in and I introduced Roberto who was grinning to himself as he watched their faces take on board Toby's announcement.

The girls saw my rings and all seemed to shriek at once. The men equally looked lost for words but were soon given a drink by the waiter. After the introductions Roberto made a speech.

'Thank you all for coming, I am Roberto, Toby's father but I believe he has already spilt the beans as you say in England'. First of all want you to know that I am honoured to meet you all. I am told that you were Jo's friends and her life support when I was thousands of miles away unaware that the woman I loved was carrying our child.

My wonderful wife of one week will no doubt fill you in with the details regarding our loss of contact, our letters that went astray, my accident and my work in Africa.

All I can say is that we will never ever be parted again. It is a highly emotional time for us and you can imagine how I felt the day I met Toby.

I am looking forward to getting to know you all individually as I have heard so much about you. I will always beholden to you and grateful that such love and warmth surrounded Jo from such special people. We were married last Saturday at Caxton Hall because I had no intention of losing her again but we are having a blessing in her local church in the Lake District at Easter so you are all invited.

He looked at me, gave me a glass and said 'To my beautiful wife and son and all of you –a toast and thank you with all of my heart. Now let's top up our drinks and start to party.'

The men gathered around and shook his hand whilst Kathy and Katy put their arms around me and started firing questions at me.

'How did you meet?'

'At the airport'

'What happened then?'

'I took him to Primrose Hill, it was Toby's birthday'

'Oh' they both said 'How lovely'

'It was, it really was and we are so happy.'

'Good looking too' they said in unison.

'Worth waiting for' I said.

I turned to Danny who was on his own with Kenny and Karen. Many hugs later I asked Danny where Eve was and he said she was joining us later when she finished work at the Maternity hospital. He was working at the University in the music dept as a lecturer.

Kenny also gave me a bear hug and said.

'You of course know my new girlfriend Karen the quiet studious one who hid herself away in her room. She is a heart surgeon now.'

I put my arms around Karen 'It's lovely to see you and its good news, and you look gorgeous (she did) Kenny is one of my heroes too.'

'Yes' she said 'I visited the flat a few weeks ago to pick up some of my things and of course they are all new people there now apart from Kenny and Danny. Kathy and Katy have new homes as you know.

My mother died about that time and Kenny offered to help me sort her out her belongings and organise her funeral. He was wonderful and we became close.'

'Yes it's a bit embarrassing having a heart surgeon for a girlfriend down at the pub but if she will have me even though I am always covered in paint she will do for me. Its time I did something about it will you marry me Karen.'

'Not yet' she said 'You have to clean yourself up a bit first and wear a green gown.' We all laughed. And so we progressed demolishing a lot of food and even more champagne.

Roberto seemed relaxed with everyone and in typically had organised a jazz band to play.

We had booked the room indefinitely and after our meal the waiters kept the drinks going. When Eve arrived Danny was happily drinking Guinness and telling Roberto about the house and Toby's birth. Eve seemed as amazed as the others and congratulated me saying that it was so lovely to see me so happy at last. She flouted an engagement ring so love was well and truly in the air. Kenny talked to Roberto later about the painting and Dino.

Roberto said 'It's safe in the flat in Edinburgh and it will take pride of place in our new home.'

'Where are you going to live' they asked'

'Beside the lake beneath the trees in the Lake District and I hope you will all come to our church blessing at Easter'.

Katy and Kathy were determined to get along side Roberto and find out more about him.

'Quite an inquisition' he said later.

'But a nice one' I said 'The verdict was that they thought you are quite suitable as a husband for me so you have passed their test.' At the first available moment they had pulled me into a corner and said

'Tell us everything and we mean everything he is gorgeous.' so I did.

The meeting at the airport, the birthday and the details about our son playing gooseberry on our honeymoon.

'Toby is besotted with him of course' and I told them about the effort Roberto had made to get to know him.

Hugh and Jim did eventually get chance to talk to him when the girls finally let him go.

They appeared to get on very well and Roberto started to explain what we hoped to achieve with our proposed Foundation.

He asked them in turn about their lives as Hugh was now a Consultant in Paediatrics.

He was keen to know about the children's clinics in the camps in Nigeria and the Congo.

Jim was now a successful builder and was building new estates all over Glasgow. He also was interested in the Foundation and asked Roberto to send him some information when it was up and running as he would be more than willing to take on some form of sponsorship.

Everyone had fun on the dance floor and Roberto dragged the girls on one by one making them laugh at his tall tales about the jungle.

I danced with all my 'A' list men who complimented me on absolutely everything including my new husband and how wonderful I looked in my bubble of joy.

The children joined in and stayed with us until about nine pm when they all went to sleep in our suite.

After the band left at 11pm Danny went to the car to collect his Guitar and sang some songs by the American singer Bob Dylan whilst the other men shared some very old malt whisky Roberto just happened to have tucked away under one of the tables.

We women sat on the floor on cushions and talked ourselves hoarse. They left at midnight picking up their sleeping children. We all agreed to meet up again when we were back to normal and visiting the shop in Edinburgh.

'Is that everybody, have I met him them all' said a sleepy Roberto as he crashed out on our bed.

'Yes and you passed their test with flying colours, you are finally forgiven.'

'And you - have you forgiven me'?

'Yes darling'. I said as he finally fell asleep.'

I pushed his hair back and kissed him.

CHAPTER 38

EDINBURGH

The next day we went to stay in our flat in Edinburgh. On the way we discussed what we would do next We decided to go back to London and spend a few days together whilst Toby was at school. We had Xmas coming up and all the stores would be busy so both of us would have to commit to our jobs until after the New Year.

Roberto said that he intended travelling down every Thursday night to have a long weekend with us and fly back early Monday. He also said that he wanted us all to be back for good in the Lake District before our wedding at Easter. He intended spending two days a week down at the old shop and it would be an excellent opportunity to get the house prepared. He talked about March 1st as our target date.

'I want you with both with me 'he said

I knew how quickly he worked now and I could imagine him getting the workmen started before they had brought the New Year in. We arrived at the flat and

Toby was so excited with the view he wanted to go down to the river so Roberto took him whilst I unpacked again and unpacked.

Roberto had left it a fortnight previously as a single man. It was reasonably tidy but there were photographs and news magazines everywhere. He had left few belongings he had not really got used to staying in one place.

Kenny's painting dominated the room. It was in different shades of orange except for my hair, which shone through it all like the sun. An ornate scarf discreetly hid my pregnancy but it was still obvious. It did really look like a genuine Pre Raphaelite painting so I can imagine Roberto's confusion.

There was another photograph of me riding Bonny and one of his two girls dressed in their leotards looking svelte like and pretty with their dark hair tied up in a snood.

As I sat there I had painful memories of being there with Ruth the night before her operation. I had a vision of her sitting on the sofa about telling me her shocking news. She would have loved having us there with Toby. I felt her around me and a sense of peace as I allowed myself to be happy.

We had lunch in the little Bistro and then visited the shop and the office. I knew that if our master plan materialised Roberto and I would have to hire some new managerial staff in each establishment. We would be looking at running each one of them as part of a bigger chain. I would keep my own Logo and have an outlet in each store.

We went into Roberto's office, which was empty. Toby went around the room with great curiosity. Betty who was out of the office suddenly arrived.

She looked flustered when she saw us.

She said 'Oh -- I did not expect you back yet Mr Grimaldi'

Then she addressed me 'Oh hello again so you finally met up with Mr Grimaldi I am so pleased'.

I smiled 'Yes Betty we met and he proposed to me, we were married a week last Friday. I said laughing showing her my ring.

She looked at Roberto in shock.

'Oh – congratulations I wondered what all the secrecy was about. There was just a message from the head office saying you were on two weeks leave. It's such a surprise but it's so exciting.'

Roberto said 'Thank you we are just calling in to the store and we will be going back to London for the rest of the week.' Toby was looking at some animal pictures in the corner of the room that Roberto had taken.

'This is our son Toby' said Roberto 'Say hello-Toby this is Betty my secretary she sometimes has chocolate biscuits in her drawer and I steal one occasionally so she makes me buy her a whole packet in return.'

Toby shook hands and said 'How do you do, have you any biscuits left.'

Betty laughed 'Of course come next door and we will raid the biscuit barrel.'

She looked at us all curiously 'He seems a handsome boy.' was all she could manage to say in her confusion.

'I know two months ago I was a lone some cowboy, now look at me it's amazing I have my own ready-made family. He put his arm around me. 'And isn't my wife still the most beautiful girl in the world.'

'She is' she said. 'Just like her photographs.'

'It's mummy in her high heels'. Toby said as he noticed some of the photographs taken from Dino's room.

'I know I will put one of you next to her I have one here in my bag and every time I look up I shall see you both. Come on help me there is a hook all ready for it.'

He lifted him up and let Toby hang it up himself. Roberto had got Karl to develop them quickly. After raiding the biscuit barrel we said goodbye to Betty obviously still reeling from our news.

Then we did a tour of the store and Roberto introduced me to the Manager, Peter Brown a native of the City. He was about Roberto's age and had been hired by him when he took over. He had been managing another Dept store in Newcastle and his sales and turnover figures had been impressive.

Roberto explained how I fitted into the family and that I was the founder of 'Toby Jo'. He also mentioned the fact that we had just got married and that I may get more involved in the future.

Peter said. 'Congratulations if I may say Roberto you are a lucky man, your new bride as well as being beautiful is a very clever woman we have all read about her success. I look forward to her involvement.'

The store on a most prestigious site looked very smart and pristine but slightly dated and not as advanced fashion wise as my own store.

As Ruth was influential in setting it up I knew I would have to carry on developing it as she would have wished.

We decided to take Toby to see 'Snow White and the Seven Dwarves' in the afternoon which he loved and so did we.

We sat holding hands like a courting couple whilst Toby sang the songs quietly to himself all the way through.

We spent the evening talking about Ruth and the day Roberto came to be with me after her death.

We both said we both knew then that we had started to love one another.

The next day we all flew back to London leaving the car behind.

Toby had never been on a plane so it was so exciting for him.

Roberto sat next to him and gave him a running commentary.

He then whispered to me 'Two weeks ago I would never had imagined that when I left the aircraft my life was about to begin again and that you would appear like an angel to make it so perfect.'

We arrived home and Toby rushed in the garden to see if Bruno was there.

He was and he disappeared.

We spent the rest of the week on honeymoon.

We lay in bed and talked for hours, got up late had lazy baths and went out to lunch. Every day Roberto bought me fresh flowers and new pieces of antique silver jewellery.

We did go out to dinner with Snowy and Mimi the night before Roberto flew back.

They were eager to hear our news so we told them about our future plans and the Foundation.

Snowy was really excited about the idea.

'I will certainly offer my services to such a cause'

Roberto said 'Thank you Snowy I will need your advice and when it is all set up I was thinking about asking you to be on the board of trustees.'

Snowy seemed pleased.

Mimi said 'Well we don't want to lose you altogether so the flats sound like a good idea. At least we shall see you every month.'

We discussed Xmas and agreed to have one party especially as we had celebrated Toby's first Xmas together.

Paulo and Helen wanted to come down too so Mimi and I ignored the men and went into Xmas planning mode.

We had an early night and the next morning Toby and I both went in the taxi to the airport.

As we said goodbye Toby said 'Come back soon daddy.' 'It will its only four days Toby look after mummy for me'.

'I will I promise' said my small son.

That was the pattern until Xmas.

We had joyful reunions and painful partings for four weeks until finally we spent our first Xmas together.

Paulo and Helen and the children were to join us so we had a large crowd with Snowy and Mimi and their children, Remy, my cousin Frances, Colin and Jill and their mother.

Roberto was as excited as the children. He rushed around as usual taking my breath away with his need to get things done at breakneck speed.

He bought the largest tree he could find and hundreds of decorations, which took us a day to put up.

We had lights in the garden and garlands all the way up the three flights of stairs.

He spent hours shopping so there were great piles of presents under the tree.

He had food delivered hampers and wine from Fortnum and Mason and Harrods.

At midnight Xmas Eve when the children were all asleep and Helen and Paulo were at midnight mass we cuddled up by our fire as I told him about my first Xmas with our son. He in turn told me about his Xmas's in the orphanages where all the aid workers made great efforts to give the children a wonderful meal and each one a gift. They had also organised football matches and other games and races.

They sang around the fire on Xmas Eve singing Christmas carols the missionaries had taught them.

He was almost in tears as he told me some of their heart breaking stories and the hopelessness of it all.

It was almost an impossible task and a lifetime's work. But he was prepared to do it and more so now he had a master plan for the Foundation.

As he finished he looked at me and said.

'And now I have you anything is possible.'

Of course our Xmas was memorable and we all shared the workload to make it perfect.

Xmas eve morning all the women prepared everything for the next day working together as a team.

The children all opened their stockings with their parents and then we all went to our respective churches leaving the Aga to deal with the cooking.

Remy stayed behind keeping an eye on things and laying our massive table.

My cousin Frances who had been away during our wedding ceremony arrived from Brighton just as we arrived back from our little church service.

We had just watched our son Toby dressed up as Joseph taking care of Mary and the baby with great tenderness in a flawless production of the St Martin's School Nativity play.

Roberto and I had never got used to weeping at such things and just held hands.

Frances finally met Roberto who gave her one of his famous hugs and handed her a glass of warm punch taking her to our large sofa by the log fire. He then had a long talk to her giving her his full attention.

He really wanted to know about my father and his brother her father.

He explained that his own parents had died when he was young and that he had been brought up in America by his uncle but had never lost contact with his brothers.

Frances in turn told him that her father and my own father were passionate about education.

Her father had been a Professor of Philosophy and died years ago. My father had been a head master but when he married my mother agreed to move up North and take a job teaching maths at the Grammar school.

They had met when he was on a canoeing holiday.

He was staying at a local farmhouse owned by my mother's friends.

She also told him about her life in the army after the war when she was stationed in Brussels and Berlin as a secretary to senior army officers at their Headquarters.

After the war she worked as a Secretary to an overseas development company which Roberto found interesting.

She was a few years older than Ruth and her red curly hair made her distinctive.

Roberto I could see was quite taken with her and as I watched them together I knew he what he would be thinking.

'My wife's cousin would fit in very well into our scheme lets invite her to the Lake District which of course he did.'

After wards she confessed to me that she could see that Roberto was irresistible and understood why I loved him so much. His total commitment and passion to us his new family and his African charity was impressive. She had worked for many high ranking Army officers of such quality and distinction she was a good judge of character.

Xmas was celebrated in true style, the lunch was perfect and Roberto and Paulo dressed as Father Xmas's gave out presents to everyone there.

The children had everything they had asked for and Toby finally had a new red bicycle. Roberto also presented him with a large envelope, which contained a photograph of one of Myra's puppies.

Toby jumped for joy when he saw it and wanted to fly straight back to see it.

The children spent all day choosing a name for him.

In the end Toby liked 'Biggles' best as Roberto had read him some stories about the flying ace. We all played games with the children afterwards and when they were worn out and bedtime beckoned we adults just sat and enjoyed the company and drinking scotch.

On Boxing Day Snowy and Mimi had a drinks party. It too was memorable not only for the West Indian cuisine and our very own jazz pianist but it was also the day we introduced two lonely people. Sandy was over from Germany and had been told about Roberto and our marriage from Snowy so he too was anxious to meet my husband.

He was even taller than Roberto and I could see him summing him up when they met.

Roberto had been challenged may times before and knew many army commanders from different countries as well as politicians, senior aid workers, bishops, pilots and company directors so he was not ill at ease with the very tough personality of this high-ranking special services officer. He told me later that he had been very subtly interrogated.

However the upshot was he gave Sandy a large glass of whisky and took him over to Frances who was near the piano laughing with Snowy and shaking her auburn curls to the rhythm of the music.

They were never lonely again.

CHAPTER 39

TEN YEARS LATER

Our lives after our marriage took off in so many directions.

We were blissfully happy.

We had our white wedding in the local church in the spring when hundreds of people from all over the world decided to accept our invitation.

The local hotels and our homes were packed. It was a great occasion.

I was also four months pregnant. Roberto's wish came true. Rosy was born nine months later. His little blonde blue eyed baby girl turned out to have lots of black curls. He adored her and still does.

BUT she was accompanied into the world by her undiagnosed twin Miles (named after Miles Davis.)

Just as Roberto in his confusion was about to rush off and phone the world my Dr shouted 'Stop! What about this little chap.'

He was bellowing for attention almost as if he was annoyed that he had been pipped at the post by a girl.

He remained the same a blonde haired, argumentative, ungainly but loveable child born to be a lawyer or a politician.

Roberto for once was lost for words and actions. Fifteen months earlier he had been a lonely man living in the bush and was suddenly the father of three more children.

He then kissed us all and never left our side all night.

Remy brought Toby in at 8am before he started school. He was as desperate to have a brother as we were to have his sister so he beamed when he saw them.

It really was the happiest time in our lives if not the busiest.

Remy wanted to stay with us. Her American boyfriend Tim was a sociology graduate and worked for Roberto. They were to be married and had secured a cottage so she continued to work for us for years. She only became a mother herself later in life. We found her some extra help. We had a night nanny and a local girl who came in daily.

At first I concerned about how I was going to continue to run our business. However I had employed so many dynamic people I came to the conclusion that I could almost leave it to them. They were all competent, creative and understood my style of management. I had handpicked most of them. Some were Italians and had worked in Italian fashion houses. I still attended the fashion weeks in Italy, Paris and London and took all of my buyers. We also had our own our own mail order service. It was a huge success as our brand was one of the most popular in the country.

The plans for the businesses worked out very well. Paulo was happy and had expanded the mail order business. He also opened a large grocery store on the outside of town where there was a new shopping mall built on similar lines to the ones in America. He became one of the most respected businessmen in the country and picked up many national awards not only for his enterprise but for his training methods and his attitude towards for his staff. In turn he rewarded excellence with shares, bonuses, and promotions.

We were all the best of friends and our adjoining houses by the lake were no longer fashionable homes for entertaining rich and influential people but comfortable homes full of laughter and fun and of course children and animals.

'The Foundation' took about a year to set up. The barn was enlarged and extra buildings were put up including an accommodation block.

When it was finished it was an exciting modernist building featured in many magazines. It had been designed to fit into the landscape using local stone but had large panoramic windows and creative lighting.

Rob's work dominated the inside. There were blown up studies of his time in Africa showing the progression of the orphanages and the work of famine relief.

There was an Italian fountain outside in the courtyard and a large sculpture of children carved in marble by a Nigerian scholarship student called David Burino.

Roberto had sponsored him and subsequently he was admitted as a student to the Royal College of Art.

Roberto developed stunning brochures advertising the work of the Foundation and the projects.

During the ten years they sponsored twenty orphanages, organised food aid and famine relief to many disaster areas. They had also set up student scholarships in several universities and succeeded in getting multiple business sponsorships.

Jim, true to his word and sponsored many students. He had expanded his business building post war housing estates as the country began to prosper.

Kathy's husband Hugh also sent some of his own medical staff to work in the orphanages and field hospitals.

Helen took over a role in the Foundation in relation to sport and became involved in setting up bursaries and scholarships at some of the new Physical Education establishments in the UK and through Roberto had useful contacts in American Universities.

As a charity they became among the leaders in emergency work in the field with children working alongside all the other major charities.

Roberto featured in two of the most prestigious magazines in America not only for his prize winning photography but for the Foundation. This all meant he led a very busy life and had to go to New York quite a lot so he was able to meet up with his daughters Poppy and Posy.

Poppy was at a dance academy there and was twenty two. She was dedicated to ballet and intended to make it her career

Roberto loved it when she joined the family for holidays.

She was enchanted with Rosy tolerated Miles and adored Toby who was as she said 'The best looking guy around'.

He was too, just like his father. Posy was still at University but came separately from Poppy and often went to Africa with whoever was going.

True to his word Paulo had allowed his staff time off for volunteering and sabbaticals for anyone wanting to work overseas.

Snowy was head of a team of legal advisors and visited us regularly with Mimi and the children. He also specialised in Human Rights and like his father ended up a barrister. He very involved with Amnesty International.

There were times when Roberto and Paulo flew out to Africa together but as they trained staff to take the responsibility there was less reason to go.

Roberto did take Toby once as promised in the early days. He was eleven and had just passed his scholarship to a large public school in the area. It was his treat and a promise Roberto had always meant to keep. They went on Safari and it was a defining moment in Toby's life. After a month of living rough, camping and taking photographs he came back with his mind made up. He was going to be a vet. When he was eighteen last year he enrolled in a famous veterinary college in Edinburgh close to where I studied. He had the flat available to him but we suggested that it would be a good idea to mix and live like a student in the residence for the first year.

Life was good. I was 37yrs and Roberto was 45.

We had everything love, warmth, work we enjoyed and three homes.

Rosy and Miles at 9 yrs were a continuous source of pleasure and amusement. They argued non-stop and Rosy competed with everything Miles did with the other children. If he climbed a tree she had to. At 14 months she climbed to the top of the slide in the garden and down again before we could stop her. She never played with dolls but insisted on playing with his cars and trucks making all the appropriate noises.

Roberto was mesmerised, as she was a potent mixture of both of us. He took amazing photographs of them all but he took some of myself and Rosy alone wearing white lace nightgowns with we had our hair falling in curls. Hers was dark as it was Miles who inherited my blonde curls.

He reminded me a little of Hugh as he was big and clumsy but as he developed his curiosity held no bounds He did manage to always come top of his class beating Rosy most of the time. At eight he decided he wanted to play an instrument and to Roberto's delight wanted to play the trumpet. They were always listening to jazz and like Toby he always wanted to be around Roberto. They were used to going to see him in the offices and looking at his new projects which made them totally involved.

Miles was a quick learner and knew all the geography of Africa and learned about the politics and the inequalities particularly in relation to South Africa.

However it was Rosy who wanted a camera for her 8th birthday. Her first picture was of us all bathing by the lake and sailing on our dingy.

Toby coped very well with the twins. He was assured of our love and was never pushed out. He was devoted to Remy so was pleased to help her do the chores. All she had to do was smile and speak to him in Italian suggesting that it would be wonderful if he could empty the bins and sweep up the mess and help her make cakes etc. He became quite a good cook.

We had Biggles for years and he was Toby's true friend. He slept by his bed and Toby talked to him and told him his secrets. Biggles allowed the twins to pull his tail and he treated them as if they were puppies. He followed the children everywhere.

Helens children were all school leavers and only Jenny wanted to go to University to read English and Italian. She was also a County tennis player.

The other two boys went into the business with Paulo at sixteen starting in the stores and driving Lorries when they were old enough. His intention was for the boys to work in every dept for six months finally ending up in the office where they could choose to specialise or leave the firm and choose another career. They were encouraged to volunteer for the Foundation. Their oldest son John decided to study economics like myself and went down to the LSE. He stayed at the flat and Snowy and Mimi welcomed him into their lives.

Bruno their son went very early on to Music College and was not only an accomplished pianist and saxophonist he also had a remarkable singing voice.

He had always sung in the Gospel choir at church. Snowy was very proud of him as he had failed to realise his own ambition to be a professional musician. Toby was his best friend and they were always together when we were down there.

Sandy and Frances became good friends and eventually married three years after they met. Sandy left the army and moved up to Scotland where he started an Adventure Training project for young people involving mountain climbing, canoeing, rock-climbing and survival techniques. A few years later he was a changed person and we gradually got to know the real Sandy. His new life and most of all Frances had a cathartic effect on him. He admitted later that his work had taken its toll in his last few years of service. He had been in Germany and then Malaya in the Special Forces. He had a job that few professional soldiers would want to do and was almost at breaking point emotionally. Nowadays they call it Post Traumatic Stress.

Although he had several medals and an MBE he never felt he deserved them.

Roberto and he communicated a lot and his expertise was valuable. He allowed some of the boys from overseas to attend the courses. He ran it successfully for the next five years and then after a heart attack he was advised to give it all up. He sold the organisation to a company who ran courses for schools, universities, and businessmen. After their retirement Frances and Sandy let their house and embarked on a world tour.

We were sorry to see them go as we had got used having them around. All of older boys and their friends had successfully completed the courses.

Sandy's leaving eventually impacted on the stability and happiness of our family life in a way that we could never have imagined.

CHAPTER 40

MILES

Miles at sixteen was strong and muscular with blonde curls, which like Roberto's fell over his foreheads defying the barber. He was a brilliant scholar and could play Saxophone, trumpet and drums. Like Toby he loved being around Bruno who at twenty-two was in demand in the music business. He had already made a lot of money doing some recording work backing other artists. Both fathers encouraged them and even joined in sometimes particularly Snowy on jazz piano. Roberto played the guitar well enough to be accepted into their jazz sessions.

Mimi told me that they had done the wisest thing by having their own sound studio in their garden. It meant that they were always around and apart from beer none of them drank much or took drugs.

They went to parties but generally seemed to hang out together watching out for one another. Girlfriends came and went but no one seemed to disturb the closeness of the group. Bruno made his parents proud when he achieved a First class honours degree at the Royal College of Music. He also attended the Gospel church and played for them regularly. To my surprise Miles often went too, as did Toby when they were down.

Both Miles and Toby went to Public schools; Miles got a scholarship to his which was the most prestigious in Scotland and went on to Oxford at eighteen.

They all went to Africa twice a year together if they could. Sometimes they met up there. Bruno was adored wherever he went. They called him 'Mr Music Man.'

He was like the Pied Piper as the children followed him everywhere. He formed choirs, bought instruments and arranged sponsors for talented children.

When Toby was at University Miles took over his role and helped in the orphanage schools teaching maths. He also took his saxophone and played for them. He had Roberto's sense of humour and taught them magic tricks and also had quite a following. And they all played football.

Miles's other hobby was sailing and he often did some serious sailing out in the Mediterranean with Remy's family and at Cowes. We had a small yacht on the lake and Roberto taught all of them the rudiments at first using a small dinghy.

Rosy would often go down to London with me and hang out with the boys and was also friendly with Emily who was a stunning girl and like myself was interested in fashion. She wanted to design and at fourteen was coming up with some original ideas. She went to ART School but also wanted to do a Business degree so did part time courses at the LSE. She would often meet up with Miles and encouraged him in his future career, which was politics.

We of course were proud of them all and their cousins.

They were all sound kids who worked hard and appreciated everything they had in life

Roberto, Snowy and Paulo were a great influence on them involving them in the Foundation as they grew up with a mission to help.

Unlike other parents we did not seem to have the teenage problems and arguments other people did. We kept them too busy. Roberto was a fabulous father who never got bad tempered with them. If anyone had to set them boundaries it was me.

He usually used his great sense of humour to diffuse any family arguments.

I knew that one of them or indeed all of them would carry on the good work at the Foundation when we could do it no longer. They were all passionate about it.

We seemed to have charmed and fulfilled lives.

The twins had their sixteenth birthday in the July

The celebrations took place in the Lake District where there was plenty of room people to stay overnight. It also meant the Glasgow crowd could come with their children.

We had our own band of course, excellent weather a swimming pool, a lake and were able to have a bonfire and fireworks. The African children from the Foundation were there and we all ended the evening gathered around the fire to sing with Bruno.

As we watched our wonderful children and friends swimming, dancing and singing Roberto and I sat holding hands and thanked God for our bounteous life where all our dreams seemed to be fulfilled.

Three weeks later everything changed when Rosy decided to fulfil her dream with dire consequences.

CHAPTER 41

ROSY

Rosy was a vibrant attractive sixteen year old popular at school and loved by our family and friends.

Toby and Miles adored her, as did her father.

In Italy his contacts asked him several times to let them sign her up for a modelling career just as they had done with me.

He had met Antonio once when we were all on holiday in Sardinia on a yacht belonging to Remy's parents.

Antonio was told of our marriage and as he was happily married to a young French film star at the time he congratulated Roberto saying 'The best man won.'

When he saw Rosy sunbathing he smiled and said 'Well I could offer her a contract anytime she is stunning with her mother's ice blue eyes and her long flowing black curly hair. She is certainly her mother's daughter and that face could launch a few thousand ships'.

Roberto replied 'My family is off limits Antonio we have other plans. He explained about his lost years in

Africa. He also told him why I had left home breaking my contract with him and the reason I had returned the diamond bracelet.

Antonio had been lied to so often by Dino that he had never found out what really happened. When he finally spoke to me later at a drinks party he complimented me on the way I had dealt with my life and built up my business disregarding the power of the family.

'Your husband is a lucky man and you are still one of the most beautiful women in the room as is your daughter. I would love to see you photographed together.'

'She is as you say and we do have lots of portraits of us taken of course by our own prize-winning photographer. She is a twin; her brother is over there with Roberto.'

Miles suited for once was a blonder version of Roberto but equally as distinctive.

He drew a crowd around him always, as he was complete extravert and had Roberto's sense of humour and fun factor.

Antonio smiled 'Can you contain him he looks quite a character'.

'He is' I said. 'However his father and brother Toby usually sort him out and he is too intelligent to get into too much trouble. He will argue black is white with absolutely anyone. He has got into fist fights over it. He chairs the debating society at school. He is also brilliant scholar and has already has an offer from Oxford.'

Antonio suggested that we kept in touch as he was still an admirer of Roberto's work and was interested in the Foundation and the stables.

Rosy was not interested in fashion and like Helen she excelled at sports and was determined to compete with her brothers and cousins. She loved tennis, swimming, riding; climbing and she would challenge them all. When the boys came back from the Outward Bound School she was determined to go and could not wait until her sixteenth birthday. We agreed to pay for her as a birthday present. She was also a keen photographer and wanted to take some action pictures of the white water rafting. Miles had already been on the course so went with Toby to stay at the flat and to play music with Bruno who had lined up a few gigs.

Sandy had sold the school so we knew none of the staff but had heard that it was still a successful establishment with a good safety record. Although the courses were mixed the girls had their own dormitories and several women mentors.

On the appointed day Roberto did an inspection and interrogated some of the staff. He wanted to be sure that all safety procedures were in place.

We dropped her off agreeing to pick her up two weeks later. It was late July and she was due to go in the Lower Sixth at her school in the September.

We all had a family hug and for some reason I felt uneasy when we drove away.

'I hope she will be ok' I said to Roberto.

'She will be fine most of those guys were SAS. They know their job.' I met some of them.'

I was quiet in the car thinking about my own experience with the Staff Sgt.

We knew that most of them were honourable men and Snowy and Sandy were exceptional and had exemplary records.

The boys had a great experience there and wanted to go again next year and develop some of their new skills particularly white-water rafting.

'Stop worrying, we can go out to dinner and enjoy a teenage free house. We can behave like teenagers ourselves tonight; we can put on the music and dance. Come on lets go I can't wait I have a bottle of Champagne in the fridge.'

So we did as he said and I lost myself in the arms of my wonderful lover uninterrupted the whole night.

Rosy rang alternate nights and said she had made some friends and that the instructors were very professional. She said that during the last few days they were going into the mountains and practising survival skills.

This meant limited food living off their wits and making their own shelter.

Toby had told her all about it and gave her some good advice. He gave her is most precious possession his knife, Roberto had bought for him in Africa.

She was due to arrive back on the last Friday night when they would pack up, have a leaving party and a presentation. We were due to pick her up on the Saturday at midday. Each time we spoke she was enjoying herself and said that they were being pushed to their limits. One of the girls had left and couldn't deal with it. Some were homesick but she appeared to be in her element.

'I want to get the Gold Medal' she said which was for the highest standard in all classes. Toby and Miles had got one and she wanted one too.

'The chief instructor is really hard on us but he is excellent and he is very safety conscious.'

Roberto seemed very happy and said he could not wait to see her on the Saturday.

I was still worried and for some reason the events in the railway station ran around in my head. I lay awake at night worrying about it, reliving it. I was restless the whole week before we were due to collect her.

My fears were not unfounded.

Late on Friday night the doorbell went. I knew before Roberto answered the door that it would be the police. It was a Sergeant who was very polite and said that Rosy and the chief instructor had not arrived back into the centre and that a search party was looking for them.

Roberto went white and put his arm around me.

'Thank you officer come in. We will go straight up there.'

Then it all became clear. I had been worrying but had not allowed myself to think the unthinkable.

'Could you tell me the name of the instructor please is it Ken Platt?'

'Yes that is his name they assure me he is very competent and it's highly likely he will bring her back to safety.'

I rushed to change whilst Roberto saw him out and when I came back he said.

'How did you know his name Jo?'

Through my tears I told him that it was the Sgt who had threatened to hold me captive all of those years ago in the waiting room and would have almost certainly abused me.'

Roberto rushed out stopped the Police Sergeant explained and asked him to contact the police in Scotland with the information.

'Come on lets go' said Roberto 'We will get the helicopter crew out of bed.

We let part of the airfield to a flying school and occasionally used the helicopter to go to Scotland. He rang Guy the owner and chief pilot who happened to be up late.

We were in the air in no time. They all had known Rosy for years. She was signed up for flying lessons the following year.

When we arrived at the centre there was only one senior instructor Mike Dowling there in charge of the other students.

They were all awake and disturbed about the incident.

The party and presentation had been cancelled and parents had already been to pick up some of them.

Mike said that he was in touch with the search and rescue team by radio and that the rest of the staff had joined the search. He confirmed that it was Ken who was with Rosy and suggested we waited in the office.

Roberto would have none of that and insisted that he either flew to the scene or went by land rover explaining quickly that he was an experienced climber himself.

In the end the search and rescue party leader agreed that he should fly there as the extra helicopter would be useful.

He left me with Mike and we sat by the stove drinking tea and waiting for news.

It then started to rain which turned into thunder and lightning.

I sat in a trance pleading with God and Ruth to look after my daughter.

I must have fallen asleep in the chair because when I came round Mike had placed a blanket over me. The sun was coming up and the rain had stopped.

It was 6 am when I woke up.

Suddenly the door opened and in came a very dirty bedraggled Rosy. Her hair was loose and wet and her clothes were torn. She was holding her shoulder, she had no shoes on and her socks were in holes. She collapsed in my arms and fell on the floor unconscious.

Mike grabbed my blanket, put it around her and checked her pulse and airway and called for an ambulance. He then alerted the rescue party.

The ambulance came first followed by the helicopter and Roberto so we were both able to go to hospital with her.

CHAPTER 42

HER STORY

She was taken to the Glasgow Infirmary where Hugh worked.

We said very little on the way. Roberto just held me as I sat and stroked my daughter's hair.

After an hour in casualty she was taken to x-ray and then to the intensive care unit. She had a head injury and a fractured shoulder. Finally after an interminable wait the Consultant in charge said that it there was no brain damage and that she would probably moved to a private room within two or three days.

She would take a while to recover and probably not remember a lot initially.

We stayed there all night and when we were told that she was out of danger allowed ourselves to go to a small hotel nearby to rest and change our clothes.

I also rang Kathy who came to join us later and insisted we stayed with them.

When we arrived back at the hospital she was sleeping peacefully and looked like our beautiful Rosy again.

A policeman joined us as did as the managing director of the Centre. We were taken into a side room and both of them told us the latest news. Ken had been found dead in a gully. He had banged his head on an overhanging rock and must have lost his balance.

They had not interrogated the rest of the children properly but it appeared that Ken favoured Rosy and insisted on being her mentor swapping with one of the female instructors. There was some concern that he was too involved with her and he kept pushing her saying he wanted her to win the gold medal as anyone he closely supervised usually got it. He kept insisting she went to his tent which was forbidden in the centres rules.

I shivered as they discussed it all and tried not to imagine the worst but his gross behaviour with me his bragging about his conquests and the control over young women in his charge made me fearful that something similar had happened to my daughter.

She was safely back with us but what had she been through. We were yet to find out.

I couldn't rule out the possibility that he knew who she was and was exacting some sort of revenge for what surely was a humiliating time he had as a result of his treatment of me. He had been demoted.

I did not say this at the time as I wanted to talk to Roberto about it first and we were all too shocked.

The detective said that the only person who could tell us anything would be Rosy when she was well enough to talk. We were also told that there would have to be an inquest and Rosy might have to make a statement.

We had not yet had a full medical report neither had the police.

We agreed to talk to them again and went back to the Hotel. I told Roberto of my fears.

He sat quietly with me holding my hand and looking at me just as he had done when Ruth had died.

'Now Jo we do not know that Ken knew that Rosy was your daughter and we do not know what happened until Rosy tells us. We have to allow her to talk us in her own time. I want you to rest tonight I will go and sit with her now. Tomorrow you can spend the day with her. We must thank God she is still alive and we will be there for her when she wakes up.'

He gave me a sedative and I slept soundly.

The next day Kathy arrived to take our luggage to her house. She had dropped Hugh off at the hospital and picked up Roberto.

He was tired but said the Rosy was sleeping and looked calm.

Hugh had been to see her and spoken to the consultant who had said that they were hoping she would regain consciousness within 24hrs. I was anxious to be there when she did.

Roberto had already contacted Snowy and the boys. Snowy said he would bring them back himself and offered to act as our lawyer if we needed help around the inquest.

Paulo and Helen had been told and Paulo said he would send a wire to the cruise line which Sandy and Frances were using.

It was about 4-30 in the afternoon when Rosy finally opened her eyes.

Roberto had just arrived looking refreshed and calm. He had an arm full of pink roses and a beautiful new night-dress and robe for her plus a case of beauty products and a hair dryer. My husband understood women very well.

We both held her hand as she opened her eyes and smiled.' Mum- Daddy where are we.'

'You are safe my darling. You had a bang on your head and are in the infirmary are you hurting anywhere.' I said.

'I have a headache and I am so thirsty, where's Miles and Toby.'

'They are in London with Bruno playing music and doing some gigs.'

I was so relieved to hear her speak.' Thank you Ruth' I said to myself quietly.

Roberto called the nurse and she called the registrar. They spent a while with her and when we were allowed back she was sitting up and drinking water.

The Dr said that they would do some more tests on her and later they may move her to a room. They wanted to sit her up in a chair as soon as possible to mobilise her.

'Try not to ask her too many questions let her tell you what she wants to tell you and perhaps you could make a note of it for us.' he said.

The police want to talk to her but I will put them off until tomorrow evening she needs 24 hours peace.'

She said very little and just smiled at us. She was calm and fragile and when she fell asleep again Roberto was in tears.

'I love her so much.' was all he could say.

We left her to sleep again for a couple of hours and went to see Kathy who lived in a larger house near our old flats.

She had told Katy and she was going to call in to see us.

We decided to stay with them until Rosy could come back home with us.

That evening Rosy had bathed and put on her new silk nightdress Roberto had bought her. The nurses had brushed her hair and she looked almost like herself. Roberto sat next to her holding her hand as if he were trying to give her some of his strength and energy.

'Mum - Dad the police want to talk to me.'

'Well can you remember anything at all'? Roberto said gently.

'I remember losing the canoe and climbing a cliff'. She said slowly.

'And then I ran. I kept falling. I lost my shoe'.

'Don't tire yourself Rosy – we will write it down as you tell us and then if you want to look at it later you can but you need to rest as much as possible.' said Roberto.

I realised then how just remarkable he was. He had experienced many situations in Africa and witnessed killings and casualties at first hand. He was like a field Dr having picked up many of their techniques. He had an ability to think quickly make decisions and act on them saving many peoples' lives over the years.

The police left their initial questioning until the next day guided by the Drs and prompted by Hugh who was in consultation with Roberto.

By this time unbeknown to us the press had become involved and for the next few months our lives were turned upside down by their intrusion in to what was until then our very private lives. At the centre of it were Rosy and her revelations which took several weeks to unravel.

CHAPTER 43

THE AFTERMATH

Rosy continued to make progress and two weeks later was allowed home.

She rested a lot helped Remy with a few chores and spent most of her time visiting her father or riding her horse.

She was also very quiet and serene which worried us a lot. She had always been bubbly, talkative with a great sense of humour like her brother Miles.

We missed that and it was almost as if we were living with another person.

Unfortunately her memory was slow in returning.

The police were frustrated in their attempts to find out what happened and had to report to the coroner. She told them very little and when they mentioned Ken and showed her his photograph she smiled and said she thought she remembered him.

Meanwhile the press had hounded us non-stop. Almost from the beginning we were headline news and some of the tabloid papers found out almost everything about our lives.

Roberto was unhappy but he knew from experience the way the news machine operated. Reporters seemed to invade every aspect of our lives and picked up gossip where and when they could. My 'infamous' picture was on page three of one newspaper claiming they had a scoop as no one had ever known who the girl in the picture was.

Then of course the fact that I owned the 'Toby' franchise gave them more to write about. When they connected it with Roberto and his wildlife photography they ran more stories featuring it in many American magazines. The Foundation did get lots of publicity that way and in the end Roberto had to insist on news conferences to get rid of journalists just turning up. They appeared to be interested more in our lives than the death of Ken Platt.

All sorts of people came forward claiming to know us and inevitably a couple of the soldiers from the waiting room saw their chance to make some money and sell their story. It then became an even longer running story in one of the tabloids.

It was all very embarrassing for me when I attended board meetings and had to speak to staff.

We had to censor the news and keep as much away from Rosy as possible.

At first it was on television but after a few days we felt it was safe for her to watch but cancelled our newspaper deliveries. Even our own broadsheet paper had carried some details.

The coroner postponed the inquest to allow for Rosy to get her memory back.

However the police had pieced together lots of information they had gleaned from the rest of the group who were out that day on the river.

They talked to Roberto a lot and it was suggested that Rosy spoke to a psychologist.

We both took her to her first session.

Hugh had offered to help us but in the end we had to see one the police used.

He was called Simon Conway and was in his 50's and had worked for the police for years. The coroner also knew him.

After her first session she seemed disturbed and for days stayed in bed a lot and said very little. Simon did not seem to have anything concrete to report to us or the police.

The boys used to go in to see her and sit on her bed playing cards and music. They all came up every other weekend John, Miles, and Bruno.

She loved to listen to Bruno playing the sax.

She lost weight and Roberto was beside himself with worry.

Hugh came over one day and we asked him to talk to her. She seemed more cheerful after talking to him and got up and went swimming with the others.

Hugh sat us down and told us what she had told him. First of all she had said that she held a lot back from the psychologist because he was pushing her too much wanting results for the police. Afterwards she had apparently unlocked a lot of her memories but she wanted to rationalise them herself and get them in order before she was interrogated. So Hugh really helped her and did what we wanted him to do in the first place. He was such a gentle kind Dr with years of experience with children and young people. She did tell him that Ken had told her about meeting me in the waiting room and that he had had too much to drink that day and acknowledged that he had been out of order. However he had played it down saying that they had made too much of it and that he had been demoted. He had asked her into his tent to tell her this.

At first Rosy said he was fine about it all and he encouraged her to exert herself in all the exercises saying he would be with her all the time mentoring her.

But after a few days he became familiar and started saying inappropriate things to her about the way she looked. When they were swimming he hid her clothes and had upset her as she had to sit by the campfire with only her swimsuit on. He joked with the others that she would have to pay a forfeit to get her clothes back.

Humiliated she had to do swim across the river five times and dive for her watch he had thrown in. It was eight in the evening and the water was cold so when she came out he put a towel round her and rubbed her dry in front of the others making jokes all the time. The others said that he had a hip flask full of whisky.

This sort of thing continued .One day he would be a fantastic leader and everyone admired the way he managed the group particularly in relation to climbing and white-water rafting. Other days he would carry on subtly taunting Rosy out of reach of the others. If he were on his own with her he would take any opportunity to make personal remarks, inferring that if she did as he said she would have the gold medal.

'Did you find out what happened then.' said Roberto, who was much shaken.

'More or less' said Hugh.

It was about 8 pm and the others had all gone back to their tents but Ken had insisted Rosy go out climbing again for an hour as she needed a few more points to pass her test. The other instructors were not happy about it.

They set off in the canoe at first and Ken was his usual professional self. They went so far into some treacherous waters. They then came to an area where they could safely leave the canoe and tie it up. Then they had to climb a steep precipice. He kept urging her to go higher and higher and she did as he told her.

When they climbed as far as they could they sat on a small plateau and had a drink. He took out his hip flask and offered her some whisky. She declined.

He lay against a rock and started relaxing.

He said 'Well you have done it Rosy you have even higher marks than your brothers'

She was very thrilled.

'But I need to see you later after the prize giving. You have to pass my final test.

Don't look so worried it won't be that bad. You look a bit of a mess now don't you? All trussed up in your climbing gear. I like girls in their party wear. I can't wait to see you all dressed up at the reception you will put on a nice frock won't you. I want to dance with you.

She stared at him wondering where the conversation was leading and started to feel anxious.

'What colour is it.'

'Black' she said

'Is it short, I like short skirts?'

'No' it's long.

'Shame you have lovely legs like your mother all the instructors are dying to see them. We take bets on things like that. What's the neckline like. You have a lot to show I have noticed you looked fabulous in your swimsuit. That's why I teased you I wanted to look at you in your bikini for as long as possible. You are not only the best looking girl here with the most fantastic figure you are sparky and I like that...

You know what I am saying don't you.

She said nothing but watched him carefully.

'Look at me, go on, we both know you have as good as offered it to me on a plate.

You have flirted with me from the beginning. You know how to tease men just like your mother. We took bets on you and guess what – I won.'

'What happened next?'

She said that she just looked at him and slowly stood up saying.

'Ken I am sorry but you are out of order. You have been a good instructor but I will not be staying for the party or the presentation, I would rather lose my medal, I am going back now.' and she got up and started to run.

She said that she had worked out that he was so comfortably stretched out with his whisky by the time her words had sunk in and he got up she would be ahead of him. She had seen a path down but did not know the terrain. It was no use going back to the canoe. She had her own compass torch and Toby's knife so she was fairly sure she could make it. It was risky as he knew the area and had all the skills so she would have to look out for a place where she could evade him for a while.

Eventually she came to a valley where there were two tracks leading down the mountain. She took the track which appeared to be the easiest. She thought she had got ahead of him. Then suddenly she saw him waiting for her blocking the narrow path. Behind him was a tree with some shelter. She froze with fear knowing he would show her no mercy. He was laughing.

'You thought you could get away did you young lady. Well not from me I know this area. I am going to have to teach you a lesson right now, you asked for it. Come on, come here and do exactly as I say. I am the teacher and you young Rosy are going to have a lesson you will never forget.' She ignored him.

'Come on and don't play any more games with me and it's no use crying for help, no one will hear. Not your mother or your father who thinks he is such a big shot.

He came to the centre checking us all out. It was my day off but if I had been there I would have given him short change.'

He reached out and grabbed her. She was trapped

'I love taming young women like you, you are like cats at first you spit a lot and then after a while you will become a soft furry little kitten.'

She could smell the whisky and see his nicotine stained teeth one of which was broken.

'Now do as you are told and don't try anything. If you do I shall hit you hard, very hard. I am trained in interrogation methods. I have worked with terrorists male and female. If I describe what I have done to women in the past you will not fight me. You will be terrified and be begging for the soft option. Right here we go. Lesson one. He hit her in the face. Then he held her by the hair twisting her arm behind her back pulling off her shirt. She kicked him hard in the shin and then managed to put her spare hand in her pocket and reach for Toby's knife. She stabbed him in his upper arm making it bleed. In pain and rage he yelled at her but had to release her to stop the bleeding.

Seizing her chance she ran. It was dangerous as there were lots of steep inclines but this time she was running for her life.

She could hear him shouting in the distance 'Rosy I will find you and you won't get away. I know this place.'

She heard him fall over and get up again giving her an advantage. She was lighter than he was. As she scrambled down she hit her head on a rock and hurt her shoulder but she continued on and on outpacing him. This went on for about an hour and she still heard him shouting at her. It was chilling. She had heard enough to realise that he was capable of being violent and sadistic.

Then suddenly it ceased.

When it began to get dark she spent the night under a rock terrified that he would find her. She tried to stay awake but her shoulder was hurting and her head was bleeding but she drifted off. At dawn there was no sign of him. She had heard the rescue helicopters in the night but had dropped her torch so could not signal them.

Exhausted she did finally manage the climb down to safety in spite of her shoulder and her head injury collapsing in front of you Jo, and you know the rest.

'Well at least we know everything now thank you Hugh' said Roberto.

My poor Rosy at least she is safe and he will never menace women and girls ever again.'

Hugh said. 'Well she will have to talk to the psychiatrist now but I will call him and tell him to give her another day. I expect the police will want to be in on it maybe listen to her in another room.'

Roberto said. 'So we can assume that he just lost his footing.'

'Yes that sounds likely' said Hugh.

The next day she seemed brighter and felt able to talk to us about it.

'Are you brave enough to stand up at the coroners' court and say what happened.' said Roberto as he sat beside her holding her hand.

'Yes Dad if I have to. I am so sorry he had to die that way. I would not want that to happen to anyone and it is so tragic for his family but he did terrify me and was going to assault me and worse.'

'Snowy will be here to help you, aren't we lucky to have such wonderful friends."

'Yes she said 'Hugh was very kind and understanding I love him dearly he was just like you Dad.'

She finally had her interview with the police. The detective was thorough and as they had investigated the area the story she told seem to be compatible with their own conclusions. It was still a cloud over our lives and the newspapers did not seem to want to let it rest. Rosy had to be questioned in court by the coroner and he had several signed statements from other people about Ken's obsession with her. It was all very upsetting the day she went to court when she had to repeat her story in detail. Ken was divorced but one of his sons was there. He was also in the army and kept asking the police to re interview Rosy.

Snowy and Hugh were both there with us.

Eventually the verdict was 'Accidental' death but the papers still persisted with the story for weeks after. Kens son was paid by one tabloid newspaper for his memories of his father who in his eyes was an unsung hero with an unblemished military record. He did not believe a word of Rosy's story and almost accused her of flaunting herself in front of him giving a distorted slant on the bikini story. He was trying open the case again convinced Rosy had pushed him as there were the knife wounds on his arm which nearly severed an artery. He was interviewed on TV and was very plausible. He had maps of the area which were shown on TV and demonstrated what he thought had really happened.

However because there was such a furore other people came forward and their stories gave credence to Rosie's version of events. The other instructors spoke up and several girls from previous courses told of their experiences. They were similar to Rosys' but in two cases there was abuse and attempted rape allegations. In both cases they were too embarrassed and frightened of telling their parents.

Then more sensation as the tabloids picked up on the treatment of female recruits as several of them also told their stories for cash. Everything Ken had told me in the station waiting room was corroborated. It went on for nearly a year.

By that time Sandy was back and we were able to get his views. He was of course appalled as the school had to close. He had set such a high standard and his staff all had fine records and references. He declared that he would never have employed Ken.

Finally were able to put it all behind us and Rosy did too. Roberto took her out to work in the orphanages for two months during the summer and she worked in the hospitals. She came back partially healed and during that time made her decision to study medicine. I think the combination of the help Hugh had given her and the suffering she witnessed in Africa sealed it for her. She saw so many unnecessary deaths from aids and many women dying in childbirth due to insufficient midwives and Doctors.

She was accepted into Glasgow medical school two years later.

CHAPTER 44

TOBY THE VET

Three years later we were all enjoying life again. I was forty six and Roberto was fifty three.

Our three stores and my franchise were still successful as I kept up to date and made sure that everything was cutting edge. Our buildings were constantly being updated and our fashions still led the way as we continued to hire only the very best designers.

Emily Snowy's daughter was one of them and I had great hopes for her as she was the only one of the young people to be interested in the business.

We had many discussions with Snowy and Mimi about it and they were pleased she had chosen it as a career.

She had an amazing grasp of the business side and I loved and trusted her .She was almost like a second daughter.

Rosy was enjoying her university and medical school.

She at nineteen was very serious and rarely socialised with anyone but our close friends. She was almost too focussed and never really relaxed. She worried us a little as she was so beautiful but insecure around the male students who paid her a lot of attention. I partly understood as I was like that myself and I knew her experience with Ken Platt had scarred her.

She was only really happy when in the company of safe men like Bruno, John, Toby, Miles, and Hugh and Kathy's boys.

Roberto and I talked about her a lot. She needs a Hugh in her life.' he said 'She adores him'.

'He will come I know and he will be a mixture of you and Hugh. You have both taught her about real love. I said. She sees it every day. Hugh with his work and you with your Foundation and just being a wonderful husband and father.'

It did come much later as I predicted and he was a perfect choice.

We were definitely north and south now as she spent most of her time with my Glasgow friends and family and Miles stayed south as he studied at the LSE and Oxford.

He was set on a career in politics and had allied himself with the labour party although he looked and behaved like a true blue.

His ambition was to get a nomination before he was thirty and the further North the better. He was also a bit of a hustler and learned quickly that he had to cultivate the right political friends. He belonged to all the important debating societies wrote many papers and did what he had to do. His charm, good looks and easy manner opened many doors for him but when they were open he was accepted for his brilliant mind and exceptional ability to adapt to all classes. All of his experience with the foundation helped him and grounded him. In many ways Antonio had been right and was quite astute when he had met him when he was 16 yrs and said that he would need firm handling.

We did however have great faith in him and Toby and Bruno knew exactly what to do, they were excellent handlers. They both loved him for what he was and were the only ones who could bring him down to size. That went on indefinitely throughout their lives. It was mainly through music as they all played regularly with Bruno who at 25 yrs was already a successful professional musician and singer.

My dear Toby lived up to all our expectations and even today when I see him with Roberto I still feel that surge of happiness and joy I experienced in the garden when they first met. He had qualified as a vet and started his own practice at Myra's farm.

She was always devoted to him from the first day she met him and when she died she left the estate to him in her will. Her other family had moved to New Zealand where they had relations and she had been instrumental in setting them up in a sheep farm.

It was wonderful to have him living next door. He was not on his own however.

When he was twenty five he got engaged after a whirl wind romance in Italy to a fine horsewoman. Three months later we had our first wedding.

She brought her horses with her and some of her fathers' too. He was of course Antonio Greco and his daughter was called Pia.Her mother was the well known French actress Simone Cilon.

Roberto and I fell in love with love all over again as we saw them experience the same joy we had in one another's company. Rosy got on well with Pia so it was another place she felt safe and loved.

The next year we had our first grandchild when Pia gave birth to a baby girl who they named Polly who looked just like her mother. Toby was overjoyed and took his little baby everywhere with him when he was at home and sometimes on his rounds. She could ride before she could walk almost.

The next major happening in our lives was the open air pop concert on the airfield that the boys had been planning for years.

Bruno knew so many recording artists and was so popular with them his charm plus his passion for the work of the Foundation soon had them on board.

CHAPTER 45

THE CONCERT

The concert was the most amazing experience for all of us. Thousands of people turned up and joined in the spirit of the evening applauding our many African children who performed amongst the famous celebrity singers. Bruno our own superstar was there and along with the rest of our boys was one of the main organisers. They had been planning it for years and all their hard work came to fruition on that August night.

All of the big name stars they wanted did turn up and gave their fee to the Foundation. It really was a joint effort and was supported by many local people, farmers, police, community councils and local businesses all profited. It was the first of many as the airfield was a perfect site.

Roberto of course worked tirelessly. The work of Foundation had carry on as it was all happening around us. The event promoters were used to it and when they arrived three weeks before we were amazed at their speed and efficiency. It was like a circus arriving with hundreds of marquees, trailers and market stalls .There was even a Merry Go Round. A week before the catering companies started to get busy as did the parking marshals and the camping organisers.

There were receptions and parties before during and after the event so the whole of our family had to be available to network and promote our Foundation. Rosy was the only one who was not able to come she was in the middle of exams. Our friends from Glasgow were all staying with us as were Mimi and Snowy. We were going to have a quiet family party with Paulo and Helen after the event to unwind whilst the younger element were going to dance the night away at Toby's house.

Bruno was now living in a different world to the rest of us. He was rapidly becoming an international star. Whenever he could however he met up with the boys. Nothing had changed in their close relationships, they were still like brothers. He hadn't changed either. After the show we only saw him briefly but then he called in on the way to Toby's party and gave us a complete surprise.

This is what he wrote down for me later to include in my family journal.

Bruno's story.

The show was finally over and I was alone in the trailer. I liked 'alone' after the hype and exhaustion of the evening especially one like that with 100,000 people on the airfield. Its significance was that there would be a few more orphanages around the world supported by the Ruth Scott Foundation.

I was alone apart from the contractor's electricians, caterers and other members of the circus that supported and sustained our concert.

It was midnight and everyone had left to party or to get back to the city some by car, some by helicopter and private plane.

Our friends and family were at the two houses owned by the Grimaldi family overlooking the lake. The younger members would be at my friend Toby's farm. He was now the local vet and had married a beautiful French girl called Pia.

I was twenty six when my Music career began to move forward .I had finished my degree and was getting plenty of backing work. I was also making a few records which also meant I was making money. My last song went straight to the top of the charts so I was asked to sing that and play jazz piano and clarinet as a finale to the concert.

My mother and father would have liked me to have pursued a classical career but gave way as jazz had always been part of their lives.

With my new found fortune I decided to buy one of the flats next door to our London house from Jo and Roberto who were our good friends and like a second family to us.

They had converted the house identical to ours into three flats as their home was in the Lake District. I had known them all my life and Toby was my best friend.

I was six and Emily my sister was four when the twins Miles and Rosy were born so we watched them grow up and we all stayed friends.

Their mother Jo is a beautiful and talented lady and owns three chain stores and a designer franchise known all over the world.

Her Italian husband Roberto is a well known wildlife photographer. He spent eight years in Africa and got caught up with relief work first in Biafra and then the Congo.

He set up a Foundation on his return to house and support orphans of these and other wars.It was named after Jo's mother Ruth who died of cancer.

My father is a human rights lawyer and acts as an advisor to Roberto.

Over the years we children went over to Africa helping out at the schools and orphanages during our holidays. We all loved it and I particularly enjoyed bringing music into their simple lives.

My success gave me lots of choices. I could go to America, get mega rich and completely change my lifestyle or stay in London.

I chose the latter. I knew I would miss everyone if left but wondered if the change would be something I needed to do.

I have reached an emotional crossroads.

I want to get married. I look around at my parents and the Grimaldis' and how happy they are and want that for myself. Toby has it too. I want to love and be with someone permanently. I have girls around me all the time. I know I can take my pick. I have some really nice ones as friends but I refuse to get caught up in the merry go round of one night stands and casual relationships that so many men seem to prefer. I am like my father in this. We talk a lot about my dilemma but I cannot tell him how I really feel. He is very wise and his message is 'Wait -she will be worth waiting for'.

It is not an easy road I choose as I am surrounded by drug addicts and all kinds of weird and crazy people that make up the music business. That is why my long standing friends keep me sane.

Tonight I am feeling more alone after such a big concert that has drained all my emotional and creative energy. So I decided to stay in the trailer for a while and clean my saxophone. I know what is at the heart of my problem but it is too personal to talk to anyone about.

I suppose if I do not resolve it I should try and talk to Emily. It is driving me insane.

I do love someone. I have loved her for years but she would never marry me.

She used to be around a lot but now she has her own friends. I think she needed me once. She probably never made it to the show. My song was for her but she doesn't know it. Twenty million people bought my single which probably meant 10 million women minus one. The message is in the song. I spoke to her as I played the melody on my sax. That same tune soon will be the one they play in a new film about lost love and innocence in a drama about displaced children in Africa. We had a lot of publicity for the Foundation and as the proceeds from my single will go to it. There was a lot of interest.

Several chat show hosts tried to probe into my private life hinting about the woman behind the song. If I talked to a woman at a party we were suddenly an item in the tabloids the next day. It is a game I refuse to play. Tonight no one I know no one in the music scene will care where I am or what I do next as by now many of them will be high on dope, heroin, or alcohol.

I finally got myself together to join the few people I care about and who care for me. At the same time someone knocked. I put my bag down and opened the door.

It was Rosy.

'Rosy'! I said. 'Did you see the show I thought you were working and doing your Finals?

'Of course I did. I changed my shift at the hospital and I have to go back tomorrow. I stood almost in front of you all night trying to wave to you but I guess you could not see me. We were all worried about you. Are you coming to Toby's? I said I would come and look for you.'

She stepped inside. She smelt of Lavender and her raven hair was gleaming in the moonlight. I held my breath. She put her arm round me to give me a hug and I hugged her back and did not let her go. She looked at me searchingly with her blue eyes. They seemed to pierce my soul.

'The show was amazing and so was your beautiful song. I shall buy it tomorrow and play it over the loudspeakers at our residence when I get back. I shall tell absolutely everyone I know that you are one of my best friends. Come on lets go.'

'Stay for a second, I haven't seen you for over a year how are you'

'I am fine I'm 4th year med student now.'

'Well you look fantastic, the last time I saw you were in purdah you denied your beauty and denied it to us too. You look gorgeous. Sit down a few minutes let's talk. I am sure I have a drop of wine in my fridge.'

She smiled shyly. 'Alright lets. I am so happy to see you again Bruno. I have missed you. You seem to have been all over the world. Every time I went to London with mum you were in another country.'

She took her coat off and put it on the couch alongside mine

She looked so pretty in her simple blue shift dress and black boots. Her long hair was loose and gleaming.

We sat on two upright chairs leaning towards one another holding hands and drinking wine.

'Play the tune for me' she said 'Please'?

'You mean a command performance'.

'Of course, right now.'

'Ok, for real or on tape'

'For real of course. I want to look at you, you handsome brute. I've missed you.'

So I played my sax that night to the girl I loved telling her without words how beautiful she was and that I had never loved anyone but her and never would. How I had dreamed about her, recreating the times I sat on her bed playing my sax when she was sixteen and had lost her memory. She had looked so fragile and crushed. I wanted to sweep her up then, take her to my castle and look after her for the rest of my life.

I looked up and she was crying.

I put down the sax and said 'Now look at your mascara it's all smudged' let me wipe it for you. I took my handkerchief and wiped her eyelid...

She smiled and eyes softened as she said

'I love you my beautiful Bruno. Come on tell me which lucky girl you wrote the song for. I am going to be so jealous. She had better deserve you.'

'Oh she does believe me but I don't deserve her.'

It's you of course'

'Me'?

She stood motionless crying.

I stood there feeling helpless and inept holding out my handkerchief.

'What would you like me to do?'

'Do! Ask me to marry you and hold me tight.' she said wiping her eyes.

AND THEN THEY CAME HOME.

CHAPTER 46

ROSY AND BRUNO

W e were all about to go to bed when they arrived with the news.

We were all astounded at first but as Snowy had always been the man I would have chosen for myself after Roberto I understood how Rosy could fall in love with his son.

We all loved him. He was certainly very handsome and strangely like a mixture of Roberto, Hugh and Snowy all in one person infinitely kind and gentle.

Rob opened the champagne and called the farm to tell the others to join us and we had a party until about 3 am in the morning.

The others were delighted. Miles and Toby made jungle noises as they came in as if they had just finished a rugby match. They grabbed Bruno lifting him shoulder high as their hero of the evening.

Mimi and Snowy beamed with pride and kissed their new daughter in law to be.

Kathy and Helen said 'Right ladies it's time we went to London to TOBYJO'S shopping for frocks.'

Roberto hugged both myself and Rosy and said to Bruno

'She is so precious I know you will always take care of her Bruno and that's all we would ever want. Next to my own boys you are like another son already.

Welcome to our family.'

Then exactly like my husband Bruno had to rush the wedding bearing in mind his bride was still a student. They both wanted to marry as soon as possible and started to make plans to reorganise their lives. Bruno decided to buy a house in Glasgow which turned out to be the one we had lived in belonging to Hugh and Kathy.

He also bought some land next door and got Jim to build him a recording studio and formed his own recording company. He wanted to create a company that would give a platform to mainly black artists.

So the wedding was in London and almost mirrored our arrangements.

They were married at Caxton Hall and had a blessing at the Gospel church which was of course dominated by music.

Rosy took me aside before the wedding and told me that she was still a virgin at twenty and Bruno was celibate.

Roberto who had suffered so much over what had happened to Rosy when she was sixteen was very pleased that they could start their lives together without baggage.

He and I discussed it a lot as we still had a perfect love life and lived for one another.

We knew how much joy was ahead of them. We of course were right.

After their honeymoon in Jamaica they came back so in love it was a joy to witness.

Bruno could not bear to be away from Rosy for a minute. He took her to University everyday and met her when she left.

When she graduated and started at the hospital working for Hugh he was so proud of her. His career was put on the back burner for a while. But he kept writing more songs for her and when three years later she gave birth to their first child he wrote one for Alberto their baby boy named after Albert of course Snowy's real name.

We all called him AL.

Of course they were overjoyed to be grandparents as we were and the sharing of little AL made us all so happy.

That meant we now had three grandchildren and loved them so much. So all of us spent as much time together as possible

Eventually not to be outdone Miles also met his bride to be which created even more surprises.

CHAPTER 47

MILES MARRIES

Mother has been writing our family story and wanted us to contribute our bit.

She is seventy now and looks pretty good. She was always beautiful and her photographs that dad has taken over the years are stunning.

Dad of course is 78 yrs. His hair gray is but he is still good looking and a great man.

We all adore them both.

They are still totally involved with one another and long may it continue.

Things have changed lately Paulo died last year and his son John and his brother have taken over the business. We all miss him very much. He was a quiet man but he was the backbone of the family and dad's best friend and brother.

Helen is still involved with the charity as is her daughter Jenny who is married with two children. Her husband is a lecturer and they live in Georgian town house near the shop.

Bruno and my other half Rosy gave us a surprise when they got married five years ago. They now have young Al who is four the image of his dad and granddad. Also a baby girl of three months called Dorcas.

They were made for one another I don't know why we didn't notice it when they were growing up. As a little girl when Rosy was stressed it wasn't me she turned to it was always Bruno.

He bought some land and built a house near the lake and during the last three years has slowly taken over 'The Foundation' from dad and runs it with Remy's husband Paul.

He still performs and records when he wants too and all the proceeds go to the Foundation. It's great having him as part of our family.

Rosy has her own surgery built for her by Bruno which serves the community and the Foundation. She has up to date facilities and it is more like a cottage hospital with and x ray dept, Physiotherapy, and Pharmacy as well as a few rooms for alternative therapies.

Toby is also going to write his chapter to record his family story.

We are all still close and do a lot of running around between houses.

Well Mum asked me to write about my love life.

She and Dad were always desperate to get us married off as they had such a good marriage. Well I suppose I had better put pen to paper on this one.

My other half is called Penny.

I bumped into her at a party when the new theatre was opened by the lake. I had known her in London and had a bit of a fling with her once. I was asked to be on the board being the local MP and all that.

I know mum has written very little about this being preoccupied with mini people in prams. I have represented the constituency for a few years now.

They say I am very outspoken. Well I guess I am. I have to be especially when surrounded by incompetent people. I am totally disciplined.

Like Dad I work hard and get up early doing hours of work before the staff arrive in the office. I do not go to lunch and waste time. I attend as many sessions in the house as I can. I am determined to be in the cabinet one day.

I will attend parties if I think I need to and if they are necessary to my career.

To relax I sail my boat in Cowes, and at home in the Lake district. When I have time in London I meet up with Toby, Bruno, and John for jazz sessions. They are my life support and keep me normal. They have stopped a few punch ups in the past when people have argued with me as I will never give in if I think I am right. They just laughed at me and told me to 'Cut the bullshit Miles.' I have had brushes with dustbin men, traffic wardens, bouncers, council officials, the odd policeman and my favourite Jehovah's Witnesses.'

What is strange I never had rows with Dad? He was and is my idol and I inherited his sense of humour and quirky personality. Like him I can turn things inside out and see the funny side of situations.

We all of course have had girl friends but mine have been fleeting and casual so far. I cannot commit but am not averse to weekends in Paris with the odd girl I meet in various sailing clubs and yachts around Cowes and the Med. I avoid mating at Party conferences and political thrashes. Too many reporters about.

I knew Penny when she was at RADA and met her at a party. We went out occasionally. She said she was in love with me but I was too selfish and I still have some commitment to the Foundation during the summer break. She found herself another boyfriend but I think something went wrong there too. I was surprised when I bumped into her at the Theatre.

She seemed pleased to see me but disappeared quickly with a gang she was with. She slipped a note into my hand inviting me to lunch the following Sunday. I shoved it in my pocket and nearly forgot.

When I changed to go out Saturday I decreased it and read her scrawly writing.

Dearest Miles
Come to lunch Sunday we meet for drinks first at 12-30.
You know where I live don't you, just across the lake.

Penn.

Well that was the problem I only knew her in London. I hadn't a clue where her home was or anything about her parents.She refused to talk about them .I assumed they lived in Scotland as she was always up there.

It was Toby who enlightened me when I told him about my invite.

'Penny' he said. 'Oh Christ Miles there is only one Penny around here and we hardly know her. Pia does though they meet up at eventing. Take a breath a minute your Penny is Lord Wesley's daughter she is an Honourable. You are about to have lunch with a Lord so make sure you wear some decent clothes not those baggy chinos you always wear.

I replied 'Well I am not so sure I want to go after all I expect I shall have to behave myself. Not much chance of a snuggle with Penny. I am sex starved.

'Do you like her?'

'She's ok as women go you know me I like being a bachelor and we don't all get to meet gorgeous French girls everyday like Pia you lucky dog.'

'Well are you going?'

I suppose I will have to there is no phone number on the note.

'Watch it mum will be on the war path she wants you safely married'

The only woman I should marry is Emily because she is gorgeous and sexy and knows how to run a business and make money in fact since she became MD of TOBYJOS she has succeeded beyond mum's wildest dreams.

It was true we had always been great mates and sometimes I had a feeling that we two could be good together. The last time I saw her she had an artist half her age trailing around after her. I could smell the lust. I felt mildly jealous which was unusual for me.

Anyway I went to the pile which I had always known was there but as I spent most of my life in London I had not met any of the family. I think Lady Wesley had been to open days at the Foundation and knew mum and dad but the old boy I gather was the Hunting shooting type. He never left the place that is why I suppose we had never met even though I was the MP.Wrong party of course.

Well before I left mum inspected me and made me wear some decent clothes and why not she knew a lot about dressing for the right occasion. I am dad's size and in spite of his tendency to walk around as if he is still in the bush Mum makes sure he has fabulous suits for the occasions when he has to do presentations. She adores it when he dresses up. She gazes at him like a love struck teenager. And that is just what they are like together. Sometimes I feel we are all in their way.

Then came her lecture.

'Miles its good for your career to network with the aristocracy'

'Nonsense mum I do ok without them you know I met a lot of them at Oxford. I am too down to earth and I find their in talk very tedious. I am happy with my own friends.

I shall be bored stiff at the lunch and you know what we all feel about hunting and shooting after living in Africa.'

Then off I went and borrowed Dads Mazerati, a beautiful machine he had courted mum in. I had an old beaten up Mini in London that had been bumped so often it was nearly falling apart.

I drove through the very large iron gates with the family crest painted on them and down the long tree lined drive to the stately home. I arrived bang on twelve thirty and Penny was standing on the steps waiting for me. 'Don't be late' were her last words.

There were lot of cars parked, big ones, 'Rollers' and so on but the old boys did cast admiring looks at Roberto's dream machine.

I did my usual bound over the top and another bound to the top of their steps into the arms of Pen who was looking rather scrumptious in a sort of blue woolly angora frock that clung in the right places.

I turned on my charm which I had inherited from my father.

I allowed Pen to push my hair out of my eyes the way mum did to dad and settled into the prospective husband mode about to be vetted by one of the most powerful and overbearing mothers in the country Lady Eleanor Wesley.

She came out to meet me ignoring the other guests who just ambled through to collect their drinks. Lady Wesley must have been desperate to inspect me with her interrogation notes at the ready. She was course used to checking the pedigree of horses. I was no horse and I for one knew 'that you can take a horse to water but you can't make him drink.'

That was my attitude throughout the lunch.

I said what I usually said to all the women I met for the first time. I told them they looked charming. I always made a joke and had them eating out of the palm of my hand. This Lady however was more the Maggie Thatcher type 'not for turning' she was smelling danger.

Her little girl was hooked. I knew it, she knew it but Penny and Lord Wesley were unaware of it. Poor thing she lost before she started. I was well prepared.

What she did not know that Pen had done all the running and was still doing so.

I personally would rather be on that boat on their lake than dining with a lot of aristocratic old fogies.

And that is just what they turned out to be. In fact I knew some of them from the House of Lords. I wished Toby and Bruno were with me. We would have enjoyed leading the conversation away from hunting and shooting to Africa.

Daddy Lord Max Wesley was indeed a powerful man in build and bluster.

As I won most of the debates at Oxford in the debating society and got a first in politics I knew I could out argue any of them if they tried it on. However I remained my jovial party self. I was polite and at ease with everyone and had come armed with my repertoire of jokes. I managed to pull it off quite well.

Unbeknown to anyone except Emily I had a speech writer who provided me with fresh jokes monthly, so I had one for most occasions.

Penny sat next to me at lunch which was roast pheasant. That did not appeal to me at all. I hated seeing the poor things being shot.

She kept touching my knee and muttering to me. 'Miles lets go for a drive later in that sexy car of yours.'

I smiled and said 'That is my dad's love machine do you like it.'

'Mmm she said nearly choking on her soufflé as I touched her knees and a bit higher up to where her stocking joined her suspenders.'

Lady Eleanor was sitting at the head of our part of the table and her father was at the other end nearer to his cronies.

She was so busy addressing everyone in turn she did not notice our under the table antics.

Then came the interrogation in front of the guests.

'Was it true I was half Italian?' Penny nearly choked again when I answered in aristocratic Italian the way Pia's father Antonio spoke.

Then there was the break through as Lady Eleanor got me going about the Foundation and on that like my father I was eloquence itself. In fact I almost had them reaching for their cheque books.

Then it was my twin's turn.

'Was it true she was married to a black musician?'

'Quite true, she is married to my friend Bruno.'

For the first time I glared at her (don't go there I thought or I shall leave instantly and your daughter will have to find another handsome prince.)

'My sister of course is the local GP'. I said. (May you never need her when you fall off your horse or indeed my brother when you ride them too hard and want them shot?) ?'

'And your brother the vet owns racehorses I gather he has a lovely French wife who rides rather well.' boomed Lord Max from the other end of the table. One of his cronies joined in.

'Perhaps she would care to hunt with us one day? She has a damned fine seat.'

The whole county had seen her out riding. She did have a good seat and that was not all she had. Hunting men were renowned for their lechery. They could spot a good 'filly' anywhere. I gather the Hunt balls were Sodom and Gomorrah country.

Thankfully it was time for coffee and Penny and I were allowed to go out for a walk whilst the older men smoked cigars.

Pen said 'I think they like you. You were very amusing. They liked your sense of humour .That last joke you told got them going. How do you remember them?'

That is my secret I thought I tell them to myself all the way to a function. Sometimes they are hot off the press from Adrian my writer friend.

BUT

It was all too exhausting. I couldn't keep this up the rest of my life. Penny darling you will have to go on the back burner.

But Penny had other ideas.

'Come on Miles lets escape in your dads car.'

'Ok where'

'Just follow my instructions' she said as we got in.

Her dress was almost up to her thigh and I got a glimpse of dark blue lace suspenders. They were Indigo my favourite colour.

We stayed in the grounds but seemed to drive quite a long way. Then we came to a cottage.

'This is my favourite place' she said. 'I am allowed to bring my friends here so come on in you're my friend.'

We jumped out. She opened the door.

Then she told me to follow her into the kitchen where she took a large bottle of champagne out of the fridge.

'Open that' she ordered in her best hunting voice. 'Here are the glasses and now you can tell me a few more of those jokes you rehearse in the car. The men only ones please.'

Meanwhile as I was about to raise my glass she took off her blue angora frock and was wearing only her blue suspender belt and sheer white stockings.

She had no bra and had the most perfect breasts,

I calmly gave her the glass of champagne.

'Have you heard the one about the-----------

'Shut up' she said as she started to undress me.

I expect her parents were used to her excesses. She went to the most expensive girl's public school and then to a Swiss finishing school where such behaviour was the norm I gather.

We had a good time in fact it was very good so we stayed there until next morning- but I did not want to marry her. So why did I.

Well if the truth be known she wanted me and in the end I succumbed after many afternoon trips to the cottage. I sort of became addicted to the indigo suspender belt, my favourite colour.

Then the wedding circus came to town. If they could have had Westminster Abbey they would have done but it was not available due to renovations.

She was their only child. The million dollar question was my 'pedigree'.

Was it good enough to father a future Baronet? No doubt it was discussed up and down the country among the higher orders.

It took them a year to plan and if it were not for the visits to the cottage I would have left the country never to return.

Lord Max took to me as he had never had a son. He even showed me off to his cronies

I had to keep turning out the jokes to keep them happy especially the blue ones which Penny loved so much.

We always managed three bottles of port when I was there and suddenly their dinner parties were the ones everyone wanted to go to. Then I was invited to join his club and on the board of his many companies. I was also given a minor cabinet post hopefully on merit.

The year dragged on and sometimes it began to feel like a nightmare.

Just before the great occasion at St Margaret's Westminster Emily called me.

She suggested we lunched at the LSE where we used to meet. I was curious but excited at the prospect of seeing her. I was there first and when she walked in I could see why men lusted after her. She was exquisite and exotic like her mother Mimi.

After exchanging our family news she went quiet.

Then she said something amazing which changed my life forever.'

'Miles I want to talk seriously to you. I am following my instincts here and I have to say it before it is too late. Come here.'

She looked at me and smiled. Then she did something that mum always did to dad.

She very slowly and gently pushed my unruly hair out of my eyes.

I was on fire.

'I don't think you want to get married do you.'

'No' I said emphatically. 'Not at all, and not now, especially not now.

But it's too late now Emily.'

'Yes it is but come back with me to my flat' she said.

She stood up and held my hand. 'Come on pay the bill and let's go now this minute. We have waited long enough.'

I knew then what I had always known if I had ever been honest with myself.

She owned the third flat in our block. We went back arm in arm past our downstairs flat and up to hers with its panoramic view of London.

I could hardly contain myself. As we stood in hallway it was all too much for us.

We made love all the afternoon, all night and most of next day.

I could have stayed there forever. I wanted her all the time after that. I really loved her and it was all too late. It was like Midsummer night's dream. She had cast a spell on me. We talked about it. I was in despair.

She said 'You are to get married and when it gets too much we can meet.

It's enough for me. I cannot have children and I enjoy my life. I want to carry on where Jo left off she trusts me. I love you Miles. I have always done so. Let's leave it this way. It's our secret and we must never let on to the family.'

I stayed another night and cancelled all my engagements. I couldn't leave. I was out of control. There were seven messages from Penny when I got back on my answer machine and I didn't care. For the next few days I bombarded Emily with gifts and flowers.

On my wedding day I had to speak to her. I called her. She came down to the family flat for a few moments. She took me into the kitchen to make me a coffee out of earshot. I had to hold her. I could hardly breathe. She rearranged my flower dragged me out and laughingly said to my mother.

'I have to have one last cuddle with him before he joins the aristocracy' then gave me a great kiss in front of all of them. They were very amused and it broke the tension.

So we had our big wedding and all the women looked fabulous. Mum and Roberto seemed so proud me and enjoyed all the massive celebrations. They were invited to the Country pile several times and introduced to many influential people. It was indeed a wonderful occasion. Half of the British aristocracy was there.

Bruno was my best man. Toby understood why I did it and agreed. There was quite an amusing incident dad told us about later. An elderly aristocratic relation of Penny's asked Bruno to get her some champagne calling him 'Bearer". She had spent most of her life in India. He roared with laughter and duly obliged.

We had our honeymoon in Mauritius and sailed a lot. Penny was a good sport and I enjoyed being with her. Emily was still in my head but I let her go occasionally.

As I settled back to work at the house I began to get more senior posts. We lived in Chelsea and to all events and purposes lived a charmed life. The blue suspender belt never lost its appeal and our son and heir was born eight months after our wedding.

We called him Louis Arthur Ronald Grimaldi after various members of the family but he was really named after my favourite black trumpeter simply to make a statement.

One day of course my dear little boy will be Lord Louis.

All in all it was all very satisfactory. I met Emily once a week for coffee sometimes with the family. We rarely had time to make love but when we did I was transported into another world. In between I felt I was living a half life. Sometimes Penny met her as she mingled very well in and amongst our family. Occasionally she visited her parents on her own and I had nocturnal visits to Emily up the stairs. I selfishly needed both women. But Emily I adored in the same way Rosy loved Bruno. Odd really as we were twins.

Occasionally I went to Africa on Government business and once Emily was there at the same with Bruno and Toby. They left two days before her. We managed to have three nights together. I had to attend functions each night but got away as soon as I could to Paradise Emily. It really was Paradise I was so in love. We never felt guilty it seemed right for us. I could not exist without her. She was the love of my life.

I was a good husband and father and Penny excelled as a political wife and hostess. I was proud of her and did love her too.

I have allowed Toby to look at my manuscript but he made me see that it was unwise to include it. He was right of course. I guess I wrote it for myself as a sort of therapy. I needed to rationalise it but couldn't. I had to come to terms with the fact that I was selfish and put my own needs first. However I could not get off the rollercoaster somehow, I needed that double life to function effectively.

So I agreed to write a special version for posterity just to keep Mum happy.

Just as well really as the tabloids would have their story of the year it had it ever got into the wrong hands as I advanced up the political ladder?

CHAPTER 48

TOBY AT 50

I was asked to write in my mother's journal to make it complete.

She wants us to start a new one which I will write. It will be about our children and I will record their lives in words, song and film.

Our family seems to have been blessed. It is all due to our parents whom we all adore. The major factor is their love for one another and their love for us.

Added to that we all have a joint interest in the work we do for the Foundation.

I only met my father for the first time when I was eight.

It was love at first sight. That tall good looking stranger walked into my life on my birthday that year and has never left it since.

He was like a magic being to me who brought not only love with him but fun, excitement, danger, daring, animals and Africa.

He eventually told me he was in fact my real father and of course it was the answer to my prayers. He was a famous wildlife photographer and we were always surrounded by his blown up pictures of Animals in the wild. From then onwards we had a wonderful family life. Mum had twins soon afterwards and we had a dog and horses and lived in the Lake District. It seemed we had everything. We still went down to London so I never lost my best friend Bruno who lived next door.

Dad started the Foundation and ran it as a charity setting up orphanages in Africa. We all liked going with him and spent most of our holidays working out there.

When I was eleven he took me on Safari. That is when I made up my mind to become a vet. Today I work from the farm which borders onto my parent's house beside the lake.

It was left to me by an old lady called Myra who befriended my mother when her own mother died. I live there with my beautiful French wife Pia whom I adore.

We have two wonderful children Polly aged ten and Ben who is eight.

I see all of our family regularly. Rosy married my friend Bruno and runs the Foundation now dad has retired. He is also an international singer and still records. He has his recording studio still in Glasgow next to the flats they own there. Rosy was particularly keen to hold on to it as she regards Kathy and Hugh and their boys as her second family. Mum often goes up there with her and sees her other friends. Hugh's sons are married but one of them was very fond of Rosy but was pipped at the post by our super hero Bruno. He is besotted with Rosy and the children Al and Dorcas.

They built a new house in the village and an adjoining surgery where Rosy is resident GP.This not only serves the village but the people who are part of our foundation and its many visitors as well as holiday makers.

Then of course there is my errant brother Miles who we all had to sort out on a regular basis due to his exuberant personality and zest for life. He would get into all sorts of fights and arguments. Bruno my cousin John and I saw ourselves as his minder. We cared about him as we knew he was a genius which made him more argumentative starting an argument sometimes with inappropriate people. He always won which made him unpopular. He went to Oxford and chaired the debating society. He was a born politician and I am proud to say is now our foreign secretary.

He married into the aristocracy which caused a stir in both families. His wife Penny was a typical spoilt daughter of very wealthy parents and one of the oldest families in England. Their wedding was attended by a minor royal.

They had a son called Louis. He was named after Louis Armstrong although the family thought it was after one of their ancestors. Typical of Miles but Penny adored him so much she enjoyed the joke at the expense of her family. It however turned out to be a successful marriage and a good career move for Miles. It was not quite the relationship our parents have but they were very happy.

Sadly Penny died of leukaemia when the Louis was four. Of course Miles was devastated and suffered terribly .He went into a deep depression for a year. Some of it was guilt. We boys were all there for him. He insisted on bringing Louis up himself with the aid of nannies". Mum helped when she was in London.

Emily Bruno's sister was always his friend and supports him emotionally. She never married. I sometimes wonder if they are ever be more than friends but it is never discussed.

However he continues to amaze us with his ability. He is tipped to be the next prime minister. If he does I think he will have to make Emily his PA or advisor.

She is so clever she could still do that and remain MD of mother's company.

I suppose he could marry her and that would cause a stir. It would be typical of him to do that but maybe they have already discussed it and she declined. He will tell me I sure one day. Apart from Bruno I am his confidante. The outgoing prime minister will be retiring next year.

Last month mother had a stroke so I do not think she will write anymore of her story. She is doing very well so will probably start dictating to me soon.

Dad never leaves her side. He is very healthy apart from a spot of angina. He walks a lot and calls on us most days after he has called in the Foundation.

They adore all of our children and are only happy when they are all here including Lord Louis. He is now aged 11yrs and about to go to Eton. His grandfather died a year ago. He is so much like Miles in behaviour but the image of Roberto. He is slim and sophisticated beyond his years. He went to a famous prep school in Oxford. I can imagine the impact he will have one day on the opposite sex. He plays piano and trumpet which pleases all the male members of our family who still jam together. Mum and Dad are enchanted with him as is his other Grandmother Lady Eleanor.

She insists he spends half his holiday with her so she can groom him and teach him their ways.

He sometimes argues with her- (I wonder where he gets that from.) He often insists his friends go with him as he gets bored. Sometimes he takes Ben.

However much she tries to brainwash him he has his own ideas. He refuses to take part in country sports including shooting and fox hunting. He makes notes all the time. I shouldn't be at all surprised if he opens a Safari Park there when takes over. He talked to me about it one day on the plane coming back from Africa.

I cannot imagine what Miles will do when Lady Eleanor dies as she is very frail. Louis may well be still under age. He will come up with something no doubt; probably let it out to the public to earn its keep. He did talk to me about moving 'THE FOUNDATION' there but it will be his son's choice. Whatever happens it will be a new and interesting chapter.

We will always look after our parents. Roberto takes total care of mum. He does her hair and dresses her. She always looks fabulous. Each night they go to sleep together locked in one another's arms. In the next ten years we know they will deteriorate and we are ready. Rosy has it all organised. They will want for nothing.

One day we shall have to say goodbye and they will join Ruth Scott in a shared grave. That will be the saddest day of our lives.

Printed in the United Kingdom by
Lightning Source UK Ltd., Milton Keynes
141454UK00001B/33/P